A Gift from Nessus

William McIlvanney's first novel, *Remedy is None*, won the Geoffrey Faber Memorial Prize and with *Docherty* he won the Whitbread Award for Fiction. *Laidlaw* and *The Papers of Tony Veitch* both gained Silver Daggers from the Crime Writers' Association. *Strange Loyalties*, the third in the Detective Laidlaw trilogy, won the *Glasgow Herald*'s People's Prize.

Also by William McIlvanney

Fiction
Remedy is None
Docherty
The Big Man
Walking Wounded
The Kiln
Weekend

The Detective Laidlaw trilogy
Laidlaw
The Papers of Tony Veitch
Strange Loyalties

Poetry
The Longships in Harbour
In Through the Head
These Words: Weddings and After

Non Fiction
Shades of Grey – Glasgow 1956–1987, with Oscar Marzaroli
Surviving the Shipwreck

A Gift from Nessus

Nessus

WILLIAM McILVANNEY

CANONGATE
Edinburgh · London

This edition published in Great Britain in 2014
by Canongate Books Ltd, 14 High Street, Edinburgh EH1 1TE

www.canongate.tv

First published in 1968 by Eyre & Spottiswoode

3

British Library Cataloguing-in-Publication Data
A catalogue record for this book is available on
request from the British Library

ISBN 978 1 78211 303 4

Printed in Great Britain by Clays Ltd, Elcograf S.p.A

For Moira

Deianeira, wife of Hercules, believing that her husband was in love with someone else, gave him a tunic which was said to have the power of restoring the wearer's love to the giver. When Hercules put it on it adhered to his body, so that when he tried to pull it off, skin came too. This tunic was a gift from Nessus.

I

Three things happened more or less at once. Cameron felt the pain in his stomach again, the car developed a strange, unidentified sound, and a passing billboard threw a jigsaw of words at him: nigh, end, is, –. The billboards sprouted along this stretch of moor road like poplars. Man-made, wisdom-bearing trees. 'The End is Nigh.' That was it. For him, for the car, for both?

The pain was beginning to enjoy itself, working out minor variations in his stomach. It seemed to start on a single pulse that multiplied itself to several, the small twinges keeping subtle time with the larger. Somehow the quiet agony that was going on inside him attached itself to the day outside so that the very sky was like an expression of pain with the last of the sunlight making the ribbed undersides of the clouds look like raw abrasions. He had the weird experience of feeling as if he was in the middle of his own pain, driving through it like a local shower, and wishing he would come to the end of it. He wondered if it was serious.

What if he was dying? He played academically with the thought, trying to outwit the pain. It was some place to die. The moor lay humped on either side of the road, stretching to miles of desolation. Towards the horizon where the air was already luminous with dusk, a row of pylons was charcoaled against the sky. Nearer the road, the heath undulated in a frozen Sargasso of grass, gorse and bracken. Winter hadn't helped. It had expurgated summer's few qualifications of flower and colour, until the moor had been restored to its fundamental statement of barren earth and bleak sky. No irrelevance was allowed to intrude for long here where growth and desolation were locked in a private Armageddon.

It was a depressing place, Cameron thought. Its vastness seemed to erase you. You felt like apologising to it for being so trivial. A pain in the guts seemed pretty insignificant here. Stop the car, walk a hundred yards off the road, and you might as well be on Mars. You could die without being noticed. Come to think of it, he could probably do that anywhere.

It had been a bad day, one of the kind he generally euphemised as a 'day for keeping in touch with my contacts'. All right, he thought. Imagine it. The perfect end to a perfect day. Car found on the moors. Up to its windscreen in a telegraph pole. Driver's body cut from the wreckage with acetylene torches. Remains later identified as those of Edward Cameron, thirty-five, salesman for Rocklight, Ltd., manufacturers of electrical equipment. So much for the formalities. Now to apportion the grief. Let's number the broken hearts. Allison? She would miss him, certainly. You didn't live with someone for eleven years and not miss him. After all, who would dig the garden for her? His mind registered that he was being unfair, but he let it pass. His children. Yes, Alice and Helen would both miss him. And that was about it. Except for Margaret. She would miss him most of all. There was a funny thing.

And here endeth the mourners' roll. Not that he blamed the absentees. He wasn't so sure he would have mourned himself. How could you live for thirty-five years and mean so little? There was something almost impressive about it. What had he achieved? Fourteen years service with Rocklight. Rising to the giddy heights of Area Salesman. A car that wasn't fully paid up but had gone beyond the guarantee, and now sounded as if it had the combustion engine's equivalent of asthma. A bungalow, in a modern development area, with modern design, modern fittings, modern mortgage. That's who would really miss him, his creditors.

He was trying to pretend that the situation was funny to

him. But mediocrity weighed dully on his mind like a migraine. He felt seedy with mundanities. In irritation, his right hand came off the steering-wheel and struck at the rib of cushioned leather below the windscreen, as if the car was to blame. In a way, it was a reasonable substitute for censure. It was one of the many financial pressures that surrounded him like beggars' cups. Part of him was in hawk to it. He felt its metal carapace enfold him like a second skin he couldn't slough. He thought of the order-books in the dash-board pocket, the list of firms' representatives with the first names underlined, the memos fixed with an elastic band to the sunshield, the samples in the back. This crummy car. It had taken him so many places, and they all led nowhere. It even cramped his dreams. These days, his wilder dreams took the shape of landing an especially big order for the firm. What had happened to the ambitions he used to have? He was ashamed to think of them, not because they had been so exaggerated, but because he had become so small.

Nothing about him mattered very much, he reflected bitterly. Not even this pain in his stomach. That would be something trivial too. It was probably indigestion. Still, it seemed to be doing its best to qualify as something bigger. He winced, slightly huddled over the steering.

The car was still giving its bronchial whir from somewhere. Some vehicle. It wasn't a car. It was a mechanical epidemic. One damn thing after another. First, the clutch wore out. Then the starter-pin broke. At least, that's what they said it was. But they could tell you anything. They were like doctors, speaking to you mysteriously through a veil of technical terms. They lost you in a maze of sprockets and gaskets and cylinder-heads. And what could you do? You were in the hands of the specialists.

Right now, he wouldn't mind being in their hands. The 'Half-way Garage' was a mile or so ahead. He decided to pull in there. He wanted petrol anyway. He could get them to look at the car and give his stomach a service. He put his foot down, heading for the garage like a pioneer making for an outpost.

Around him, a luminous stillness held the moor itself. Every tuft, every hillock took on sharper lines. But on the road the traffic was getting heavier as tea-time approached, with cars that traversed the moor like noisy profanations.

On top of the hill ahead of him, he saw the garage stand up squat and ugly against the sky, a piece of architectural litter in the countryside. He swung off the road and pulled up at the petrol-pump. As he turned off the ignition, he realised that the pain in his stomach had subsided. Perhaps it had come out in sympathy with the car, he thought. It was probably indigestion right enough, or cramp. Whatever it was, he was getting it too often.

He stepped out of the car. At his feet engine-oil made small mother-of-pearl pools. A rag blew across the yard in front of the garage. Far in the distance he could see cars crawl across the moor like maggots. Nobody came out. He heard laughter somewhere. Opening the car door, he leaned briefly on the horn.

A mechanic who looked about nineteen or so emerged from the garage, wiping his hands on a rag.

'Well, sir,' he said. 'What can we do ye for?'

'Four of the middle one,' Cameron said. 'And would you check the oil and the water, please?'

The mechanic held the nozzle in the tank, whistling and watching the revolving needle.

'No' a bad day, then. For the time o' the year. A bit blowy, mind ye. Ah've seen ye in here before, have Ah no'?'

'I come in now and again.'

'Ah thought that.'

There must be something memorable about me, Cameron thought.

'It's the car Ah recognise actually. Funny number-plate. Funny how ye remember a thing like that.'

The petrol-pump clicked to silence.

'Release the bonnet then, will ye, sir?'

Cameron did so.

'There's something wrong with the engine, I think,' Cameron said, watching.

'How's that then?'

'A noise, I mean.'

'Your water an' oil's all right. Switch 'er on.'

The mechanic listened for a moment. He made a couple of mystic passes at something under the bonnet.

'Nah,' he said. 'Ah don't know. Canny be anything serious.'

'Listen!' Cameron said.

The mechanic listened some more. He rubbed his hand across his cheek, leaving an oil-streak that, taken along with his acne and his gangling figure, made him look like a grubby schoolboy. He's too young to know what's wrong, Cameron thought, and felt briefly envious of him. It must be nice to be like that, to be nobody in particular yet, with all your mistakes to make. That was what trapped you, made you what you were, narrowed the permutations of your potential – your mistakes. Cameron felt his own mistakes like jailers beside him.

'There's something right enough,' the mechanic said. 'But it'd take too long tae find it just now. It'll see ye home all right. That's for sure.'

Cameron was going to argue, but the mechanic clipped the bonnet-rod into place and bumped the bonnet shut. Accepting the finality of his action, Cameron gave him two pounds. Better not to argue with him. He needed his goodwill. Cameron switched off the engine.

'Ah'll get yer change.'

While he was inside for the change, Cameron took a scribbling-pad from the car and wrote on it.

'Keep a bob for yourself,' Cameron said, taking his change.

'Ta.'

'By the way, would you just sign this chit on behalf of the garage? Just a check for my firm, you know?'

'Dae they no' trust ye?'

The mechanic laughed. He took the slip of paper, signed it,

and was handing it back when he suddenly withdrew it again from Cameron's open hand. He looked at it more closely.

'Ye've made a wee mistake here, sir,' he said. 'Ye've wrote doon eight gallons. Instead of four. Ah'll just correct it for ye.'

He superimposed '4', making the figure about quarter of an inch thick all round.

'There we are,' he said, handing the paper back with the biro. He stood leering knowingly, and Cameron was suddenly conscious of his antagonism. Against what? His smart clothes? His thinning hair? His accent? The mechanic stood opposite Cameron wearing his boilersuit, his acne, and his rangy youth like an enemy uniform. He was taking obvious pleasure in having found Cameron out. In spite of his expensive suit, Cameron felt shabby with fakery, scruffy with petty deceit.

'Dae ye want yer bob back now, sir?' the mechanic added.

'That's all right,' Cameron said. 'Sorry about the mistake.'

He came back out onto the road so fast that he nearly collided with another car. The hooting of the other car's horn echoed the derision he felt for himself. Bloody stupid, he kept saying to himself, bloody stupid. He took the piece of paper containing the mechanic's emendation, crumpled it, and pushed it out of the window. He wished he could get rid of his embarrassment as easily.

Why had he done it? It was pointless. He didn't usually bother keeping a check on minor expenses like that. Morton. That's what it was. Morton had been suspicious lately. Especially since the Simpson and Auld contract hadn't materialised yet. Maybe that was an Area Manager's job. But Cameron didn't like it. It rattled him to think of Morton padding mentally behind him like a lynx in a Hector Powe suit.

Hell, Cameron's mind said, and one wheel overran the shoulder of the road before he righted the car. He despised the picture of himself he had seen in that garage mechanic's eyes, especially since it was probably accurate. He felt trapped by it. Everywhere he looked, it was there. In Morton's eyes. In the eyes of the businessmen he dealt with. Even in Allison's eyes. They all gave him back small financial worries, expense accounts, business contracts, mortgages. It seemed to him that all the things he did every day were no more than the semblance of his existence, the reality of which took the form of figures that appeared in books and ledgers he never saw, numbers that proliferated infinitely, increasing or diminishing in accordance with his hieroglyphic destiny. Sums of money swam around in his head like corpuscles, the dynamic of his existence. He wrenched the car into a lay-by and before it had stopped moving his eyes were shut. His left hand applied the handbrake, his right switched off the engine, and then both fell into his lap.

After a while, he got out of the car and walked round in front of it, looking across the moor. The sunset had frozen. It seemed no darker now than it had been ten minutes ago. The daylight was distilled to a last pellucid essence except where dusk had gathered like a sediment in hollows. He stood miniscule against the moor and the sunset, feeling himself dwindle into the vast statement of earth and sky. He didn't move, as if his stillness were a kind of camouflage, making him acceptable to the scene, giving him roots here.

Closing his eyes, he was unaware of the van that pulled into the lay-by behind his own car. A young man stepped out and bent down over Cameron's car before coming towards him. Cameron heard the crunching noise made by the young man's feet on the whinstone chips, but had not deciphered the sound before he felt the fingers prod his shoulder.

'Heh, you!' Focusing on the sound, Cameron saw a faceful of anonymous anger. 'Yes, you!'

It was like opening a poison-pen letter. The hatred expressed in that face was addressed to him. There could be no doubt about that. But where it came from and why, he couldn't understand.

'Lay off. D'ye hear me?'

Cameron had no reaction. The pure malice in the eyes

15

transfixed him like a snake's head, and he waited for more venom.

'Lay off Margaret Sutton. For if you don't, you'll be the sorriest man in the world. I'm not the only one who knows. You'll find that out.'

Cameron felt his stomach keel. It wasn't the threat. It was the knowledge others had of him. It was the thought that he existed in the minds of people he didn't know. It was a primal dread, a sudden sickening sense that he could be destroyed in effigy by other people.

'Cut it out, will you?'

The young man seemed momentarily put out by his own change of tone. They both stood looking rather crestfallen, as if neither of them liked the script but they were stuck with it.

'You better keep your trousers buttoned after this.'

He turned and walked away. The crunching of his feet on the whinstones seemed the most truly irrevocable sound that Cameron had ever heard. As the van pulled out, the gears crashed like an omen.

The moor seemed fouled by his presence. Walking awkwardly back to the car, as if any movement that was too quick would make him vomit, Cameron switched on his sidelights and drove out onto the road again. It was as if he was following the van at a pre-arranged distance, but they would meet at a common destination. Instinctively, he slowed down. He played a game that he had for making things seem less important. You pretended you were telling someone else about the incident, and you made it sound funny. 'He went away as if he'd just brought the good news from Ghent to Aix,' Cameron thought. And, 'Anyway, I always use zip-fasteners.' But it didn't work. The whole thing felt about as funny as gangrene.

At the outskirts of the city, a light fog was joining forces with the darkness. Cameron didn't know whether to curse or welcome it. It made visibility poorer for him, but then it made it poorer for everybody else too. And at the moment, Cameron had a nightmarish feeling that the city teemed with

16

people in mysterious conspiracy against him, a secret club, two of whose members he had just met. The young man at the lay-by had hinted at a bigger membership. Cameron might meet a third member anytime, anywhere, and not even know it. He drove carefully through the streets, wearing the fog like an alias.

17

2

It was hot in the office. Morton crossed to the window but didn't open it, content merely to watch the people in the cold air outside and cool down by proxy. There was no more than a faint wash of fog, just enough to blur edges and make traffic and pedestrians move in a poetic greyness where the lamp-standards flowered gently. Nice, Morton thought, from his window in Olympus, a study in degrees of confusion. The general greyness was intensified wherever people moved, each one's breath creating a private fog about his head. Having things to do, Morton took in the sensuous pleasure of the scene quickly, swallowed it like a pill. Then he crossed to the door, opened it, and spoke into the small outer office.

'Annette. You can bring me in that file on Mr Cameron now.'

He came back in and sat on the edge of his desk, adjusting his mind like a microscope with Cameron under it. But as soon as Annette entered the office, his concentration misted. It wasn't just the smell of her, although her perfume, strong without being obtrusive, proclaimed her femininity in a whisper. It was more complex than that. Annette attracted indirectly, as a sort of emotional *agent provocateur*. Not particularly pretty, she managed to make prettiness seem a fortuitous accessory, like earrings. Wherever she moved among the men in the office, she created small skirmishes on the borders of their attention. Many a business-like thought had found itself dissipated by the rustle of her nylons, many a sombre decision had been ambushed by her scent. She had learned to live with the fact that she was proposition-prone, and spent her days pleasantly side-stepping careless hands and avoiding knees that seemed magnetically attracted to hers and innocently staring innuendoes into stone. Disillusioned juniors maintained that she was merely saving herself for lechers of more elevated rank.

Morton wondered about it as he took the file from her. He thought there was a secret submissiveness about her that only needed the right password. But he hadn't time to play at Ali Babas just now. He opened the file.

'Tidy up a bit in here, Annette, will you? There's a good girl. It needs a woman's touch.'

He wondered at once why he had said that. Certainly not because he wanted the office tidied. The simple statement, emerging without apparent reason, added a new dimension to the atmosphere in the room. Annette obeyed without comment, going through a ritual of shifting things about on his desk. Morton felt as if he had made a remark in code, the true significance of which only the two of them could have understood.

Cameron's file. Graph of one man's deterioration. As the sales figures degenerated, the expenses increased, as if Cameron could compensate imaginatively for the shortcomings of reality. Morton shook his head. There was only one conclusion to be reached.

'All right to put this stuff in the basket?' Annette asked.

'What's that?'

She came round beside him and held the papers in front of him while he riffled through them. He was more conscious of the fine white hairs on her arm than of the writing on the papers. The shape of her bosom affected him like an astigmatism.

'Okay,' he said, not sure himself whether he was passing judgment on the contents of the papers or the contents of Annette's blouse, and he watched her cross to the wastebasket.

There was only one conclusion to be reached. He couldn't help wondering about Annette, though.

'These ones here, Annette. Put them in the left-hand drawer.'

Although he wasn't in her way, he made a show of moving to let her pass, settling nearer to her than he had been. She was in no hurry to move away, tapping the edges of the sheets of paper on the desk-top.

'A second,' while his hand rested on her forearm. In leaning over to see the top sheet, he felt her hair brush his cheek. Her skin against the blouse sighed infinitesimally, as if deputizing for an emotion. His fingers made a small gesture of contraction on her arm. 'Yes. They're the ones,' leaving pale fingermarks like a rubber-stamp on her flesh.

Only one conclusion to be reached, his mind repeated to him like a patient secretary. But duty came to him as his mother's voice had through countless dusks when he had been involved in timeless games, distant and unreal. This was becoming an absorbing game. Annette, with the drawer closed, wasn't so much standing as hanging, marionette on loose threads.

'You could empty the ashtray if you've time.'

It was so ridiculous he almost laughed, but she did it. For a manic moment, he had a wild spatial sense that this room had broken off from everything else, was spinning in a private orbit, surrounded by eternal fog. Even more absurd requests were improvising themselves in his head. Brush my shoes. Stand on your head in the corner. He decided to halt on the verge of megalomania. He might just be suffering from over-work. After all, what signs had she given? Also, there was an uneasy ambiguity about who was the ringmaster in this subtle circus. He wasn't sure whether he held the whip or responded to it, for he couldn't take his eyes off her. One thing he hated was to let other people get the upper hand. This was enough for one performance.

'All right, Annette,' he said. 'Thanks. You can knock off now.'

'I'll see you tomorrow, Mr Morton.' She invested the words with a lot of weight, like a walk-on actress trying to

20

make her name on the strength of a line. 'Goodbye,' pouting on the plosive, as if she was extinguishing a delicate candle.

'Night,' Morton called, the unnecessary volume of his voice seeming to intimate the distance she should have been from him. But his mind noted her departing buttocks like a memorandum.

Only one conclusion to be reached. He glanced at the file again. It was ludicrously obvious that Cameron was at it. A fiddle was one thing, but this lot amounted to an orchestra. Morton didn't want to do anything too drastic. For old time's sake, he thought. And other things. But there was this additional information. Margaret Sutton. You couldn't expect to run a mistress on expenses. No. Steps would have to be taken.

Morton flipped the file shut and locked it in the right-hand drawer of his desk. Having decided to act, he felt better. It was now only a question of how, and Morton was good at the mechanics of a situation. He lit a cigarette. He was seeing Cameron tonight. But their wives would be there, as well as Jim Forbes and his wife. (Morton's mind donated a smile like a penny to the image the name of Forbes always called up to him.) He decided he would merely mention to Cameron that he wanted to see him in his office first thing in the morning. Give him some doubt to sip on overnight, like black coffee.

Morton stood as still as bronze in the middle of the office and listened. He relished this moment of soft limbo when the office-building ceased to be a factory of noises and addressed itself to murmured sounds, muted as prayers. The clank of a pail, melted by distance to a coin of sound dropped into a large silence; the closing of a door, a small hardness that healed in a second; footsteps like a message in morse; the preoccupied moan of the lift complaining to itself; all sounds that were movingly self-absorbed, confined to the confessional of their private purpose. In the glare of his small linoleum sanctum, Morton smiled self-sufficiently and to himself, graven out of his own preoccupations, wreathing smoke down his nostrils like a lonely bull that manufactures its own incense.

The small cubicle adjoining his office contained a wash-hand-basin and a rack where his coat and hat hung. He washed his hands slowly and the question of how Allison Cameron would react if she knew became involved with the suds. He kneaded the issue to the point of her forced moral indignation and then washed it down the sink.

At the door of the office, he paused with his coat on, looking round. All was in order. The office looked small with familiarity and Morton felt he had all but outgrown it. He noted in the general drabness the small prophetic pockets of luxury – oriental letter-opener, expensive desk-lighter. London was next. The future lay like tracks towards it. Suddenly Cameron clicked in his mind like a signal standing against him. Morton resolved in that second that Cameron would give neither him nor the company one more day's trouble. He would bring him out into the open. Softly, wisping up out of dim Glasgow backstreets where children stuck like flies to a lamp-post that dropped a grey bell of light over them, threaded with memories of endless games of tig and scuffed shoes and tin-can football and snot-hardened jersey-cuffs, came the words of a game they used to play: 'Come out, come out, wherever you are, the game's abogey'. Morton nodded in answer to their echo, closing the door.

3

Although the fog might have seemed an adequate safeguard in itself, Cameron adhered scrupulously to the complicated rules he had evolved for visiting Margaret's flat. This evening, as always, he parked the car a couple of streets away from where Margaret lived, but not in the same place as he had left it the time before. He had four habitual parking spots and he permutated them moodily. Having locked the car, he went in the opposite direction from his destination.

It was a compulsive performance with him and, like most rites, was not quite rational. The dread of leaving the car two nights running in the one place had the strength of a taboo over him, as if such carelessness would bring discovery inevitably upon him. And the erratic course he took towards Margaret's flat was not designed simply to foil the rubber soles of followers or elude the eyes of passers-by. For him it had almost the power of a spell, woven by his own feet, and proof against more than mere people. It was as if by pacing out a deliberately devious route he could shake off his sense of guilt, give his own conscience the slip, and create a charmed context for his meeting with Margaret, a private room that excluded the fears that scuttled in the cupboards of his mind, the shame that snuffled to get at him in his sleep. This evening especially he needed such a secret place to be, a shelter from drab realities.

The fog did its best to countermand the hardness of the truth, touching the gaunt dullness of the buildings with a brief, grey mystery. Cameron was glad of it, although he knew what lay beneath it well enough. This part of Glasgow was tucked and folded in his heart like a map of himself.

Since he had known Margaret, it had taken hold of him with that relentlessness places have. Pointless images from it formed insistent lumber in his memory – the house in the corner sporting the potted plant whose leaves reached wanly after growth that never came; the newsagent's window where handwritten postcards advertising rooms made illegible offers in the rain. That grubby plexus of streets formed a knot that tied him somehow to himself, meant more than masonry, so that sometimes in a dream he was running down one of those streets away from something, but found that one street doubled back endlessly into another, while around him rose the familiar tall black buildings where the starlings alighted to defecate in cheeky insult to the architecture.

But tonight the fog helped him to generate the atmosphere he wanted, neutralising time and place. He was amoeba swimming through a grey infinity. For the time that he was with Margaret, there would only be two people in a room and nothing else would matter. Someone lurched past him greyly, drowning in his own dream.

The light in the entry burned stale on the dank walls. As soon as Cameron's foot clanged on the cold stone floor, the small dream he was nurturing died on him. This dim corridor admitted no deviation from the fact itself, led to nothing more than the bleak stairway at the end of it. On the two doors he passed, unknown names were dissolving in polished brass.

Margaret lived in one of the top flats, three storeys up. The stairs had been hollowed down the middle by a river of feet, and greasespots showed here and there like domesticated bloodstains. Behind one of the doors as he went by, an argument raged faintly; the words, audible but incomprehensible, made small explosions of futility. He opened the door to Margaret's flat with his key and went in.

'Oh. Eddie. Hullo,' she said.

She was genuinely surprised to see him. Obviously she had assumed it was too late now for him to come today. There was a pile of jotters on the arm of her chair and she had a red pen

24

in her hand, marking. She must have taken a very early tea. Cameron was embarrassed to see the tea-dishes still on the table and the fire not cleaned out, grey ash showing round the edges of the electric heater she had placed in the hearth. All that sloppiness was somehow like advertising her loneliness, seemed to be saying: See, nobody cares. She hadn't even drawn the curtains.

'I can't wait long,' Cameron said.

At once he was angry with himself for saying that. It was unnecessarily brutal, so much more clumsy than the deft scene of mutual seduction that he had imagined. Margaret said nothing but her eyes were a reprimand he could hardly bear, like small wounds. Within himself he felt a response stir like a small haemorrhage, and the thing that bled in him was a complex tissue of shame and lust and hunger and pity.

'I've just been doing some correction.'

Margaret put the words between them like a screen until she could find herself, separate her thoughts from irregular French verbs. She stood up, gathered the jotters together and laid them on the floor beside her open briefcase.

'The fog slowed me down a bit.'

'Yes. It would. I think it'll lift soon, though.'

She was hesitant a moment in the middle of the room before she went to the window and drew the curtains. In taking off his jacket and hanging it over a chair, Cameron became vulnerable, like a tortoise without its shell. The white shirt-sleeves seemed ridiculous, a symbol of domesticity that was out of context here. The anonymity of the room swamped him. The bulb that hung from its fraying flex was shadeless, giving off the dull, cold light that seems to be stored in the waiting-rooms of railway stations. The whole place gave a sense of being in transit. Books were piled in several places, and two of them lay open, as if they had been abandoned by people in a hurry. On the arm of Margaret's chair was a half-eaten biscuit. The wallpaper was ancient, and parts of its motif asserted themselves here and there, like graffiti.

Cameron found himself wondering what he was doing in

25

this room, and what he and this woman drawing curtains had in common. Margaret didn't help to make the situation seem more natural. She crossed awkwardly from the window to the fireplace and became preoccupied in a contest with her own untidiness. She lifted an empty cup from the hearth and put it on the mantlepiece, as if that was where it belonged. She took the jotters from the chair and placed them neatly on the floor beside it. Trapped in her own chaos like a complicated chess problem, all she could do was shift the fragments of it around into different patterns, searching vaguely for some way out.

The particles of her confusion seemed to settle like dust on Cameron, fouling his taste for this moment. He had an impulse to put his jacket back on and get out for good, leaving his key on the table, as if this room was a locker he had no further use for. It was hopeless for him too, he suddenly realised. He was like Margaret, forever pushing the refuse of his life from one place to another, as if it made a difference. He had been coming to this room for over a year now, and yet he felt it was pointless. Every time he turned his key in the lock, his own shame and self-deception fell out on him, smothering him. It was as if he kept his relationship with Margaret locked up in this room, like luggage he was always just about to use. But he hadn't used it so far. He came back from time to time to check that it was still in the same place and still available to him. But he wasn't sure he had the guts to take it any further. He wasn't even sure he wanted to. Almost every morning, he woke into the same question: would he do it? Would he ever break with Allison and go to Margaret? Emotionally, he lived each day with his case packed in the hall. All he had to do was save enough resolution to buy a ticket. But it only needed Alice to cut her finger or Helen to touch his hand with questions, and he was robbed of resolution. It would be more honest just to leave now, and for good.

But turning from the fireplace, Margaret showed him her face in familiar half-profile, the high forehead, the straight

26

nose, the large mouth, the brown eyes that went opaque with secret thoughts, the dark hair in which even this light found veins of sudden amber. He inventoried her features painfully, like a clerk recording someone else's wealth.

'I wanted to come tonight,' he said. 'I had to see you.'

It was spoken like a recrimination.

'I'm glad you did.'

'It's been some day. What a day! Disaster day.' He wanted to give all the tawdry weariness of it to her, as if she could expunge it.

'I know what you mean. It's been like that for me too. But you've salvaged some of it for me.'

'You were going to do some work?'

'That doesn't matter. The past participles can wait. How long have you got?'

'Not very long. I'm going out tonight. *We're* going out. With friends. Damn them.'

'At least you're here.'

'I wish I could stay.'

'I wish you could.'

A small hammer of blood tapped at Cameron's temple. They stood in mute commiseration with each other, reluctant to give more. They had fed that demanding pain that grew out of their mutual presence, dropped a few words into it, and the jaws of it only widened. Taut and painfully dignified they waited for it to swallow them, transcending the little drabness of the place. Formally, solemnly, quietly, like someone articulating the first words of a ceremony, Cameron spoke.

'I want you,' he said and, walking over, flicked the switch, erasing the room.

The place seemed to roar with darkness. They found themselves clumsily in the dark, their fingers relearning each other's bodies in frantic braille. Unskilfully, Cameron released Margaret from her dress, patches of skin blooming palely. She keened slightly, the sound a minute descant to the muffled traffic of the city.

27

'Love me, love me, love me,' Margaret said, and the words swam weakly through her breathing. 'Take me through, take me through.'

They moved across the dark room like some impossible animal that had wandered out of prehistory. In the bedroom the curtains had not been drawn, and the fog washed on the window-pane, making the room seem to drift in a heaving void. Cameron felt angry at his clothes for shackling the urgency of his desire with the ludicrousness of trousers, the mundanity of laces. As he lay down beside Margaret, lust sprang her like a trap.

'I wish there could be more,' she was saying. 'Why can't we be together?'

'I love you,' offering the words as if they were some sort of absolution. Then he gagged her mouth with his.

Beyond the moilings of their bodies, the city churned and hooted faintly like a factory, busily engaged in manufacturing their futures, making arrangements, constructing situations, precipitating choices. Again Margaret made to speak, but Cameron smothered her words, for her voice gave access to the needs that waited for him to finish, illumined the faces that watched him from the darkness of his own head. Allison, their children, Morton, the young man. Inexplicably, one irrelevant thought hovered over him like a vulture, waiting to glut on the guilt of his exhaustion: was this Allison's day for going to Elmpark? He wondered if it was. He hoped it wasn't. Somehow, that would make his action worse.

But he drove that thought off with all the others, repelling it with the force of his involvement. He mined desperately at her body, as if he could transmute them both into something different and escape what waited for them, or could admit them to some small, private eternity, while the luminous dial that burned like a cancer on his wrist kept an ironic record of his efforts.

4

The clock showed half-past three. Mrs Dawson had already slipped out, unobtrusive as an earthquake, to brew the tea. Just time for a rousing finale before biscuits were served.

'These are just a few samples of some of the things that have happened to our Guild Members while on hospital visitation. I hope I haven't painted too rosy a picture. Nor one that is too black. It is sometimes amusing, sometimes depressing. But I think I can safely say it is always useful. Illness is a lonely condition. And the sick can always benefit from pleasant conversation, friends, a little warmth.'

Which would be quite useful here too, Allison thought. The church hall was very cold. The walls were ascetically bare and painted a shiver-inspiring off-white. Igloo Grey. The four old-fashioned radiators that defaced the walls gurgled encouragingly from time to time, threatening heat that never came. Perhaps they had abdicated in favour of the spiritual warmth of the legend painted in huge letters below the clock: 'I am the Way, the Truth, and the Life'.

'This is one small way in which we can try to show the truth of a Christian life. It is easy to forget in our own comfortable lives the quiet suffering that a lot of people less fortunate have to put up with. It's not asking too much for us to sacrifice a little of our time for their sake. We mustn't let our own comforts blind us to the needs of others.'

'Comforts' was an understatement. Looking round them, she could well understand why this was said to be one of the richest congregations in Glasgow. It showed, especially in the small inner circle of older women who sat at the back of the hall – Mrs Gilchrist, Mrs Cartwright, and Mrs Anderson.

She had often wondered why they attended these 'Young Wives' meetings at all. The only thing that qualified them was their noseyness. It was strange. With their money, they could have been doing anything they wanted. But they preferred to come here. Perhaps it was just that they liked to be where their influence could be felt. And in this room it was almost tangible.

While she was speaking, she watched them sitting there, a little trinity of their own, doing a modest trade in social destinies. She felt she knew them well, having memorised each the way one would memorise an important telephone number that might be useful some day. Mrs Cartwright was the most obtrusive, as blatant about her money as if she had been dressed in hand-stitched fivers. One of her more memorable remarks had been: 'I find food always catches in these gold fillings. Don't you?' Mrs Anderson was much more bearable. Her husband was a coal-merchant who had built up his own business, and her bad grammar, which antedated her wealth, she bore around with her like a cheerful mark of Cain. The most influential of the three was Mrs Gilchrist. She never touched upon anything connected with money, just as other people seldom point out that they have blood. She spoke very little altogether, but was eloquent with diamonds.

'Perhaps the best way to appreciate how these people can benefit from our visits is to think of someone near to you being in their position.' She decided she had better shut up soon, because she had reached the stage where she couldn't see any connection herself between the ends of her sentences and their beginnings. 'Myself, I have a sister who knows what it is to have been in this situation. To depend on the charity of other people for company. And it has made me determined to try to comfort other people in the same predicament. In tribute to her, as it were.' She was hunting desperately for a way to finish. She felt they might just have to pull her into her seat. 'Anyway, I hope I haven't bored you too much in telling you about this. Because, really, if there is one thing this activity is not, it is 'boring''. She paused, sensing that she had devised an unintentional conundrum. Write your answers on a postcard and send them to. . . . 'And those young wives who are at the moment completely involved in seeing their children past their first few years might like to bear this in mind. As something they might like to do once their children begin school. Thank you.'

There was a smatter of genteel applause before Mrs McKendrick, the minister's wife, stood up.

'I'm sure we're all very grateful to Mrs Cameron for her most interesting little talk. I feel certain that her words have not fallen on stony gound. And I want to express my personal thanks for the way she bravely stepped in at short notice to fill the gap. Thank you, Mrs Cameron. By the way, Mrs Gilchrist has very kindly agreed to help in the running of our Daffodil Tea. And any ladies wishing to be of assistance, either with baking or labour, should roll up their sleeves and give their names to Mrs Gilchrist. Now, tea will be served.'

Mrs Dawson re-entered, armed with an enormous tea-pot.

'Thanks, Allison. You saved a life,' Mrs McKendrick said.

The christian name was a concession. Mrs McKendrick only used it on special occasions as a sign of favour. Pleased at their temporary intimacy, Allison left her and went straight to where Mrs Gilchrist was sitting. She expressed her willingness to help with the Daffodil Tea and gave her name to Mrs Gilchrist, who took it as if she had been the angel who appeared to Abou Ben Adam.

'Won't you join us, dear?' she said. 'I must say I found your talk very interesting.'

'Thank you very much,' Allison said, making it serve for the compliment and the chair proffered by Mrs Anderson.

She felt slightly overwhelmed for a moment among their upholstered effigies. When you got close to Mrs Cartwright, she became a concerto of subterranean sounds. Stays creaked, cloth sighed, breath fluted faintly in her throat – all clamouring minutely against the injustice of the demands made upon her corpulence by her vanity. She had drawn up the final lines beyond which there was no surrender. Her makeup was a death-mask, her corset a catafalque.

She epitomised the impression that all three of them made on Allison. They were initiated into a coldness, a finality that excluded others. Even the way they stirred the tea given to them by Mrs Dawson and her assistants was ritual, as the first sip was ritual. They enclosed the simplest actions in a kind of stateliness, like canonical brocade. Allison thought with a shiver that she would one day be one of them, a high-priestess of the menopause.

'Thank you, Mrs Dawson,' said Mrs Anderson.

'Pleasure, Mrs Anderson,' said Mrs Dawson. 'Try a butter-fly cake. They're lovely.'

Then Mrs Dawson lumbered off among the talking ladies, a pleasant pack-horse harnessed to her own willingness.

'That woman always takes the full honours of making the tea upon herself,' Mrs Anderson observed obscurely.

'She's a very willing worker,' Mrs Gilchrist agreed.

'Ah well. Martha and Mary,' said Mrs Cartwright. 'Some of us are talkers. Some of us are doers.'

They all did neither for a little while. Mrs Cartwright levered herself down in a series of compromises with her scaffolding, and gently rubbed a puffy ankle.

'My ankle's so *sore*,' she said. 'Tripped going into the Directors' Box on Saturday afternoon.'

Allison was trying to think of how to convey her impressed condolences when Mrs Gilchrist saved her the trouble.

'I didn't know you had a sister,' she said to Allison.

'Well, yes.'

'Does she live in Glasgow?'

'No. Not exactly.'

'Near?'

'Fairly near.'

'You must bring her along some time.'

'Perhaps I will.'

Allison drank off her tea and decided to leave before they could ask her any more questions. The entrance of Mr

32

McKendrick gave her an opportunity. He was a handsome man and because his even features were safely framed in a clerical collar, his female parishioners enjoyed engaging in a sort of bowdlerised coquetry with him.

'I'll really have to go,' Allison said. 'We're eating at the 'Regent' tonight. And I'll have to get the children attended to early.'

'Of course,' Mrs Gilchrist said. 'I must have you and your husband over some evening.'

The remark made Allison wish she could stay and consolidate the promise. But she had committed her self to departure and Mrs Gilchrist left it at that. As she took her leave, pausing to talk to Mrs McKendrick, as she travelled home on the bus, and as she gave Alice and Helen an early tea, she continued to build imaginatively on Mrs Gilchrist's remark.

By the time Cameron came in after seven o'clock she had convinced herself that they were as good as invited to Mrs Gilchrist's. It seemed to her a definite achievement. It wasn't easy to penetrate that social fortress, round which circulated stories of luxury, hints of flunkeys. She felt that an otherwise futile afternoon had been given point, that she had been somehow vindicated in giving up her visit to Elmpark to speak to the Young Wives.

Cameron was aware that she was preoccupied as soon as he entered. Round the siege Helen immediately laid to his attention, Cameron exchanged a few meaningless phrases with Allison, while she washed up the children's dishes. Having prepared himself to endure her reprimands for his lateness, he found that he was depressed that her objections should be so perfunctory. They weren't talking to each other at all, merely sending out habitual words like sentries that guarded their thoughts and feelings, keeping them from coming into contact with each other.

'Had a good day?' Allison asked, having gone through the drill of the annoyed wife.

'All right.'

But he suddenly revolted against the nonsense they were

33

talking. Why should everything they said to each other be a lie?

'Actually, it wasn't a good day,' he said. 'It never is. There's something else too.'

The tremor in his voice opened a door between them. She turned from the sink. The cup she had put down skated along the draining-board and clinked against another into a silence, across which they met for the first time since he had come in. He noticed something small happen in her eyes, like a momentary dilation, the widening of a trapdoor, down which he could push all their lives with the weight of one sentence. All it needed to do it was the truth. And everyone, he thought, has a right to the truth. It's all we have a right to.

'What's wrong?' she said.

We have to face each other sometime, he was thinking. Moments of honesty are rare, elusive residues of living that must be panned with infinite patience. And this was one, a bright second of clarity riddled by chance out of a day of dross, and presented to them. When would they find another? He had to be honest now. Helen was making patterns in his hand with her finger. In the next room, Alice was singing tunelessly.

'The car's on the bum,' he said, stopping his mouth with a biscuit the children had left and pulling a droll, clown's face.

He felt as if that mask would freeze onto his features, and become himself.

5

'I mean I was only eighteen,' Jim Forbes was saying. 'This was the first girl I had *really* fancied. And here she was, you know? Telling me to give her five minutes to go into the house, let her parents think that was her in for the night. And then slip back out, you know?' Eileen Forbes was gazing interestedly into her husband's face as if she hadn't heard the story a hundred times, but her dessert-fork moved like a conductor's baton. Elspeth Morton kept her eyebrows arched in interest while her jaws busied themselves with the gâteau. Allison noticed that either Elspeth was wearing a new ring or her diamonds were putting on weight. Morton was toasting himself in secret with the last of his wine. Cameron watched a girl three tables away, fascinated by the versatility she showed in being able to eat, talk, pat her companion's hand and run a survey of her audience-rating, all at the same time. He wondered what her feet were doing. Tramping grapes? Knitting? 'So there I was. With Eden five minutes away. I'm telling you. My knees were knocking like a one-man band. I was standing in their back garden. About ten yards away from the house. And my breath was misting their windows. I was ready to show Romeo one or two tricks. Her window was the one above the kitchen. She'd told me that. Five minutes. And then the signal was to be the light going on in her room. A second, and then off again. I cleaned my teeth with my hanky. Combed my hair. Flexed my arms for the clinches. I mean, she was a lovely bit of stuff. And I waited. Nothing. Not a sausage. Five minutes. Ten. I thought maybe her watch is slow. But hell, it would have to be going backwards. I thought of everything. A power-cut. Her old man had coughed it kissing her goodnight. She couldn't find the light-switch in the dark.'

'You were always a bit of an optimist, Jim,' Morton said.

' 'Ope spregs 'ternal,' Elspeth said suddenly, giving voice to her gâteau.

'A new ring, Elspeth?' Allison asked, under the impression that Forbes's anecdote was concluded.

Eileen dropped her fork on the floor.

Meanwhile, back at the asylum, Cameron thought. An incidental profundity occurred to him: perhaps Elspeth had accidentally revealed the machinery behind the unfathomable ambiguity of utterance achieved by the priestesses of Delphi. They spoke with their mouths full. Then he said: 'And then, Jim?'

'Well, anyway,' Forbes continued, experiencing the sedentary equivalent of an audience walkout, for Eileen was cleaning her fork with a paper napkin and Elspeth was nodding in delayed action response to Allison's question. 'Fifteen minutes. And I thought: right! Some communication is called for. I had seen it done in the pictures. I lifted a piece of clay and chucked it cautiously at her window. Nothing. So I went on doing it. I was hissing: Linda! Linda! all the time. That was her name. And all the time my ammunition was getting bigger. Till I was really on the heavy bore stuff.' And you still are, thought Morton. 'Then, smash! Right through the window. I put in a full pane of glass. What happened after that was strictly Keystone Cops. Lights seemed to go on in every room but hers. I heard footsteps running downstairs. It sounded like a centipede with hobnailed boots. And a dog was barking. I didn't know what the hell was happening. I was running four ways at once. Then the back-door opened and I hears this voice shouting: 'Seize 'im, boy!' Seize 'im? This thing like a Shetland pony comes out, going like a racehorse. I was off. I was wishing they had cut their damned hedges more often. Five feet if they were an inch. I went over with this thing hanging to my bum like a booster-rocket. It must've been with me for about a hundred yards. Before I broke free. Never again. I left my arse in San Francisco, right enough. That's when I took up golf.'

They laughed.

'It's a lovely ring, Elspeth.' Eileen was first with a follow-up, since she had recognised the golfing remark as epilogue.

'Do you like it?' Elspeth smiled, her hand turning like a lighthouse.

'It's beautiful,' Allison said. 'A good bit bigger than the other one, isn't it?'

'Yes. The other one's about the size of yours, Allison. Sid's been promising me another one for years. And this is it.'

'Very good too,' Allison said. 'Though I always think nothing can replace the sentimental value of the first one. Don't you? I mean that's the one you got engaged with, isn't it?'

'Oh, I'd never part with mine.' Eileen looked nostalgically at her own ring, each diamond of which was like a facet of the ones on Elspeth's ring.

The women withdrew behind the purdah of diamond talk. The men lit Forbes's cigarettes and blew out smoke signals of satiety.

He took too long, Morton was thinking. Could have taken at least two minutes off the telling. But that was typical. Forbes was one of those people who nearly always pull the punchline too late, so that the joke explodes in their face. His ego bore the marks. He kept trying. But he was one of life's natural casualties. Amen.

They're always against himself, Cameron thought. He watched Jim's face brood upon the moment, hatching another anecdote perhaps. Cameron felt a tremendous liking for him. He tried so damned hard. But it was embarrassing the way he was always so funny about himself – like a cripple whose party piece was balancing on his crutches. He kept showing you his scars and asking you to laugh. Cameron remembered irrelevantly how at school Jim could walk for fifteen yards on his hands. He held the record. They had measured it. He had also been able to skid pebbles on the water more times than anybody else. That was another record. And he could weep anytime at sad films. All the qualities that weren't viable, he had. It was sad to think that perhaps there were some men who passed their prime with conkers. He had wanted to be a missionary. Now he worked with the Electricity Board. That was a funnier joke than any he could tell – the irony that each of them had to some extent become. Hadn't idealism festered in every one of them and healed into indifference? Only some of them, like Cameron himself, kept picking off the scab to contemplate the diminishing wound.

What happens to us? Cameron thought. We start out as real people. What makes us hide from our own dreams, submit to a cage cliché, refuse to face each other?

He looked round their table, round the restaurant. He saw them as if under glass cases. Genus suburbanus: found only in semi-detached houses. The sexual behaviour of these creatures is their only interesting feature. After mating, two off-spring are produced at intervals mathematically calculated by the female. Whereupon, the female swallows the male whole and re-emits him in the form of a bank-balance. Homo aquaticus: this creature hibernates for fifty weeks of every year. For the other two weeks, it can be seen at coastal resorts being buried by its young. Unfortunately they usually dig it back up. Genus Cameron: this creature is believed to be extinct.

'Did you hear about Charlie Slade, Eddie?' Morton asked.

'What was that?'

'Died two days ago. Complained of pain in his chest. Doctor thought it was indigestion. Put him to bed with a hot water bottle. Wife called him in the morning. Dead. Thrombosis.'

The three syllables halted talk for a second, left them listening into the dissipation of the rhythmic word, imperative as a tribal tom-tom. Message received, Allison and Elspeth finished what they had been saying. And that was it, Cameron thought. Morton had delivered his cryptic, cosmic message as anonymously and impassively as a telegram boy.

38

They had all drawn curtains for a moment to watch him, and then shut them again before the reality of it could impinge on them. But Morton wasn't finished.

'Funny thing is,' he said. 'They've been telling me he didn't have any insurance policy. Nothing. Imagine that. A bloke like Charlie. Always so methodical. Canny. And leaves his wife in dire straits.'

A nice, sanitary cliché: 'He left his wife in dire straits'. Our lives are intricately plumbed with clichés, a vast network of ready-made words to pipe away inconvenient feelings, dispose hygienically of responses: 'It'll all come all right in the end', 'It comes to us all', 'Why worry?' Faced with the reality of experience, all you had to do was consign it to a cliché and flush it out of your life. How old was Charlie? Thirty-seven, thirty-eight. Three children, two marriages, years of work and worry, holidays by the seaside, plans and failures had worked patiently on his body towards that moment in the night when his heart would burst like an evil seed and flower into his dying. Offended by the clumsy pointlessness of his corpse, you covered it with a comment: 'He left his wife in dire straits.' And nobody need bother any further. Except Eileen.

'His wife's left with the three children? They still had the child from his previous marriage, didn't they?'

'Yes,' Morton said. 'Charlie got custody. His wife had committed misconduct.'

'My God! Three children. The youngest one's only about two. How is she going to live? My God, it's terrible.'

Eileen was attacking her gâteau as if it was a pain-killer. Her manifestation of sympathy was mechanical and controlled and didn't disturb the élan with which she ate. Cameron had known her as a girl, very sensitive and emotional. But time had corroded her sentiment to sentimentality and rusted her reactions into gestures. Perhaps it was because she had never had any children that she had developed a vaguely maternal affection for any kind of pain that crossed her path. She moved about her life as responsive to every touch as a

39

barrel-organ, and whatever event might turn the handle, dead relative or limping dog, it was the same worn and tinny tune it summoned forth, fretted indelibly on her heart by the dull uniformity of her life.

'He used to work with Auld and Simpson,' Morton ruminated. 'By the way, Eddie. How are things going with you and them?'

'All right. Should have something definite fairly soon. That reminds me. I've got a phone-call to make. Business before pleasure. Excuse me.'

'I'll get you out,' Jim said, getting up. 'I think I've got a watering-can for a bladder.'

Cameron had invented the phone-call as an escape hatch but Forbes's presence trapped him in it. He had to phone somebody.

'Have you got change?' Jim waited with him, generously sacrificing the demands of his bladder to those of friendship.

'Yes, thanks.'

Cameron lifted the receiver as Jim went off. He dialled TIM. 'Pip. Pip. At the third stroke it will be nine thirty-five and ten seconds. Pip. Pip. Pip. At the third stroke it will be nine thirty-five and twenty seconds.' The voice was cold, remote – talking marble. The pips were thawing ice. It was like being tuned in to the core of all erosion, the dripping of an unquenchable wound. When Jim patted his shoulder on the way back into the dining-room, Cameron was still listening blankly: . . . 'it will be nine thirty-eight and forty seconds. Pip. Pip. Pip.'

He put down the receiver. He couldn't face going back into the restaurant just yet to listen to their perfunctory voices. He wondered what Margaret was doing. Why couldn't he be with her now, the curtains drawn, and only the two of them together, growing again into people in each other's presence. It only needed one big, positive action to reorientate his life. To walk out now and drive to Margaret's would be enough. He turned and made towards the door. The design of foliage on the carpet stretched before him like

40

a jungle. The thick glass doors gave him back the hotel lobby as if the night outside was only an extension of this room. Voices came from the lounge-bar on his left and he turned desperately towards them, losing himself among them, knowing as he did so that the voice locked in the recesses of the phone was coldly deducting every second from his life.

The air of the lounge was meshed with smoke and every table was fortified by earnest talk against intrusion. Cameron saw a space at the bar beside a large balding man who stared into his drink as if he was angling it. Cameron won to the space and asked for a double whisky.

He couldn't just walk out on Allison at a time like this. It wasn't even practical. He was the only one with a housekey, for one thing. And he hadn't paid his share of the bill. It was ridiculous how circumstances held the grandest intentions trapped like a staked bear while trivia snapped at it like terriers until they wore it into submission. Just when you were about to jump the moon, you tramped on your turnups.

'Do you have any children?'

Cameron thought he was overhearing someone's conversation and his glance was automatic. But it was at him that the large balding man was staring, his eyes muddied with drink. Cameron realised at once why there had been a space beside him at the bar. An aggressive gloom surrounded him like a railing.

'Have you any children? I've got children.'

He was so drunk you could almost see each thought well to the surface of his eyes like a dead fish. Cameron decided that talk was the best method of defence.

'Yes,' he said. 'I've got two.'

'I've got children. I've got three children. Two daughters and a son. The boy's only ten.'

Silence followed and Cameron began to think it was finished, that the big man had been concerned merely to deliver a brief bulletin on progeny.

'How many children have you got?'

'I've got two.'

41

'See that they take their sugar.'

'They always do. Plenty of it.'

'Their polio sugar. The vaccine. See that they take it. They've got to take their sugar. Ralph was taking his. One lump to go. One bloody lump. And he got polio. Calliper. His leg's no thicker than that.' He held up a wavering forefinger. 'That's him for the rest of his life. The bastards. That's a good break to give a boy. Because there was one lump to go. One lump of sugar between him and a full life.'

The big man's massive futility swelled Cameron's, towered into a wave that swamped him. Surfacing for a second, Cameron reached for the first thought that came to him, and said, 'Do you want a drink?'

'I don't want your bloody drink.'

The big man's face pitched close for a second and then receded into the distance of its private storm.

Cameron came out of the lounge and stood for a moment, as if he had lost his way. It wasn't that he had been particularly moved by the big man's dilemma. He even doubted that what he had heard was medically feasible. But it seemed to have a certain poetic truth. In the large, pulpy face he recognised the fist-marks of his own world. That's what he was up against too – a world in which the omission of a sugar-lump could wither your leg, where the infinite ways of losing nullified all the permutations of precaution. Each day chance was infiltrating its bacilli: brakes wore; blood clotted; feet slipped; smoke tarred the lungs; worries gnawed at the struts of the mind. Some time one or more of these would win. Meanwhile the calendars hung in rooms, icons of emptiness, computing coincidence. He felt years sifting away from him, and he was left with no more concrete measurement of their passing than the spaces in his diary, bleak tundras of paper on which survived a few skeletal facts, fragile as moth's bones, crumbling to shapelessness in a month's turning: 'Remember shoes – collect', 'Sales conference', 'Helen's birthday – doll – talking or dressing', 'See Auld'.

It isn't me, he thought. None of it is me. Nor is any of this –

42

Jim Forbes's jokes, Morton's complacency, Eileen's sympathy. Yet he went on acting as if they were. For how long? Until Charlie Slade's epitaph became his own? Pass round the conversation, boys, and put a sentence in. In memory of Eddie Cameron. No. He wasn't finished yet, he told himself. It would be nice to know who you were before you died. He felt a need to hurry. But there was nowhere to hurry to. The rest of the evening waited for him, talk and jokes and drinks in a conspiracy of slow motion, designed to strangle his urgency. So, nursing his desperation like a time-bomb, he went back to them to become part of the conspiracy again, to nod and smile and not hear what was said.

The rest of the night drifted past him in a meaningless debris of aimless actions and fragments of conversation: the banter when he came back into the dining-room and Jim Forbes's joke about its being a fine time to phone his fancy-woman, at which Morton didn't laugh; the journey back home in the car (Jim and Eileen were travelling with them); tailors' dummies in eerie conclave in bright windows, a cinema disgorging anonymous gobbets of humanity onto the street; Allison and Eileen talking brightly in the back, Jim intoning the respective merits of front- and back-wheel drive (banish technicalities from the language, and what would we find to talk about?), and Morton's car following a yard from the back fender; thanking Mrs Davis from across the road for baby-sitting; giving out drinks; eating Allison's delicate supper; giving out drinks.

They were using the living-room because it was warm from the fire kept on for Mrs Davis. Jim's pleas to have the children brought out of their beds had been swiftly squashed by Allison.

The new cushion interested them, gave rise to jokes. Allison had only bought it the other day. It sat on the settee, too big for it. Too big to be a cushion, really. A hybrid form. As if a car-seat had been crossed with a mattress. And this was their scion. A luxurious deformity.

'Chinese?' Forbes was asking.

Because of the huge dragon depicted on it. Did that make it Chinese? Do the Chinese have a monopoly on dragons?

'Japanese. Naturally,' Morton pronounced.

Thank you, Morton, san. Purveyor of Culture to Ignorant Masses.

'Here's how you should really use it.'

Morton put the cushion on the floor, pulled up his trouser-legs, and squatted cross-legged, his hands inside his jacket-sleeves.

'All lightee?'

Sedate fountains of jolly laughter from the ladies. Morton bathing in it. May you do yourself an injury with your chop-sticks.

'We've got one almost exactly like that,' Elspeth said. 'I would say you had been copying. Except that you can't have seen ours. It's in the bedroom.'

Satanic oh-hos from Jim Forbes. Why did Allison buy these things anyway? Every so often the fever took her and she went forth to buy, armed only in a vague sort of covetousness. Her sorties had won them a motley assortment of booty. Her trophies were uniform only in their uselessness and their spurious 'classiness'. One had been a painting – an abstract of bilious ugliness, which Cameron detested and which Allison could only defend wanly as being 'really contemporary'. She had wanted to hang it in the girls' bedroom but when Cameron objected, implying that Spock wouldn't like it, it had been shunted to their room, where it hung above their bed like an invitation to a nightmare. Another buy had been what Allison claimed was an African mask. The face it depicted looked as if it came from darkest Gallowgate. And now the Chinese (Cameron preferred Jim Forbes's theory) cushion. Soon they wouldn't be able to see each other for status symbols.

'Eddie!' Jim's voice was confidential. He was taking advantage of the preoccupation of the others. 'I've got a very good night fixed up for us. Next week. Can you make it? Thursday.'

44

To judge by the furtive excitement of Jim's tones it should be at least a free run of a harem.

'I think so, Jim. What is it?'

'You're okay for Thursday?'

'Yes.'

'Dalmeath Burns Supper. Some night. Special invitations only. We'll have a great time.'

Cameron couldn't think of any excuse to make.

'Drink's tremendous. Stag night. Good speeches. It's tough to swing admission. But I've managed to get tickets. Only two, though. So keep it quiet just now. You know?'

Jim indicated with a nod to Cameron that Morton's luck was out and then chimed in with the laughter of the others, deftly camouflaging their transaction in case there should be a stampede for tickets.

'Fine!' Cameron muttered, the low pitch of his voice keeping it conveniently neutral. That was another night dead. Even time came pre-packaged. In convenient capsules. To be taken like tranquillisers. Morton reminded him of more.

'You're not forgetting next month are you, Eddie?' he asked.

'What's that?'

' "What's that?" he says. Some salesmen I've got. The conference. In London. The Big Dinner. How could you forget? Different hotel this time. That place last year was a dead loss.'

'You salesmen have a great life right enough,' Allison said. 'Any excuse for a good time.'

'It's all business, though,' Morton said, mock-serious. 'Mind you, we do manage to squeeze in the odd orgy afterwards. Nero had nothing on us. Talking of orgies. An office-party next month as well. After we get back from London. You'd better lay in a heavy stock of Alka-Seltzer, Eddie. Two of the girls leaving to get married. An epidemic. And then we didn't have our party at New Year. Thought we'd better celebrate.'

'Now there's a thing I'd fancy,' Jim said. 'A genuine swing-

45

ing office-party. The only kind we have are tea and buns. Three old maids discussing knitting patterns. And the blokes arguing about eight-iron shots. Your place should be able to generate some action.'

'It has been known to,' Morton agreed. 'Fill in an application form and we might get you a ticket.'

Maybe Jim was regretting rashly promising the extra ticket for Dalmeath to Cameron. He could have used it to influence Morton. Strange how boyishly enthusiastic Jim was about anything that could be construed, however mildly, as a male adventure.

Cameron's inattention scrambled their talk for several minutes before he tuned in again to Allison and Morton arguing about immigration. How did they get onto that? They were kidding each other clumsily, aware of their audience.

'West Indians have been exploited long enough by us,' Allison was saying. 'We owe them something.'

'Allison!' Morton remonstrated. 'Noble sentiments. But you can't run a country on them. You're too generous for your own good.'

'And you're too efficient to be altogether human. You can't streamline human affairs the way you do your work.'

They both laughed. It wasn't so much an argument as an exercise in verbal back-scratching.

'How can you live with somebody as efficient as this, Elspeth?'

'No. But seriously,' Morton said. 'We owe them nothing. We gave them the greatest culture in the world. We educated them. Gave them religion. Taught them democracy. Anything we took in return was what they didn't want. Or couldn't use. They're *our* debtors. And now they want to come over here in hordes. No go. They haven't reached our level of civilisation yet. They'll only upset the balance.'

'Rubbish!' Cameron said suddenly, surprised to find that his time-bomb had exploded and was after all only a squib. 'I have seldom heard so much bollocks in such a short space of time. Who the hell are you to set yourself above anybody else? And what have we got that's so sacrosanct nobody else can share it? Folk like you are so bigoted you could use a thimble for a hat. It's true that my uncle's a negro, but that's not why I'm defending them.'

The last remark was a weak attempt to change the tenor of what he had said, make it seem funny. But nobody was laughing. There was a strained silence until Morton saw fit to break it.

'Report to my office first thing in the morning,' he said.

They all laughed thankfully. It could be treated as a joke, a rather feeble one. Cameron became the butt of a few jocular remarks at which he betrayed himself so far as to smile. Morton rounded it all off by telling Cameron that he really did want to see him in the morning in his office. 'But purely on business,' he laughed. 'And not necessarily first thing. Nine-thirty will do.' How could Morton always contrive to make Cameron feel as if he was wearing short trousers?

6

Cameron knew that Allison was going to quarrel with him. Although she was in the kitchen and he stood in the living-room, the fact transmitted itself with absolute clarity. Roger. Over and out. He accepted it with tired resignation, not even bothering to wonder why. Obviously he had once again said or done something that offended Allison's delicate code of hypocrisy. It was one of those things you couldn't escape.

You could postpone it, though. He lit a cigarette, moving slowly about the room to gather up the debris of empty coffee-cups and sticky glasses. Bring out your dead, he thought, heaping them carelessly on the tray he had brought from the kitchen. They made a sad, cluttered little still life, and he sat down in front of it as if it was a shrine, smoking. What a waste of a night! They should give lessons, the lot of them. How to kill your nights stone dead. How to talk with-out saying anything. Bore life into submission. Cameron's Simplified Course in Catalepsy. Instant futility. He had a quiet moment of panic wondering if it was scientifically true that each night dedicated to being nobody in particular meant that there was less of you to be realised in the future.

He felt an urge to make some grand gesture of purification. Instead, he rose and emptied the ashtray into the fire. There were no large actions available to him, he reflected. Necessity lay on him like handcuffs, curtailing every sweeping move-ment to a tic. He was the servant to his own life. Throwing his cigarette in the fire, he lifted the tray and carried it through to the kitchen like a waiter.

'Nice of you to look in,' Allison said, standing rubber-gloved like a surgeon by the sink.

48

Cameron let the remark pass. It was just a scalpel-sharpener. He unloaded his cargo on the draining-board, wiped the tray, and selected one of the left-over petit-fours. As he bit it, the clove in the centre prickled like a disturbed hedgehog, stinging his mouth. He grabbed a handy bottle of milk and drank from it.

'Oh please!' Allison said as she submerged the dishes in water.

Cameron saw that there was no way to avoid the quarrel. He hated these trip-wire situations that Allison rigged up, where no matter what you did or said, there had to be an explosion. But this was to be one of them, and he consciously donned indifference like a steel helmet.

'Must you be so crude?' she persisted.

'When you're putting out a fire, you don't worry about the etiquette of hose-holding. That's what you call an aphorism.'

Allison smiled, her teeth showing like a row of icicles.

'Clever,' she said. 'You're very clever for a boor. Did you have to drink it out of the bottle?'

'Well, it's handier than an udder, isn't it?'

'I don't suppose you'd ever think of cups? That's what they're for, you know.'

'Is it really? Judging by the brew you put in them, I always thought they were for holding specimens of urine.'

'You are utterly disgusting.'

Let this chalice be taken from my lips, Cameron prayed irreverently. Let this stop at the preliminary exchanges. But at the same time he felt his own bitterness and malice gather on his tongue, as potent as anything she could give him. He lifted the dishcloth and started to dry the dishes.

'You're so boorish you would be black-balled from Old Macdonald's farm.'

That was an insult à la carte, speciality of the house, and Cameron answered in kind.

'Any moment now,' he answered, 'you are due to announce for the umpteen-millionth time that you went to a finishing

49

school. Which is a good name for it. They certainly finished you. Sent you out with a hermetically sealed head.'

'If I have said it before, it's only because it's true. I *did* go to a finishing school.'

'Tell me. I'm really interested. What do they do in a finishing school? What did they do at *your* finishing school? Teach you to say 'It's a nice day' in half-a-dozen languages? So that you could become an all-round, cosmopolitan idiot? How to curtsey without showing your knickers? Have classes in tea-cup-holding? I bet you passed "magna cum laude" in pinky-sticking-out.'

'At least they taught us how to conduct ourselves decently in the company of other human beings. That's something you've never learned. Look at what happened tonight.'

This was it. The rest had only been range-finders. Now the real reasons for the quarrel were about to be brought into play. They would be of no consequence, he decided, but he retracted a little inside himself just the same. Nobody is ever immune to the criticism of others. Cameron slowly polished a coffee-cup dry, making a dugout of the action.

'You were so rude to Sid and Elspeth. Don't you realise he's your *boss*?'

'I should. The way he keeps striking matches on my forehead. And using my breast-pocket as an ashtray.'

'He's the very man who could help you to make something out of yourself.'

'What he wants to make out of me, you could make out of a Woolworth's plastic kit and a tube of glue.'

Allison was washing the same cup over and over again as if it was Cameron's brain.

'You're so stupid for yourself, I can hardly believe it. Why can't you be nicer to people who matter?'

'Next time I'll unroll at the door and he can walk all over me.'

'You'll never be anything. Never. Not until you learn to cultivate the right friends.'

'I'll never be anything. Period. Look, Allison. For God's

sake put a match to your dreams of having married Charles
Clore, heavily disguised as me. I'm not disguised as a bum. I
am a bum. In terms of business, I'll never be more than a tea-
boy. Let's face it now. For a time, I could make a show of it.
Getting mentioned in the magazine and what not. But we're
too old to kid ourselves. Me. I couldn't sell pound notes at a
shilling a time. So lay off it, will you?'

Cameron parted the curtains and looked out of the window
to meet his own reflection staring in, a taut and discontented
ghost. All the houses within his vision were in darkness. Only
Allison and he were still awake, guarding their enmities.
Wake up, he wanted to shout. You're in this too.

'It's so unnecessary to be like that. What does it achieve?
"Rubbish!" you said. Even just the very fact that they're your
guests. That should've been enough.'

The treadmill was turning, bringing them back to the same
place. Cameron couldn't see anything he could do about it.

'They can have the use of my chairs. Borrow my ears.
Drink my whisky. But my mouth's my own.'

'But more than that – he's your *boss*. Have you no sense at
all? He's your *boss*.'

'He's also a conceited bigot. He's also about as sensitive as
cement. The way he talks and talks. He makes the pope seem
diffident.'

'Don't run people down just because you can't keep up
with them. You're a fine one to talk about Sid Morton.
You're just making excuses for yourself. It's always the same.'

Allison emptied the basin and peeled off her rubber gloves.
But the operation wasn't over yet.

'You're always the same. You actually go out of your way
to offend people.'

'Yes, I know.'

'How can you be so boorish?'

'For Christ's sake.'

'Listen to yourself.'

'You should never've married me. You know that? You
should've hired a husband from Moss Bros.'

51

'Will you never learn to be just a little nicer to people?'

'Every night I pray for God to make me a normal healthy sycophant.'

'I think you do it to spite yourself,' Allison went on round the corner of his last remark. At such times, she spoke in spasmodic monologue, treating anything Cameron said like an incidental noise that merely prevented her from being heard for the moment. 'I think it's because you've given up. You've accepted failure. So you snipe at everybody else. You don't care what they think of you. It won't be any less than you think of yourself.'

Cameron suddenly realised how quietly they had been speaking. It was amazing when you thought of it. He took time off to ponder the fact, like a galley slave listening aesthetically to the sound the oars made in the water. There was something almost admirable about the skill with which they administered discreet mouthfuls of poison to each other. They were moving back and forth in the kitchen, neatly side-stepping, lifting and laying dishes, and at the same time deftly knocking nails into each other with velvet hammers, while their children were able to dream undisturbed a few feet away. It deserved some kind of award, Cameron reflected. Say, a certificate from the Institute of Masochists.

'You can never make any prolonged attempt to be just a little better than you are. Your stamina always runs out. And you fall back on being nasty. It's so much easier.'

Cameron stacked away the coffee-dishes and returned the leftovers to their respective tins. He became aware sadly that he knew where everything went. Everything in this house had its place, including him. He was labelled indelibly and it was too late to change his destination. He collected two teacups that had strayed from a previous meal and hung them up on their hooks beside the others. The completed row of cups glittered with malice. They waited, along with the biscuit-tins and the paper-rack and the aspirin-bottle, to measure out his life for him. The future came up before him like a fantastic conundrum. How many cups of tea? How many

52

headaches? How many strokes of the brush across his teeth? For what? He seemed caught in a million measurements of his transient futility. Tubes of toothpaste. Rusting razor-blades. Hair-cuts. Nail-parings. Wearing heels, recording a loss that couldn't be recouped with leather. And Allison's voice, patient as a river, eroding him.

'You've always been the same. If I hadn't pushed you, we'd never have got anywhere.'

She was laying the table for breakfast. She did it swiftly and expertly, as she had done it countless times before. Cameron watched the pattern of the four set places emerge on the formica tabletop like a coat-of-arms he could never disown. He wanted to sweep the dishes onto the floor. But he noticed the small pools of water left on the draining-board by the crockery and his hand wiped them with the sponge, locking him into a small necessity. And when that was finished there would be another, and then another, each small necessity opening into another, endlessly.

'Put out the light when you come through,' Allison said.

She put off the gas at the main. That's right, Cameron thought. Keep us safe from other harms. Never be hurt by anything but me. And I'll save all my blood for you. Allison checked off the kitchen with her eyes and went through to the living-room.

Cameron lingered on a moment. He filled a glass with water, drank, and spat into the sink. His mouth still felt scummed. Putting out the light, he walked through to the living-room, where Allison stood, waiting patiently.

As soon as he came in, she started to undress, draping her clothes over the chair that tradition had made hers. The moment he pokered the fire she spoke, as if he had inaugurated the next phase of a ritual.

'When are you going to see about the gas-fire, by the way?'

'I already have.'

'So where is it?'

'Look. You can stuff the domestic catechism. You know damn well. They can't supply the one you want. Remember?'

53

'But when will they?'

'We'll have to wait. They'll install one when they have them in stock.'

'But you haven't even been back in to see them. Of course, you'd rather have a coal-fire anyway.'

'That's right. I prefer the naked flame. Me and the cavemen both. I'm a primitive.'

He was undressing too now, and he padded through to their room in his stockinged feet and fetched his pyjamas and her nightdress.

'It's nothing so romantic,' she said. 'You're just lazy. Look at that last place we were in. I was never as glad to get out of anywhere. Nothing worked. The toilet only flushed when it took the notion. Half the doors didn't shut properly. But you were quite happy with it.'

'I like houses that are humanised with flaws. Anyway, it's too late at night. Don't go into your Rosetta stone routine just now. Fragments of pre-history.'

Cameron stood stripped to the waist, contemplating his stomach. It had softened, though not too much. But at his sides small folds of fat overhung his trousers, an ominous fifth-column. He exercised fitfully for a few seconds before putting on the jacket of his pyjamas.

'I intend to see that everything in this house is the best, anyway. The very best. Even if I have to do it without your help. You would think even for the sake of your children, you would care more. Don't you want the best for them, and for us?'

'Oh yes. For your birthday I'm going to get you a gold-plated thumbscrew. And you can buy me a monogrammed flagella. So I can keep my self-disgust fresh in your absence.'

She was combing her hair. Cameron lit another cigarette. The flame from the match seemed to shoot up like a flare, illuminating a future that stretched infinitely before them, an unbroken plain of such petty quarrels. The thought of it was almost comfortable. There would never be any need for them to find new weaknesses in each other. They knew them all and where to hit them. Similarly, having been hit so often in the same places, they were largely immune to each other. It meant that while they gnawed away they could get on with other things, brushing shoes, drinking tea, reading a paper.

'For one thing, Alice and Helen should be at a fee-paying school. Like Hutchie's. They really should.'

I've had enough, Cameron thought calmly. You'd better stop.

'But you won't hear of it. Why not? Is it just because I want them at one? Is it? Why do you want to spite all of us at every turn? You deprive us of so much. Like a vampire.'

Cameron laughed incredulously.

'Say that again,' he said.

'You're like a vampire,' Allison said defiantly, but she couldn't quite see herself how it applied to him.

Having her attention for a moment, Cameron started to dial on an invisible phone. After a second or so, he lifted the receiver.

'Hello,' he said. 'Doctor? Yes. She's having them again. Same old hallucinations. The old family trait reasserting itself, I'm afraid. Fine, you'll be right round. Will you bring the strait-jacket or shall I?'

The silence that followed seemed as if it would be endless. Allison laid down her comb, sat in her chair, composed herself, and started to cry. Her carefully made up face unfolded like a withered flower. Running mascara spiked her eyes.

Cameron looked at her impassively. His timing had been perfect, his aim flawless. It was the sort of expertise that could only come with long acquaintance. The history of a relationship was a bit like the history of a society. At first it's pretty disorganised. You hurt each other only fitfully. But through time everything gets categorised, centralised. Specialisation sets in. You know exactly where each pain is. Agony is on tap. Grief by the gallon, at the turn of a phrase.

'You know exactly what to say, don't you?'

She looked very ugly. Her voice lisped with slaver and her breathing was noisy. To Cameron, her face seemed no more

55

than a breaking dyke that could barely hold back the snot and phlegm that shifted behind it. Her skin looked about to thaw into a watery pulp.

'I've had to learn,' he said.

It had achieved two things, anyway: it had finished their quarrel, and it proved they were still alive. Her tears were a bitter sort of manna, falling from her eyes like the grace of God. At least they were still sufficiently alive to be hurt by each other. Not all their words were powerless. They weren't quite immune to every truth. Perhaps there was hope for them.

Allison still sat weeping in her underwear like an X-certificate Victorian etching: The Discarded Wife. The ludicrousness of her grief touched a nerve of sympathy that the grief itself had missed. Cameron felt guilty that such bitter tears should seem ridiculous to him. The reason for them was real enough to her, and perhaps his indifference was a measurement of the distance they had put between each other. The chasms that people cleft between themselves were awful, giddy, hardly to be crossed. Sifting, eroding, lives changed irrevocably, stranding people in themselves. It happened imperceptibly, grain by grain, too subtle to be noticed. But hearts were precise seismometers, and every mood, every pain, every disillusion was meticulously recorded, so that people who had once been near enough to touch could turn round and find each other miles away, with gorges that seemed impassable between them. And he and Allison had once been in love with each other. And somehow they still were. Looking at her, he could see one reason why. Her body was marvellously fluent yet. Two children had done no more than soften her hard nubility, add a nuance of more flesh. At thirty-four, her body seemed not to have yielded a pore of its prime. What a waste, he thought, remembering too those other things, of which that body seemed the last survivor, the naturalness, the quick laughter, the easy happiness, the honesty. Those other gifts had not been easily surrendered, had been won from her by long attrition, and partly by his help. What both were, both of them had helped to make, and each was responsible in some sense for the other. Feeling that, he wanted to make love to her, locking them together. All they could do was surrender to each other, go on again and again making that ultimate act of mutual submission, in the hope that from the recurrent ashes of their passion would come some kind of benediction, some kind of grace in the coolness of whose shadow they could meet. If they couldn't irrigate the desert, at least they could lay the dust. Intermittent truce was a sort of substitute for reconciliation. But even as he made to move to her, she spoke.

'It's not for my own sake I worry so much. I can bear it. It's for the children. It's them I want to have everything.'

The mock stoicism blighted his intention instantly, the hypocrisy of it made dust of his desire. He stayed where he was. The game demanded that you forgot temporarily those things about each other you despised. She had pushed her dishonesty in his face, like a scab. He had to wait for disgust to ebb. So passion is schooled by time, chastised by circumstance, and the honesty of lust must learn the devious manners of love. Perhaps that was all love meant: teaching lust to be patient and to work towards the achievement of mutual moments. In the meantime, all he could do in the way of union with her was to acknowledge his own part in what she had become, to admit that he must share it with her, as she must take her share in what he was. As she spoke again, he felt that she was setting up an echo that would never end for him.

'My only worry is the children. And what we can do for them.'

There was the sound of bare feet in the hall and the door opened the way doors do at moments of tension in a film, inching towards revelation. Helen stood there, her hands grubbing in her eyesockets for wakefulness. She unearthed enough vision to see her father and then ran blindly towards him, sticking to him like a burr.

57

'I had a bad dream, daddy,' she said, offering him her defencelessness like a trophy.

She was too sleepy to notice that her mother had been crying. Cameron held her to him for a second, savouring the release of her arrival like a *deus ex machina*, a divine simplification of all their seedy complexities.

'Come on, love,' he said. 'It's all right now.'

He scooped her off her feet and took her out. In the hall, she found she needed the toilet. She let him put on the light for her but closed the door on him, having learned dignity young. As he brought her back, Allison was waiting composedly in the hall and the two of them touched briefly over Helen, as if she was neutral territory.

In her bedroom, Cameron tripped over one of Alice's slippers. When he laid Helen down, she still held on to his neck and her voice disturbed Alice, who wakened briefly, touched her father's arm, and promptly fell asleep again. Cameron remained crouched over the bed while Helen drowsed. The weight of her arms on his neck reminded him of Alice's arms and of Allison's, and of Margaret's. He felt weighted down and trapped by his strangely alloyed loves for all of them, caught in them like golden shackles. And he couldn't imagine any event that would ever provide him with a hammer strong enough to free himself.

7

The clatter of typewriter keys in the main office punctured his concentration like buckshot. He was sitting in Annette's glorified cubicle adjoining Morton's sanctum. Through the glass partition that separated him from the main office, he could see the rows of well groomed girls chained to their tasks, an industrial harem. That noise was all he needed. He had wakened with a head like an open wound, and every sound was salt to it. Now the pain in his stomach was starting up again. It promised to be quite a day.

If Morton breathed on him too heavily, he would break. Whatever he had to say was not going to be pleasant, and Cameron wasn't feeling very fleet of word. It was unfair somehow, Cameron thought. There should be some special dimension in which meetings like this could take place, outside the jurisdiction of headaches, dyspepsia, and tiredness. How could any reasonableness and clarity be achieved through the media of the faulty mechanisms we find ourselves housed in? Sheer physical discomfort must have been the major factor in a lot of decisions. How many courtiers had died of a royal headache? Memo to heaven: revise the rules.

Even the chair he sat in was becoming an instrument of torture. The ribs along the bottom felt as if they were made out of sharpened metal. It would have been ideal furniture for a fakir. If Morton didn't hurry up, the chair would go in with him when he rose. He looked at his watch: half-past nine.

'What time do you make it, Annette?' he asked.

She corroborated his watch, speaking as if she were bestowing the last rites.

'Do you think he's fallen asleep?' he asked, laughing.

59

'*Does* he sleep?' Annette said, and went on working.

She had been about as talkative as a waxwork since he had come in. Perhaps she knew something that he didn't, and thought that disaster was contagious.

The door of Morton's office opened and he smiled affably at Cameron.

'Morning, Mr Cameron. Sorry to keep you waiting. Do come in.' And then, on the other side of the door, 'How are we, Eddie? Sit down. Cigarette?'

The reversible man, morning-coated Mr Morton on the one side, sports suit Sid on the other. He lit Cameron's cigarette and then his own.

'Damn good time last night, by the way. Elspeth enjoyed it thoroughly as well. I like that place of yours.'

'Thanks,' said Cameron; and come out fighting.

But the preliminaries weren't over yet.

'Here. What whisky is that you use again? Lovely stuff.'

Cameron told him, and then let him enthuse some more. The sun was bothering Cameron. It was surprisingly strong, and shone right into his eyes like a searchlight that Morton had hired. His eyes were starting to water. He was glad when Morton wandered to the side of the office, and he could angle his head away from the sun.

'Well then,' Morton said, having decorously interred yesterday. 'Business is business. I thought we'd have a wee get-together this morning. Beat a few things about. Before I forget, Eddie. No sign of that contract from Simpson and Auld yet?'

Cameron's brain shot to attention at the sound of the firm's name, ready with a parade of glib reasons.

'You know how they are,' he laughed, man-to-man.

'Auld you're dealing with, isn't it?'

'That's right, Sid.' He whipped his mind into working. 'Nice wee bloke. Actually, I think I've just about got him to see it my way. But oh dear. Plymouth Brethren, you know. It's like trying to date a nun. I mean, there's nothing he seems to *do*. He eats, right enough. I know that because I've

60

seen him do it. Otherwise, I wouldn't be so sure. But *what* he eats. The last time there. Big restaurant. Plush décor. Scene set. Menu. Wine list. So what does he take? Cheese omelette! Washed down with a flagon of water. Vintage '67. How much bonhomie can you generate on that?'

They both laughed, but Morton's laughter disappeared almost at once into Cameron's so that Cameron was aware of himself laughing alone.

'Yes, I can see what you mean, Eddie,' Morton said. 'But.'

He made no attempt to supply the qualification the conjunction heralded, leaving the word to enlarge in isolation – fanfare without a follow-up. Cameron's mind strained into the inconclusiveness, trying to gain some fore-warning. He felt the silence point at him like a gun, under the menace of which his conscience was emptying its pockets.

'Eddie,' Morton said, and his voice redefined their relationship, its tone no longer chummy, but a chastisement to the wayward. 'Are you happy enough with us?' The sunlight in the room seemed suddenly glacial.

'Sure, Sid. This is a good firm to work with. Really good.'

Cameron tried to convey as much fervour as he could without standing to attention and singing, 'Onward, Christian Salesmen.'

'Uh-huh. And how do you feel things have been going lately? I mean, your work.'

'Oh well. You hit these patches. You know? A bit sticky here and there. But in the main all right.' His laugh was ignored by Morton, as if it had been an alms-cup. 'I'll pull through, I think.'

'Did you know that somebody from Raylex had been seeing Auld?'

'If we don't get the contract, they won't. That's for sure.'

'Where do you get your information, Eddie? A weighing-machine?'

'Look! What do you want me to do? Sleep with him? It wouldn't work. He's Plymouth Brethren.'

'Just sell to him, Eddie. You're sleeping with enough as it is, I imagine.'

The last remark didn't register properly with Cameron because he was busy biting his tongue. He regretted the turn the conversation had taken, feeling he had allowed Morton a chance for open hostility. Even yet, he wasn't very sure how it had happened. Why hadn't he tried to maintain the amicable atmosphere? Betrayed by his headache? It was too late now.

'I'll give it to you square,' Morton was saying, standing now with his back to the window, seeming to Cameron's bruised eyes bigger than any man had any right to be. 'You've been a good man with us, Eddie. Made a lot of contacts. And I like you personally. But two things you'd better realise. One: a salesman who doesn't sell is a liability. That Simpson and Auld contract, for example. A couple of new buildings they're going to have. That's a lot of light, Eddie. You should've had that contract buttoned up.' He went straight on, precluding interruption: 'Two: don't charge your private life to our account, will you?'

'What?'

'Come off it, Eddie. You know what I mean.'

'I haven't a clue what you mean.'

Morton lifted some sheets of paper, flashed them at Cameron, and threw them back on the desk as if it was a litter-bin.

'These expenses. They would do Hans Andersen credit. You've even lost your touch with *them*. I've seen the day when they made convincing reading.'

'Everyone of those damned items is justified.'

'Like hell they are! Don't come scout's honour with me. So a man pares off a wee bit here and there. Fair enough! It's in the game. But this lot. What's this in aid of? You saving up to buy a hotel?'

'I can't operate on a shoe-string.'

'It costs nothing to sell nothing. And that's what you've

62

been selling. Sweet damn all. Right? So it follows that most of these figures belong to your imagination. Right?'

'Rubbish!'

'Hell. When are you going to admit it? I'll have to check my mirror. I must look bloody stupid. I didn't come up the Clyde in a banana-skin. Look! After this, why don't you be honest? Instead of wracking your brain for inspiration: lunch here, a drink there, a book of matches to Messrs This-one-and-that-one – why not just be honest? And write the one expense to which all this money is due. Write it in block bloody capitals: MARGARET SUTTON.'

The name came to Cameron like a translation of something he had heard minutes ago and hadn't understood: 'sleeping with enough as it is'. The familiar room became strange in a second, peopled now with a part of his life he had always kept separate from it. He stood up desperately, as if he could still prevent that fatal confrontation between the halves of himself.

'Margaret Sutton?' he said, and he was sick at the tone of his own voice, which was a betrayal.

Morton said nothing.

'What the hell's she got to do with it?' Cameron followed up, remembering to be angry. 'Who told you about that?'

Cameron suddenly realised that what he had said was confession by default of a denial.

'Her brother. He came to see me. He was trying to be straight about it. Didn't want to queer your pitch at home. So he thought of me. Her family know about it. And they don't like it. It's some mess, Eddie. You'd better get out of it while you can.'

'Mind your own bloody business.'

'That's just what I'm doing. You're obviously not going to do it for me. Get sense, Eddie.'

'Why don't you? It takes a pretty crummy imagination to see any connection between Margaret and my expense sheet. What do you think I do? Pay her thirty bob a time?'

'Listen, Eddie –'

63

'Knock off! Go away and slaver over your Hank Jansen books.'

'Listen! Normally I wouldn't care if one of my blokes was having affairs with half of Sauchiehall Street. A few things make this different. For one, whatever's going on between you and this girl is ballsing you up. You make less and want more. For another, I think I owe it to Allison to try to set you right.'

'Owe it to Allison? What the hell is Allison to you?'

'She's a nice person for a start.'

'Pardon me while I puke. You'll be handing out hymn-sheets in a minute.'

'Don't make it any stickier for yourself than you can help. I'm telling you. Her brother's trying to give you a break. But if you don't drop it, his next stop's Allison. Do you want that? I don't want to see Allison bombed out because some silly wee lassie with itchy knickers fancies herself as Juliet. Think what you're doing, Eddie. And if it does blow up on you, you're out. Don't make any mistake on that score. I've got enough justification here to put you out. And I'll do it. I'm warning you. You'd better ditch her.'

Cameron sat back down, saying nothing. For a moment he thought he was going to be sick. Shame made mush of his stomach. He had thought of shutting Morton's mouth with his fist. But he knew why he hadn't. This lousy job was all the compass he had in his present confusion. Without the assistance of the mechanical sense of direction it gave him, he was paralysed. Perhaps once he had found out where he was and what he had to do, perhaps once he had some kind of landmark to move towards, he could loosen his frantic hold on this job. But not now, not just yet.

So he hung on to it at the cost of so much else: his self-respect, what was left of his dignity, his very self, it seemed. He felt just about small enough to walk out of the room without opening the door. He sat tautly, clenched with self-disgust which had pursued him from that dim lay-by to this room. Its forerunner in both places had been the same young man – a zealous houndsman who was bringing the hounds of Cameron's own contempt nearer and nearer to the centre of his life. Now they had tracked him into this room to tear at him.

Dully he saw what the last few minutes had cost him, and felt weak, as if his loss was measured in his own blood. He had witnessed his secret image of Margaret being fouled in Morton's mouth, and had allowed the small private passion they had generated between them to be scaled down to the terms of a paragaph in the *News of the World*. He had seen his petty deceitfulness laid bare to its ugly, quivering nerves. He had had his grubby, private offal held up to his own nose. That it was Morton's hand which had held it depressed him the more.

He knew with an awful finality that this room marked the point where the two mutually exclusive parts of his life narrowed to meeting, where he was run to earth and had nowhere else to hide. He could only turn and face his own ravening contempt for himself.

'Look, Eddie,' Morton said in his diplomatic voice, reading capitulation in his silence. 'I'm trying to do you a favour. You could still be the best man on our books. I remember you when you started. I should do. I introduced you to this job. I mean I feel as if I've got a stake in you.'

Round about the heart, Cameron thought.

'And I've always helped you in the past, haven't I? Every way I could. You know, you owe me something too.'

'I wish there was some way I could repay you,' Cameron said. 'Like giving you share of my insomnia.'

But it was a remark that gave him no satisfaction, a last upsurge of petty rancour, a sop to his own bitterness, soaked in the vinegar of his disgust with himself. Morton magnanimously ignored it.

'I'll tell you something else,' he said. 'My own job is going to be vacant. Not very long from now, either. Prove yourself, and I'm with you. I tell you what. Get back to form. Land this contract with Simpson and Auld. And there's another job I want you to tackle. Dumfries. But after this one. You see, I've still got confidence in you.'

'Who knows? You might even give me a proficiency badge.'

'Save the clever talk for the customers. That's what I don't get about you, Eddie. Your one commodity's your mouth. And you only use it in all the wrong places. That's it, anyway. I've been fair with you. Take it or leave it.'

The parley was over. Cameron was now quite calm. He knew that he was taking it, although what he was taking was not necessarily what Morton was giving. Morton's glibness was translated for Cameron into his own desperate discontent. What he was taking at Morton's hands was simply himself as he had been forced to acknowledge himself to be. He realised that what he had been angry at and bitter about was not Morton or what he had said, but himself. His anger had been merely a denial of that self, and now he accepted it to make what he could of it. He would have to face his life honestly and try to put the pieces of it together into a coherent pattern in which he could see himself.

'I'll be getting in touch with Auld today,' Cameron said quietly.

'Fine!' Morton said. 'That's the boy.'

Morton went on talking for a little while, reestablishing a semblance of normal contact between Cameron and himself. Cameron nodded and agreed a lot. When Morton finally showed him out of the office, Annette could see nothing significant in the way they parted from each other, although she was looking closely enough. But when she tried to add her smile to Morton's cheerio, Cameron didn't seem to notice it.

Outside, Cameron wandered aimlessly about the streets for a time, taking a detour to duty, as if he was paying a nostalgic tribute to himself as he had been. The hammer had hit. Already the shackles were weakening. He was finding that he was terrified of freedom.

66

8

'Sutton and Son – Colour Printers.' The traffic-warden couldn't remember having seen the van before. It was pulled in about thirty yards from the school gates. The driver had come out a few minutes ago and tested the tyres with a kick. Twenty-four, -five. Turtle-necked sweater. Better-wear hair-style. They should never have done away with National Service. Would have made a man of him. Probably waiting for a pupil. Plenty of room in the back of that van. The things the young people thought of nowadays. Old men before their fathers. There was the bell. Prepare to repel boarders. The warden took up his position at once, knowing that the first onslaught was always the worst.

School came out according to a spontaneous caste system. First were the junior classes, storming freedom, whooping like Highlanders, skirmishing with schoolbags, while the warden stood like Canute, a lollipop for a sceptre. Behind them came pupils of about third year, talking loudly in cliques, a few boys shouting rough nothings at girls from a safe distance, courting by megaphone. Minutes later, when the playground was sufficiently cleared, the senior pupils emerged, many of them in couples, one with a copy of Kafka sticking out of his pocket, another holding an L.P. of Joan Baez like a shield. Throughout it all, teachers had been hurrying to catch buses or edging their cars through the gate.

Margaret was one of the last to leave the building. She felt rather tired. Her last class had been IC. They were quite good but inclined to be irrepressible at the end of a day, sensing release. They could knock holes in your discipline if you weren't careful and she had felt a bit like the Dutch boy plugging the dyke. By the end of the period she had been running out of fingers.

She thanked the warden for conducting her across the road. He was very nice, and that gesture of seeing her to the other pavement had become part of her day. The latest grapplings of IC with the French language weighed heavy in her brief-case. She didn't notice the van but as she passed it the near-side door slid open and a voice said, 'Margaret!'

'John?' she asked herself.

He was leaning across the passenger seat with his hand on the door-handle.

'Come in,' he said.

'I've got a bus to catch round the corner, John.'

'Come in. You'll catch your bus.'

She looked round automatically to see Dawson of fourth year watching her. She got in. John started up the van and pulled away.

The sensation of abduction that surrounded the whole inci-dent fitted in with the rest of her day. Shunted from class to class, from textbook to textbook, from question to question, she felt as if she had lost herself in transit. She had passed like a refugee through a series of alien impressions, none of which seemed to belong significantly to her. The uses of 'qui'. An extract from *Lettres de Mon Moulin*. Gibberish in the staff-room: 'They expect to pass without doing any work. It's the same old story.' Shepherd's Pie cooling in the clamour of the dining-hall. Mary Sim crying because someone called her 'four eyes'. And now this musty van, with John sitting sourly beside her, venting his spleen on the gear-stick. And the back of the van containing a couple of incomprehensible packages, and a smell of new print, sinister in the memories it evoked. What was she doing here? Presumably John knew and would tell her. As they turned the corner, she saw her bus-stop ahead.

'That's where I get my bus, John,' she said.

He pulled up about twenty yards before it and stopped the

68

engine. A bus overtook them and halted at the stop, but she didn't move.

'Well,' he said. 'Are you not even going to ask how they're keeping?'

It took a moment for her mind to focus.

'Mother and father? How are they?'

'In a terrible state. That's how they are.'

'Does my mother's back still bother her?'

'Oh, we can do without the polite questions. You know what I mean. They know about you. Did you know that? They know about you.'

'I wonder who could've told them.'

'I told them. All right. Do you think I enjoyed doing it? But I'd rather it came from me than somebody else. That would've killed them. So don't blame me. I had to do what I did.'

'It doesn't really matter, anyway.'

'It doesn't really matter, anyway.' He mimicked her voice like a schoolboy. That and the melodrama of his belief in the lethal capacities of the word 'adultery' made her feel a lot more than five years older than he was. 'How can you say that? This thing's split up our family.'

'That's not true, John. I was out of the house long before I met Eddie.'

'You would've been back by now.'

'You can believe that if you want.'

'You would've been back, all right. You would've been back.'

The words were a door slammed in the face of reason. There was no point in bruising her knuckles. She recognised their father's mode of argument in John. A mystic belief in the power of repetition. Keep saying it and it would become true. She had suffered too much already from conflict with it to want to engage it again. It still shook her to remember how close she had come to surrendering, and accepting the dogma that came from her father's mouth. It wasn't that her father's manic repetition of the laws of life made them come true, but

69

it certainly made them seem to come true, so that you found yourself almost acknowledging them automatically.

'I saw him, you know.' John's thumb played across the horn as if longing to blast it in sheer anger. 'Your boy-friend. I saw him close-up. He's no oil-painting.'

It was sad to listen to your own brother talking like this. She had never heard him being as petty or as stupid before. Why was he doing it? He sat morosely twiddling his thumb, thinking up more fourth-form insults. She was surprised at the length of his hair. That was something new. Perhaps he was beginning to rebel against their father, too. From small beginnings. . . . But then there was nothing in the scriptures about the length of your hair.

She wondered for a moment if her father had sent him. But it didn't seem likely. Too much like weakness. Her mother perhaps. But when she thought of that wan water-colour of a woman, paling with every year that went by, she couldn't imagine her forming a decision that wasn't her husband's first, let alone one that went contrary to his wishes.

'I spoke to him too. Told him exactly what I thought of him.'

The self-righteousness was a replica of his father's, blotching him like a birthmark.

'You did what?' The anger in her voice flustered him, but he went on, defiant as a wayward child.

'I told him what I thought of him. I didn't miss him. He had nothing to say for himself either.'

Eddie hadn't told her. She felt a need to apologise to him.

'What right have you got to speak to him?' She struggled for words to fit her humiliation and anger. 'Keep your mealy mouth off anything concerning me. Did your daddy tell you what to say?'

'You can't talk. You're just a whore!'

The word had a fine biblical ring in his mouth. She felt he would have liked to add 'of Babylon'. She slid open the door. A woman was passing with a small child who dangled from her mother's hand like an afterthought, hopping between the lines of the paving-stones.

'Margaret!' His voice was lost between pleading and hatred of himself for having to plead. 'Please don't. Please. I'm sorry.'

The woman with the child was looking back and Margaret slid the door shut again. He really wanted her to stay. Why? What was going on behind that crumpled face? He looked utterly crestfallen. The apology must have been hard for him. Where had he learned to do it? Not from his father. She felt sorry for him and angry with him at the same time. She had invested a lot of affection in him for many years and it came to this. She couldn't look at him without embarrassment. He was so stunted somehow, nowhere near to being a man, a waste of unexplored ideas and unsounded longings. It occurred to her that he might be getting a vicarious thrill out of being involved in all this, and she loathed herself for thinking of it. But he inspired such thoughts.

'You should come back home, Margaret,' he said forlornly. 'For your own sake.'

The last words were like a motto learned from their father. Slogan of the self-righteous: 'It's all for your own good.' They brought back so much to her. Oh, why was he talking to her at all? Didn't he know that he couldn't influence her? All he was doing was bringing that past back into her present. And God knows she had fought hard enough to get away from it. 'Come back home.' Where he lived wasn't a home. It was a hothouse for neuroses. He was a living warning against going back there. It had almost driven her mad before. Once was enough.

She wished he hadn't come here at all today. All he had achieved was to remind her that she couldn't look at her own brother without seeing an oddity. Her eyes filled suddenly with tears, as much for her own disillusionment as for anything else. For she realised that she saw her family with irrevocable objectivity. And that was a frightening thing, begetting a terrible loneliness. For no one, she knew, should

71

ever look upon his own from completely outside love. That was the thing she could never forgive them for. They had driven her out of the range of their love to make peace with herself in a cold place, from which she saw with ice-cold clarity her father's bigoted cruelty, her mother's futility, and her brother's incurable weakness. She had had to understand these things to survive in herself. And the knowledge had excluded her from them for good, and from much more than them.

'He'll never marry you, you know.'

'Oh stop it, John. Don't talk about things you know nothing about.'

'Perhaps I don't know a lot. We're not all university graduates. But I know the difference between right and wrong.'

Why did he have to keep shoving his private pains in her face? Every sentence uncovered another wound. He still smarted under the magnified misfortune of not having gone to university. Memories came to her of the gloom in the house at the time and her father's brave face on things, as if it was all a divine visitation on them. She didn't want to remember. She couldn't bear to sit any longer watching John struggle feebly in his self-imposed strait-jacket, cutting himself on imaginary obstacles.

'I've missed another bus already,' she said. 'I'll have to go, John.'

'Listen,' he said. 'My mother and I want you to come back home. That's why I came here today. We can still make it all right with my father. But this is your last chance, Margaret. It's your last chance.'

'Goodbye, John,' she said. 'I hope my mother's all right.'

As she went blindly away from him, he called after her, 'It's a sin! It's a sin you're committing!' She kept staring ahead, not wanting to see if anyone had heard him.

At the bus-stop she set down her brief-case. She looked up as he went past, but he avoided seeing her. She was thankful he hadn't stopped again. She felt abandoned standing alone at the bus-stop and in her sadness only one thought sustained her: Eddie. She let the thought of him swell until it filled the vacuum of her life. Instead of a family, Eddie. Instead of a husband, Eddie. Instead of emptiness, Eddie. Eddie. Eddie.

9

'You're next, Mister,' the fat woman said, her cigarette snowing another fall of ash across her coat. The 'No Smoking' sign hung officiously above her head, but nobody offered to enforce it.

Cameron looked round the others to see if there were any rivals for precedence.

'Oh, it's you, right enough,' she reassured him. 'An' Ah'm efter ye. Then it's you, hen. Then the young fella. An' the rest o' ye can fight it oot among yersel's.'

They all met her remark with a laugh, a united front in which each one's personal contribution – malice, mockery or embarrassment – was expunged in anonymity. Sly, masonic smiles were exchanged. A big man, drumming on his knees with hands that looked as if they had been acquired in a quarry, nodded at the placard forbidding smoking and winked to Cameron. Cameron produced a smile like a blank cheque, not sure what he was subscribing to. All he could think of was that the big man saw some sort of Damoclean potential in the sign.

'He should hiv the appointments thingmy by noo, anyway,' the fat woman went on through the medium of a girl who was sitting beside her. The girl was unresponsive enough to be almost inanimate but the fat woman had taken to using her as a kind of microphone through which she could make her announcements to the company. 'The rest o' the doctors is using appointments noo. A lot less bother an' time. The time it takes tae see a doctor noo. Ye could come in here wi' the hives an' be sufferin' fae the chinge o' life by the time yer turn come.'

The big man elected to champion their tacit distaste.

'He'll no' need an appointments system as long as you're here tae keep us a' right,' he said, looking round for applause.

'Aye. True enough. Ah keep ma een open. You came in last, didn't ye?'

The retort, intrinsically feeble, was dynamised by the fat woman's decisiveness. She had the kind of conviction that some people inherit with their pores. Hers was that regal manner that seems to make a natural law out of what would merely be an attitude in someone else. Now her raucous voice set up in the room a small sirocco of scorn before which the big man's challenge had to wither. The silence of the others seemed to constrain them to be a synod that ratified her ruling: one of the most shameful roles that human nature could assume was that of being last in a doctor's surgery. One or two secretly and selfishly gave thanks that they hadn't come in last. The big man crept in behind his crushed smile, bleeding self-esteem.

Cameron could sense the conspiracy of distaste regrouping round the fat woman. They were all mutely linking prejudices against her untidy, obtrusive presence. There wasn't a tremor of response to register her next few remarks. Their tight-lipped unity was almost tangible, and as solid as a wall, one mortared out of mediocrity. That was the basis of their resentment. They had come to wait with one another in this room where the yellow light lay on them like leprosy and they wished to remain anonymous, not to be impinged upon, not to have any share in anyone else. That was their right. They weren't here as themselves but merely as portmanteaux for their illnesses.

The attitude these strangers took towards the fat woman was merely a lower form of the one that Margaret's brother and Sid Morton had adopted towards him. The latter was more sophisticated, represented a further stage of evolution, but both had their origins in the same primeval social slime, the noxiousness of which must have permeated the doings of the first men who came darkly and uncertainly together,

75

underpinning them like the law of a bastard divinity: death to the different. Margaret's brother might convince himself that he was motivated by brotherly love or Christian morality; Morton might plead disinterested concern for Allison or the demands of business competence. But the malevolence that had burned in the eyes of both was the same fire, though the fuel might differ.

Cameron felt a sense of kinship with the fat woman that he could hardly have articulated for her. But he felt also one overwhelming difference. Her certainty in herself was impervious to external influences. In contrast, his own somnolent sense of identity had wakened to find itself paralysed with compromise, bound by minor commitments like a million threads, trapped in an accidental context that fitted as close as a coffin. For the past week he had been struggling futilely, unable to make a positive move. He had painstakingly tried to separate the strands of his confusion and only succeeded in snarling it further. Every time he moved towards a decision, he was baulked by another question. Was it escape from himself that he was looking for in Margaret? Was it better for Alice and Helen to live in a covertly rotten marriage or grow up through an overtly broken one? Was it humanity or cowardice that paralysed him? The convolutions of such questions compounded themselves with others until no values seemed extricable from their complexity. Concepts like 'love' and 'identity' and 'right' and 'decision' became enfeebled in the face of his recalcitrant situation, were meaningless simplifications, paper principles, incapable of shearing through the toughness of reality, crumbling on contact.

He could see no meaning, nothing that fixed a significant pattern on his problem. There were only the accidental fragments of his life, marriage to Allison, meetings with Margaret, a job to do, Alice and Helen to care for, a gnawing discontent, rattling together in a cosmic void, colliding but never connecting. The only unifying force was time, imposing a kind of order with fragile arbitrary rivets that shut out chaos. Tomorrow the men were coming to install a gas fire. Sometime this week he was to see Auld again. Alice was soon to have a birthday party. When he was out of here, he would visit his father, as he did once a week. After that, he would collect Jim Forbes and they would go to the Dalmeath Burns Supper.

The familiar urge came on him to get up and go somewhere, do something, as if mere movement could conjure up direction. But where was there that he could go? To see his father? To collect Jim Forbes? Dalmeath? Every other place seemed as pointless as this one. His life was like a series of ante-rooms through which he wandered, seeking admittance to the place where the real decisions were being made and he might be able to influence their course, while commitments interceded like petty officials, diverting him from room to aimless room. Like this one. Cold and remote, irrelevant as a star. Dispensing instant anonymity from its distempered walls. From behind the closed door of the doctor's surgery came murmured voices, pain or worry, perhaps incipient death, reduced to a decorous incomprehensibility while the others waited their turn, patient as cattle, having divested individuality at the door. Except for the fat woman.

She nodded now to Cameron as the door of the surgery opened and a young woman came out. Cameron smiled to the fat woman, seeing in her squat assurance hope for his own uncertainty, went in and closed the door. The doctor had his back to him, washing his hands.

'Please sit down,' he said without turning round to the anatomy that had entered. Cameron sat down on the black leather couch along the wall. He reflected that if what he had was a cancer his situation would be simplified.

'Ah, it's yourself,' Dr Culley said incontrovertibly.

Having had him as his doctor for as long as he could remember, Cameron recognised prevarication in the decisive tones. Behind their glasses, Dr Culley's tired eyes were sifting Cameron's face for an old symptom to remember him by. Cameron felt like flashing his appendix scar.

'Edward Cameron, esquire.' Dr Culley laughed, as if

77

formality was wit. 'And what brings you out on a night like this? Not the same complaint as your wife, I hope. Or non-complaint. That's a long time ago. Could hardly be. She'll be relieved, eh? Have you in *The Lancet* then, all right. Eh? You look fit enough. But appearances can be deceptive. Eh?'

Cameron didn't understand Dr Culley's references to his wife. Had Allison been here? He couldn't remember her mentioning such a thing within the past couple of years. But there was no point in trying to pursue it. Besides the fact that Dr Culley could be mistaking him for five other people, his professional small talk was as generalised as an income tax form. It must have been more or less standard for everyone and it was bound to contain a lot that had no relevance to the person in immediate receipt of it. It was up to his listener to delete mentally whatever did not apply.

'It's my stomach again,' Cameron said, helpless to prevent a fleeting sense of personal failure at the doctor's expression, as if he should have had better control of his mutinous anatomy.

'Playing you up,' the doctor confirmed, applying a euphemism to his fears like a salve. 'Uh-huh. Spasmodic pains. I see. Heartburn quite frequently. Of course. Nothing that can't be dealt with.'

The doctor had just wrapped Cameron's vague dread in his own confidence like a polythene bag, ready for disposal. His reassurances were so deft that they unnerved. There was a frightening neutrality about the eyes as if they inhabited a place where all facts were of equal stature and could be reacted to on the same standard issue terms. It was as if the layman's rabble of uncertain responses to sickness – fear, pity, desperation, awe – had been replaced by a bureaucracy of competence – diagnosis, reassurance, prognosis – that would broadcast its instructions from his brain in the same relentless tone of mechanical sanity regardless of the circumstances. Since he was a man who worked the borderline between the ordinary and the terrible, who could translate a commonplace into a death, and could translate death into a commonplace, through long usage sickness had imparted some of its callousness, its deadening monotony to him, but he had also taught sickness some of his own calmness, his practicality, his smallness.

'Sometimes better not to fuss these things too much. A lot of the time surgery's better left. But this has been a while. A long time. Eh?'

Again he ended with that trick of speech that Cameron had learned to respond to like a dotted line: answer should be inserted here.

'Yes. Years anyway. I don't know how many. Seven? Eight?'

'Long enough. And you've watched what you were eating. The way I told you. It's a while since you were here. Eh?'

'Well, I've been feeling pretty good for a long time. Until just lately. Worse than ever now.'

'Lie down on the couch and pull up your shirt, please.'

While the doctor's fingers pressed coldly around his rib-cage, Cameron stared up at a tree leafing out of the darkness beyond the surgery window. It was raining again and one leaf like the green tongue of a gargoyle was vomiting a steady trajectory of raindrops against the window.

'Just say where you feel it sore. Some night. Bang goes my golf tomorrow if it's like this. Do you play? Nothing there? I see there's been flooding in the south of England.'

The soft fingers manipulated an appropriate gasp from Cameron.

'Yes. Well, you can make yourself respectable again.'

As Cameron stuffed his shirt back into his trousers, he felt some obligation to add his own pennyworth of platitudes to the occasion.

'Do you never think of using an appointments system, Dr Culley? Save a lot of waiting.'

Dr Culley, who was seated again over a form, looked up at Cameron pityingly.

'Here?' He nodded towards the waiting-room. 'Most of the patients I have wouldn't know what that meant. If you'd

79

dealt with them as long as I have, you'd know. Completely irresponsible. They'd put it off for the bingo if it suited them. No. Better to have them wait out there. Queues are something they understand.'

Cameron had unwittingly brushed a sore. It surprised him to watch about thirty years of disillusionment well out of it. Something happened to you when you observed people too long from a professional standpoint. The persistence of your gaze dehumanised them until their individualities froze into generalisations, which were easier to cope with.

'Address?' the doctor asked.

Cameron told him and gave him the rest of the information he wanted. Dr Culley completed the form, licked the gummed edges, sealed it, and handed it across.

'Post this when you go out, eh? You'll get word back. A few days or so. To report for an x-ray. For the time being, eat often and little. You know what to avoid. Eh? Don't bother about your will just now. You'll live.'

'Right, doctor. Thank you.'

As Cameron came out, the doctor was back over his wash-hand-basin, kneading at his hands as ineffectually as Lady Macbeth, while the fat woman lumbered in to soil them again.

There was a postbox near his father's house and Cameron decided to post his form there. When he got out of the car, it was still raining. Protecting the address with his hand he dropped the letter into the box, despatching one worry along with it. He had done all he could do about that for the time being. His case was being considered.

His father took some time to answer the door. Cameron knew why. His father was in the basement, working. The thought came to Cameron like the first stage of a scientific reaction, given which, the rest could be calculated to within a few phrases of variability. Past experience had proven that the proportion of vocal silences to actual silences would remain more or less constant. He and his father, Cameron reflected on his dry island of doorstep, were like a formula for vapourising time. The door opened.

'Hullo, Eddie. I'm in the workshop.'

Cameron closed the door and followed his father along the hall and down the home-made staircase into his improvised workroom, which was a cement square salvaged from the foundations. The lowness of the wooden ceiling (a floor in reverse) enforced a bowed posture of humility that fitted Cameron's body round his mood. For this place had always shamed him a little, as if he were a eunuch in a harem. Rough lengths of timber lay bedded together, disappearing into the darkness below the house, a dormitory of sleeping purposes that his father's fingers would awaken; a rack of tools above the workbench waited for uses Cameron could barely imagine; remnants of old furniture, bits of metal, subtractions from broken implements lay all round like challenges to ingenuity – all indicted Cameron's own manual incompetence, made his hands feel like redundancies, only good for wearing gloves. As if in self-justification, his hands automatically took out a cigarette and lit it.

'How are you coming along then?' he asked.

His father hadn't looked up from the oblong of wood he was chiselling.

'Fine, Eddie. Fine.'

Cameron hadn't bothered to finalise the application of his question in his own mind, and therefore didn't know whether he had been asking his father about the work he was doing or about something more general, like his life. But it didn't really matter. Their voices were no more than a kind of background music, inarticulate as whistling. That was how his father used words, to take up the slack of his attention, a necessary residue of waste, as incidental to his purpose as the falling slivers of wood.

'What's this you're making then?'

'What do you think?'

As far as Cameron could see, he was making a smaller piece of wood out of a bigger one.

81

'Tray?'

'Table. Occasional table. It's for Allison. Don't tell her though. Lovely bit of wood I got. Feel it.'

Leaning over, Cameron hit the light-bulb with his head, and shadows raged suddenly around them.

'Terrific,' Cameron said, bringing off a pollen of wood on his fingers. 'Lovely grain.'

His father's raised hand exorcised the furious shadows with one sacerdotal gesture.

'Wee ones all right?'

'Yes. Great. Badly behaved as ever. Everything okay at the work?'

Cameron used the chisel-strokes for punctuation.

'It's still there.'

The wind was moaning like a foundling outside the house and Cameron could imagine the rain sheeting between here and Dalmeath. The night was roughening. But in the basement there was only the occasional quivering of the light-flex, small as the tremor in a barometer-needle.

'You seen Stan Gilbertson lately?' His father pared the question off slowly from the centre of his involvement and let it fall like a wood-flake.

'Is he still about?'

'Saw him this week. Tuesday, I think.' Knowing his father was going to say more, Cameron let him work on in silence as if he was teasing his next comment out of the timber. 'Still has his wee bookshop. Says he would have you back again anytime.'

Cameron wasn't normally nostalgic but there were parts of his past that certain memories kept haloed in light like lamp-posts. Looking back, it was these patches of clarity that he remembered. Working for Stan Gilbertson was one of them. He had been almost a year in the bookshop, having just finished National Service. Coming back from the rarified atmosphere of post-war Berlin, he had experienced a sort of weightlessness without his uniform that had detached him from his life, left him floating ineffectually among solidities that he could not grasp. Berlin had been a weird occurrence in his life, insubstantial as a dream in which there material-ised strange faces that had no background, strange rooms that had no history, in which there happened copulations so casual and so numerous that features melted like candle-grease to a blurred and pallid anonymity, in which the only identity was a common wick of hunger that burned in every body. He still came across stray moments from those times that had remained scribbled across his mind like hieroglyphs of human suffering; waking into a room that he had never seen before, in which a small boy dressed only in a vest stood laughing through the bars of his cot to where Cameron and his mother lay together; a young girl leaving a dance-hall, submitting to the anticipatory maulings of two soldiers; a mother rousing him with a cup of tea after he had made love to her daughter. Returning from that limbo, he had been lost in a world of solid relationships, and glad of Stan Gilbertson's offer – made because he knew his father – to come and work in his bookshop. The bookshop had provided a temporary refuge from which Cameron had managed to get in touch with himself again. There hadn't been much to do and Cameron had read and thought towards himself more than he had ever done since. In many ways he seemed paradoxically to have been nearer to himself than he had ever been again. Until Morton, whom he had known at school, re-appeared like Mephistopheles, promising him more money.

'Of course, he couldn't pay you anything like you're getting now.' His father whittled cautiously towards whatever point he was trying to make. 'But then Stan's wearing on too. I think he would like somebody like you to carry on the shop. A good wee business.'

His father seemed reluctant to leave the subject. Cameron wondered if his father knew how much he hated being a sales-man. It was impossible to tell. There wasn't much you could tell about Cameron's father. The externals of his life formed a succession of smooth surfaces like closed doors, behind which his privacy dwelt unmolested. He had worked in the offices of the same firm for forty-odd years; he had served in Italy during the war; he had married late; he had always provided well for his wife and son; he attended church regularly, but had refused an eldership. Cameron had never been close to him. Shortly after his mother's death thirteen years before, Cameron had heard during the night a sound like weeping from his father's room. Next morning whatever wounds there were ached invisibly behind a bland face. He vaguely suspected that his father was disappointed in him. But perhaps his father's disappointment was less local. Certainly he seemed always to present that air of distracted patience to most situations, as if the world was a funeral which he had been forced to attend.

Only in this room was he ever fully involved. It was the shadowy stithy to which he brought all his crippled frustrations and hammered them out into pleasant shapes, trays, tables, picture-frames, step-ladders, toys for the children. That was why he wouldn't sell this house, though it was now far bigger than he needed. It was full of himself, a museum of the forms he had given to his private pains.

Cameron wondered about those pains. He had never known what they were. His father had found his personal language for them. Perhaps that's what everyone had to do. But Cameron knew that he had no such language, no means by which to express his own frustrations, to externalise his hunger. All he could do was to hire them out to the successive situations that crossed his path as aimlessly as tarts, let them drain his energy, dissipate it in pointlessness. There was always such a situation to hand. The past week had been full of them enabling him to avoid facing Margaret. Dalmeath was another one.

He watched his father for a moment longer, fascinated by that complete preoccupation of others which always mesmerizes.

'I'll have to go, father,' he said.

'Already? You don't want anything? Tea or what?'

His father didn't really want to leave what he was doing.

'No. Thanks. I've got a Burns Supper tonight. A bloke to pick up.'

'All right then.'

'I'll see myself out. See you. All right?'

'Right, Eddie. Cheerio.'

He left his father still smoothing the edges of the wood. As he prepared to head for Dalmeath, he didn't feel that he was going towards anything at all, but merely away, always away, away from Margaret, away from Allison, from himself. As he opened the door, the rain made a grey void of the night.

I O

Dalmeath was a small town the two big mills of which materialised suddenly out of green Ayrshire countryside like a William Blake nightmare. Originally agrarian, it had industrialised suddenly and dramatically, the two mills dwarfing the rustic church, hailing the millennium of Mammon. But the new god had proved no less dilatory than the old and the place had frozen into a dreamy ambivalence, part village, part town. Men working the machines in the mills could look out of the dusty windows and see cattle gnaw the hillsides, the herds shifting by the hour into changing patterns of perpetuity. Grass infiltrated the flagstones of outlying pavements. Dalmeath, like a hopeless lover, embraced contrarities simultaneously, daily cleansed the waste wool with its river, held dogrose dying of fumes, was a cankered idyll.

Towards the end of January in every year the small town hall was ceremonially prepared for the Burns Supper. Tables shrouded in white table-cloths made up three sides of an oblong. A cyclostyled sheet containing programme and menu lay amid the cutlery at each place. Both menu and programme were invariable from year to year, like sacrament and sermon. Beginning with the 'tappit hen' (a free drink from the pub next door), it proceeded through a plain meal of haggis, champit tatties and bashed neeps, to a series of speeches of soporific banality. Yet each year the hall was crowded and each year men left bearing word of uproariously pleasurable evenings that could stir envy in the absentees. The same faces were trained, attentive as spaniels, year after year on speakers whose features might vary but whose words were interchangeable. The secret lay perhaps in the bottles of whisky

86

that had been brought in from the pub. The disappearance of their contents, mixed with milk, water, or nothing more mitigating than air, offered an incidental measurement of the evening's passing that was in inverse ratio to the amount of uncritical goodwill in the hall. As the levels of the whisky bottles dropped, spirits rose. Platitudes were solemnly expounded and applauded as revelations. Men who never contemplated poetry from one year to the next listened to reciters as if they were so many burning bushes. The image of Burns, Scotland's own Jack of all men, would recede further and further until it vanished altogether, leaving a roomful of men wallowing in a vague euphoria, secreted out of themselves, with smiles tacky as molasses stuck to their teeth.

This night was no exception. Cameron, alienated from the others by his mood and confined to moderation by his need to drive, looked with bread-and-water coldness upon the orgiastic degeneration of the rest. He felt like an adult obliged to supervise the rumpus of a children's party, and Jim Forbes proved to be one of his more objectionable charges. Jim performed a one-man opera of reactions throughout the night: table-thumping in tune to the chairman's eulogies, staring determinedly into clichés like crystal balls, hear-hearing at the heels of small quotations, his gestures enlarging towards climax until the toast to 'The Lassies' brought him to a crescendo of appreciation, guffawing, burbling, choking, defenceless against the deft assaults of wit, raped by whimsy.

Cameron, adrift in his own worries, never let his attention wander for long from the clock on the opposite wall. He watched the slow swathe of the minute-hand reap the evening and took satisfaction from the inexorably following hour-hand, stacking time away in neat units of boredom. By eight o'clock his half-cold haggis still cooled on his plate, seeming to enlarge with every incision, like a culinary hydra. He stapped it into his mouth in defiant forkfuls till his craw capitulated. At half-past eight the big man who was proposing 'The Immortal Memory' was in full flutter. 'And that lad who was born in Kyle, that self-same lad, no different – it must have seemed – from you or me, that farmer has since sown his words throughout the length and breadth of the world and today, more than 160 years later, the nations of the world still discuss them.' The crop, of course, is corn. Depreciating yield. A ton of chaff to every grain of sense. Five minutes to nine produced an omen. A short, florid man (farmer, Cameron had decided) his nose a dull ember of past alcoholic excesses, applauded his whisky glass onto the floor and muttered 'Skol!' The incident was notice of eviction served on sobriety. By ten past nine a guttural rendering of *Tam O' Shanter* was being given. The gestures that accompanied every line were comprehensive enough to convey the gist of the text to a deaf-mute. The poem emerged immortal as Venus from a sea of saliva. At twenty-five past nine the singing started. Three solos, then what appeared to be spontaneous choric singing. A vocal foxhunt, a yelp of voices tilting in full cry after elusive notes. Somewhere, at the other end of the hall from Cameron, a singing sapper, persistent subterranean base, vanishing from time to time to reappear on another octave and undermine a high note. In the middle of the second chorus of 'A man's a man for a' that,' the roseate farmer, his nose now stoked to a glow of incandescent veins, quaffed down a farewell dram, set his glass ceremoniously on the table, and crashed, chair and all, onto his back, where he lay in well-earned repose, mission accomplished. The clock counted ten. When they had finished the song, those nearest him set up his chair and tried to fit him into it. But his bones were in oblivion. He ran liquidly through their fingers, a suitful of quicksilver, resolving himself into various mocking poses on the floor. In the end they left him there, carried back a bit from the table so that their feet wouldn't disturb him, his hands crossed peacefully on his chest giving him a vaguely Pharaonic look. His premature departure cost him what was later to be called the 'highlight' of the evening by those who remained to enjoy it – the toast to 'The Lassies'. This was delivered in short sniping bursts that evoked answering cannonades of laughter. The speaker was obese, putty face mounted on acres of rolling cloth, and a lot of the laughter came from his posing as a lady's man. One enormous fore-finger upraised perpetually, a chubby phallus, he seemed to hang from it, quivering under the flagella of his own dirty jokes. Cameron reflected, not for the first time, that obscenity only becomes offensive when chaperoned by gentility. By twenty to eleven it was over except for a few groups dividing out the remains of the night in drunken dollops of conversation. In a weary voice, basted with drink and loud singing, someone was urging Mary Morison to be at her window. At ten to eleven Cameron suggested to Jim, who was engaged in a duet of monologues with a stranger, that they should go. By eleven o'clock they were standing in the doorway of the town hall, contemplating the weather.

A man who was sitting behind them in the doorway as if that was where he lived said, 'The storm withoot might rair and rustle, eh?'

Cameron said, 'Yes.'

'Weather by courtesy of Alfred Hitchcock,' Jim said to the resident of the doorway but he appeared not to hear.

The wind rampaged around them in fitful, tidal fury, threatening to break the two trees in front of the town hall from their moorings, drifting glintering shoals of raindrops past the lampposts. A dustbin-lid cymballed climax to an unseen gust.

'Wait till you hear Eileen,' Jim said. 'She wanted me to bring a coat.'

His voice was mournful, his shoulders hunched elegiacally against the rain. The rutting odour of the mead-hall was behind him. Ahead was the nagging monotony of domesticity.

'You wait and I'll fetch the car over,' Cameron consoled.

He sprinted through the crystal flak of rain across the road to the car-park. When he stopped outside the town hall with the door open, Jim skittered through puddles, cowled in his jacket, into the car in a whiff of damp cloth.

'Still,' Jim said as they moved off. 'Rain or no rain. What a night! Man, what a night!'

89

Cameron silently agreed. The wipers swished wearily, sluggish as oars in a heavy sea. Since he knew this part of Ayrshire, having been born a few miles from Dalmeath, Jim was navigator.

'The right fork, Eddie,' he said. 'It's quicker.'

'This isn't the way we came, is it?'

'No, but it's quicker.'

The headlights tore a tunnel of light out of the darkness ahead of them where the raindrops dizzied like motes of diamond. Into that never-ending, self-made tunnel they moved, creating a way for themselves out of nothing as they went. The rest was a suspirating canopy of darkness, gnash of branches, wind sough, enclosing in quick oblivion those fragments of itself their lights revealed, tree-thresh, blown grasses, white ghost of a gate barring the way to nothing.

Demisting the windscreen periodically with his hand, Cameron felt a sense of rightness about the way the night had peeled to this black kernel. The quips, the leers, the instant camaraderie, the mush of small talk, all had fallen away to bring him to this moment with his headlights drilling him through the darkness to the core of his problem, where the worm of disgust was gnawing. The rest was rind. With whatever mattered, with whatever he had to decide, he was alone. Let him decide now in his loneliness.

'Wait till you hear Eileen, though,' Jim said, slumped thoughtfully beside Cameron.

His tone was preface to a soul-baring. Cameron resented Jim's encroachment on that tight area of private pain which was his mind at the moment. Keep off, he wanted to say. You have your worries. Let me have mine. But he said nothing, though he knew that the car, a compartment of nowhere, its windows blind with their breaths, had too much the quality of a confessional for Jim to be deterred.

'She will wait up too. That's the bit. In her dressing-gown and a headful of curlers. It's like a bloody cartoon. Ten minutes late and she's imagining bloodstained bodies at the crossroads. Half-an-hour and she's looking out the insurance policies. Allison like that?'

Cameron concentrated on cornering.

'I don't suppose there can be two like Eileen. You go in and she's sitting with that Jane Wyman look on her face. Gone with the Random Harvest. I don't know what it is. It's about the only time she ever comes alive. Moans about you being late and then keeps you up till about three in the morning. Analysing our married life. Chewing nerve-pills like caramels. Most other nights it's meet the zombies. Madame Tussaud's with words. Not too many words, either. In case you disturb the telly. She's the only person I know who watches both channels simultaneously. She must knock the TAM folk daft. Other night there. Watching two films at once. Two bloody films at the one time. One minute Gregory Peck's kissing some bird in a bustle. Next minute Robert Mitchum's putting the glove on a Chinaman. You don't know where the hell you are. Switching back and forward. I know what it is, though. Straight through here, Eddie.'

A puddle they passed through sawed the underside of the car.

'No kids.' The trite words forced their way out of Jim's mouth with difficulty, enlarged by his experience. 'That's what it is. She needs to have children. You wouldn't believe how much not having kids can foul you up. It's a bastard. It really is. They're the things that put a marriage in perspective. Eileen spends her time worrying about nothings. Fagash on the carpet. Whether the cat's constipated. We've been going to adopt. But they say there's no reason why we shouldn't have our own.' Cameron, measuring Jim's lack against how much his own children mattered to him, felt his resentment unflower in sudden sympathy. Still, he hoped Jim would leave it at that. Any elaboration was redundant. But Jim was intent in ravelling out the whole tapeworm of it for the thousandth time, never to find the head. 'They put us through the mill. At their bloody hatchery. Found nothing.

No reason why we couldn't have children. I began to think I was working on the wrong orifice. Some place right enough. Some place.' Cameron realised that Jim was about to supply full details, which he had always witheld in talking about it before now. ' "Sub-fertility Clinic." Nice name. Boy, that makes you feel good for a start. They might as well have 'Sexual Scrubbers' above the door. Have miniature urinals in the cludgie. There was a bunch of us in this waiting-room. They took the women out first. Left the men exchanging symptoms. It made you feel seedy just looking at each other. Ten minutes more in that atmosphere and I would have been impotent. Then you get to see the doctor. Chats you up about how often you're at it. Checks the equipment. Sends you into the toilet for a sample. Took me about three weeks to get it. Eileen had the worst of it, though. She was crying when she came out. Wasn't the doctor. He had been helluva nice. Just what they have to do. Blow the fallopian tubes. Seems to be bloody sore. But it wasn't that, I don't think. Not the pain that made her cry. More the whole test-tubey atmosphere that made her cry. It was hard to be romantic for a wee while after that. Keeping charts and things. Like filling in your coupon. Which square wins the treble chance. And what good has it done?'

A trough in the road contracted visibility to a few yards. Cameron noted how lugubrious Jim's voice had been. These memories were genuinely painful to him still. Why did he deck them out in absurd images? He never allowed his pains out until they were dressed in red noses and baggy clothes. He only let his feelings stand straight long enough to be knocked down. The small moving tent of the car became unexpectedly for Cameron a crucible in which many particles of insight into Jim, haphazardly acquired over years, instantly fused and resolved into comprehension. Remembering how desperately sensitive he had been as a young man, Cameron saw how far Jim's plot against the world had gone. Jim's manner was the callous developed by long contact with what hurts. He deliberately compounded the sad with the funny, and the funny with the sad, till they were neutralised by each other. His was the hairline equilibrium of the clown, never quite prostrate, never quite upright. He cynicised all his ideals into illusions before they were tested, so that any fall was a fake fall. If you were deft enough in taking the mickey out of yourself, you could forestall the world from doing it to you. On with the motley.

'First left from here, Eddie. Know who I would adopt though. Alice and Helen. You've got great children. No kidding. If you ever find the demands of fatherhood too much for you, you can farm them out to me. That's straight up. I'm serious. I would adopt them tomorrow.'

'I'll send away for the forms. Here, Jim, is this the right road? Beginning to look like a set for *Wuthering Heights*.'

'You're all right. It's first left from here. I'll let you know when.' The road twisted wetly up at Cameron in stuttering stretches and spontaneous loops, improvised on his headlights. 'Only one thing missing tonight. Some women. Should have a couple in the back, eh? You to drive and me to entertain them. 'Twice round the Shire, Charles.' Got no hanging straps in your car, Eddie? This can't be the new Roué Model. Handy for tying them to.'

Cameron's mental image of Jim was now complete. The mask of pathos: one side dropping with depression, the other frozen into implacable mirthfulness: the mouth that starts out as a moan ending in a leer. Both sides set in mutual mockery. The other cheek always ready to be turned.

'Hell. Thirty-six and never strayed. Opportunity. That's what I lack. That's where you salesmen score. Mobile. Here today, gone tomorrow. I wouldn't mind some of it. Left, Eddie. Left. Sometimes I feel that. . . .'

Cameron swung hard left, drove through an open gate, realised it too late, and braked a couple of yards into a field. The engine stalled.

'That's not the turning I thought it was,' Jim explained. 'Away!'

The rain horded into the silence, stampeded finely across

the roof of the car. Cameron turned the ignition and the car gave a garrotted whine. He tried again. Engine-gasps spiralling into silence. Jim breathing prayerfully. At the third attempt the engine sparked and Cameron worked the accelerator like bellows, pumping it to a roar. He put the car into reverse and revved madly. They juddered in a bog of motionlessness. Opening his door, still pedalling, Cameron looked back to see his rear wheel grinding the ground to a chaff of muck. They had come down a fair incline into the field. Cameron put on the handbrake.

'Have to get wood or something. For under the wheels. Give them grip.'

He came out leaving the engine running and was joined by Jim. The rain seemed to drench them in seconds as they groped about the field. Dripping rainwater, Cameron moved out of the range of the headlights, his hands brushing blindly against wet grass in search of something solid. It seemed the final comment on the inconsequential nature of his evening, of his life. What was he doing squelching about an empty field in the middle of the night?

'Why can't they shut their bloody gates, anyway?' Jim's voice mooed melancholy out of nowhere. 'Watch your feet.'

The field was mined with cow-dung, great plateaux of turd the rain had irrigated to softness.

'I've got it!' Jim's shout made Archimedes seem restrained.

He came back from foraging along the hedge with what looked like the bottom of a box, jointed through the middle. They broke it in two and put a splint beneath each of the back wheels.

'I'll push from the front,' Jim said with compensatory heroism.

Back in the car, Cameron revved and Jim heaved and nothing happened. Then suddenly the car lurched free and shot upwards onto the road. Preoccupied though he was in straightening out the car, Cameron was conscious of Jim's fractured shout. Looking down into the field, he could see Jim caught in his headlights, rising up with the knees of his trousers covered in cow-dung. Jim tore up fistfuls of grass and rubbed at his trousers. Sitting in the car, Cameron stuttered into a mild hysteria of laughter, watching the manic figure gesturing to itself in the field, sowing wild handfuls of grass in green filaments that fused gently into the darkness. Jim ran up and into the car. As they drove on, Jim worked with dedication on a complex and comprehensive series of curses until he had anathematised farmers, five-bar gates, dark nights, cars, cattle, and the fact that earthly life should have anal manifestations. Only when they were safely onto the main road did his rage subside.

'I've had enough drink to brass it out tonight,' he said. 'But it's humble pie for breakfast tomorrow morning.'

They went on in soggy silence until the suburbs skeined glistening streets and pompous brick around them. A new supermarket, hushed as a mausoleum.

'Here, Eddie. I've been meaning to ask you. Remember that office party Sid Morton mentioned. How about an invite to it? How about that?'

'Office-party? Oh, that one.'

Cameron glanced sideways at Jim. It was the last stage of a plan, Cameron was sure. An extra onto the price of the ticket for the Burns Supper. Jim sat staring expectantly at Cameron, his hair runnelled into ragged peaks by the rain, completely unconscious of the greaves of cowshit on his legs. No matter how assiduously Jim might labour to mock the comicality of his own life, the final irony of himself lay bless-edly beyond his grasp. Life monotonised into existence, self anonymised into species, love banalised into sex. Relation-ships turned into a circus performance. And seeing himself distorted in the image of Jim, Cameron made his decision: off with the motley. He was going to see Margaret tomorrow.

'Wouldn't mind some action. Can you swing it?'

'Action? No. But I can get you along to the office-party. If that's what you want.'

'Great. I can fix an afternoon off. If you just let me know nearer the time. Thanks a lot, Eddie.'

95

Jim completed the journey in restrained anticipation. Cameron felt fraudulent in the role of benefactor. Jim's situation seemed to nullify any help he could give him. It was like giving Sisyphus a hoist up with his stone. But what could you do except help each other to fulfil your mutual loneliness? The rest was private business. Cameron had his own to bother about.

Next morning he did. Having put the car into the garage. Cameron walked along to a public phone-box. Last night's storminess seemed temporarily to have exhausted the weather, leaving it in a mood of fretful whimsy. The wind doodled the sky with limber racks of cloud. The sun ignited random panes. The day teased with contradictions, went bright and dull by turns, and Cameron, freed from duty by the absence of his car, reflected its mood, enjoyed the nip of the weather, worried about Margaret. The door of the booth nudged him towards the phone. He found the number of Margaret's school in the book and rang.

The voice that answered was brusque with preoccupation. He asked for Miss Sutton. She had a class. Could he speak to her just the same? Well, he couldn't leave a message? He couldn't leave a message. It *was* urgent? He thought it was. Who was it speaking? It was her uncle. He was to hold on. Uncle would oblige.

'Hello?' Margaret's voice, estranged by doubt and the lurking presence of the secretary. Cameron imagined the secretary in veldtschoen and hebe sportsuit.

'Uncle speaking. Uncle Eddie Cameron.'

'Oh, I see.'

'I just called up to commiserate with you. That's a helluva headache you're going to have ten minutes from now.'

'I beg your pardon?'

'Your headache. Head. Ache. It's going to be a stormer. You follow me?'

'I'm not sure.'

'On top of that three of your aunties have been run over by a dromedary. We're burying the bits at Partick Cross.

96

They've all asked for you to be there. What I mean, Margaret, is, is there any chance of you wangling the afternoon off? I'm free today. I would like to see you. Feel free to use any of Cameron's Patent Excuses.'

'Actually, we have a half-holiday today, anyway. There's a textbook exhibition on in Glasgow.'

'Great. Well, look. Can I see you for lunch?'

'Of course.'

'Right. I'll see you in Central Station. Where the Shell used to be. Okay?'

'Right. Thanks for phoning. Uncle.'

'Don't mention it. By the way, Margaret, you're my favourite niece.'

He put down the phone. Where had all the funny talk come from? Habits never know when they're not wanted. Today might teach them.

I I

Like the menu, everything seemed familiar to Cameron. It was the restaurant in which they had first met, chosen not from any reasons of nostalgia but simply because it was the most natural place for them to be, the décor a part of their relationship. Even the waitress was in some sense theirs, having been an unintentional purveyor of discretion from the beginning. When she came up to their table today, the whole situation became immediately for Cameron both repetitive and new. It was like a ceremony often witnessed but only for the first time understood. With understanding came the certain knowledge of what he had to do, though it expressed itself not so much as a rational decision as a spontaneous conversion. The day seemed to intersect so many other days that the smallest actions were both heavy with the past and implicit with the future. Aware in his heightened concern of the ramifications of their actions, he was by an inevitable progression aware also of their conclusion, seemed to understand finally the necessity which enclosed them like this room. The way Margaret recited the soups was part of their personal ritual, and he knew which one she would choose before she said it.

'Minestrone.'

Strange the expanses of memory that can hide behind a triviality. That was the first word he had heard her speak. In this same room. His memory repeopled the restaurant to that busy teatime. The persistent click of knives and forks, a Wimbledon of competitive remarks.

He was aware first of all of her legs, seen over a forkful of omelette.

'Excuse me. Is anyone sitting here?'

'No. Not at all.'

Romeo to Juliet, while each still wears the mask of anonymity. What strange alchemy is in small words that their exchange can generate two strangers into fusion? He had felt nothing at the sight of her. His eyes took in her face as if it were a small ad offering something in which he had no interest, and flicked it into forgetfulness. She was banality wearing make-up. And not wearing it very well.

His attention returned to his omelette while he went on with whatever he had been thinking about, patiently hoeing a few weeds from his mind. The waitress came up to take her order.

'Minestrone, please.'

The waitress's pencil twirled above her pad, pivoting on itself the attention of the others at the table.

'You're looking at the luncheon menu, dear. High teas just now. Dinners don't start till after seven.'

'Oh. Well . . .'

Confusion betrayed in her face an attractiveness which its formal repose had concealed. It was like the opaque facet of a surface which becomes transparent when held at a certain angle. Cameron found himself staring into a sensitivity which withdrew shyly before his eyes, drawing him after it. She was searching the menu.

'You don't want to wait for dinner, do you, dear?'

'Haddock. Please. Haddock'll be fine.'

'Haddock it is, dear. Tea and toast for one? All right.'

Cameron tried to infiltrate a smile that would relieve the embarrassment from which she was under siege. Failing to get through to her, he turned for help to the other couple at the table. But the middle-aged woman was staring at the girl, recording her condition like a camera, while her husband glanced round the room, talking in a married monotone: 'It was obvious they would have to close it down. Two pet shops within fifty yards. Stands to reason. Folk are going to stick to their old one. And all those monkeys. Who buys monkeys nowadays? Remember I told you at the time.' Cameron felt an anger so disproportionate to whatever offence the couple were supposed to be committing that it was perhaps a sign of something. He had already allied himself with the girl. He knew his reaction was ridiculous, quixotic in its intensity. Knight of the knife and fork. But still he watched her almost protectively as she took a paper napkin from the tumbler in the centre of the table and involved herself completely in cleaning her knife, polishing it with a circumscription that excluded everything else.

The same circumscription with which she now broke up and buttered her dinner roll. For familiarity had taught him that Margaret approached everything with the same sort of child-like intensity. She locked herself inside every action, made a temporary home of it.

He watched her now, realising how time alters its perspectives around us so that the background of the past becomes the foreground of the present. The seeds of yesterday's casual moments become forests we wander lost in today. Past oak trees yield themselves into acorns, too small to be recovered. That evening in this restaurant, for example. What had he been doing in here at tea-time? There must have been some strong reason for his not having the meal at home. There was. He was sure of it. But it appeared in his mind like the outline left on a wall by a picture which has been removed, an irritating blank testifying to its own absence. Whatever had brought him here, it seemed to him now an accident of mind-paralysing improbability. They didn't even live in the same city, except for the purposes of the census. In the wastes of cities, each had to make his own tracks, pioneer his own routes, small personal patterns worn out of anonymity like clay paths in long grass and as easily lost. Cameron's Glasgow was superficially wide, a travelling man's itinerary with known faces to be found in many parts. But the city was essentially something that unreeled across his windscreen, unsubstantial as a travelogue. Margaret's Glasgow was a dislocated village, among the parts of which she commuted across deserts of grime by bus and underground. Most of her locales were private: a bench in the Kelvin Park, a seat in the Cosmo, a book in the Mitchell Library, her flat. Her city was a few corners, hidden behind the glib façade of Glasgow Cameron knew. Both their cities converged only in Margaret's room, found mutual plexus on her bed. But all he could remember of the evening which led to that plexus was the chance occurrence which now brought him back to this place with this woman facing him, and a crisis that was being fuelled further towards combustion with every prevarication, with every pretence of its non-existence.

'How's the soup?' he asked.

'Fine. I'm good and hungry too. Could use a little salt though.'

He passed the condiments. She rejected the pepper automatically and the small action, so simple on the surface, had, like an iceberg, unseen extensions which hit below the level of his consciousness. She never used pepper. She took no sugar in her tea. The only alcohol he had ever known her to drink was Advocaat and lemonade. Aimless pieces of her that he came across from time to time, a persistent confetti, celebrating an intimacy begun casually in this room on that past evening.

Remembering that situation now, he saw it with an almost frightening clarity that moved him to sympathy, a sympathy that included himself as well as Margaret, as if he were no longer the person who had sat with her then. Watching himself and Margaret in retrospect, he was aware of their words and actions taking place as a kind of rite, vehicles of a sad compulsion, touchingly decorous. Was it possible they hadn't understood the implications of the ceremony in which they allowed themselves to participate?

'Don't let it bother you,' he had said.

'I beg your pardon?'

The mildly aggressive question made them reverse roles momentarily, Cameron now being the embarrassed one. He saw the woman who had just left their table staring at him from the doorway while her husband paid at the cash-desk. Her suspicion formed an accidental alliance with the girl's. Already he was beginning to regret having taken advantage of the couple's departure.

'The business with the menu,' he said feebly. 'You seemed bothered about it.'

'Oh that. It was just a bit embarrassing.'

'I know what you mean,' he went on, not willing to let silence settle on their exchanges just yet, since the moment would be frozen for good into the form of his failure. He wanted merely to bring their conversation to the point where he could opt out more honourably. 'Mistakes get magnified when there's an audience.'

'Oh my,' she said. 'Philosophy with my haddock. I hope they're not going to put it on my bill.'

It was a dual purpose remark, one which could either be construed as sarcasm, shutting off their conversation, or be turned to levity, prolonging it. Cameron laughed.

'Just a thought I happened to have on me. I always carry a spare profundity about with me. In case of injuries to the ego. Like a first-aid kit.'

'Thanks for the bandage then. But I don't really think I needed it.'

'I'm beginning to think I do. In future I'll keep my wise sayings for my own comfort.'

'Including: 'Never engage strange women in conversation'?'

'Where I come from, we don't call this sort of thing a conversation. Pogrom's the word we use. For a shy girl, you're pretty tough. What's your name, by the way? Irma Grazie?'

'Nice to be called a 'girl' anyway.'

I could think of other terms, Cameron thought. Anyway, he felt he had made a reasonably dignified retreat. Napoleonic almost, except that his losses were fewer. He consulted his cigarette like a script. When it burned to the butt, he would make his exit. Limping stoically to the cash-desk, trailing a little spoor of blood. Dignified to the death. And span his nose at her from the door. He was right about her, though, he thought. There was a hardness, a tensility about her responses, that didn't seem to match her shyness. Later he was to feel that this hardness was an ancillary feature of her shyness, in the way that qualities often grow an unnatural opposite like a Siamese twin. Her natural sensitivity was shadowed by an acquired toughnness, practised and aggressive, that would come forward in a crisis, like a bodyguard. But at the time his powers of analysis went no further than his own rejected protectiveness. She must have sensed it.

'I hope I haven't hurt you,' she said.

'Far from it. Oh, excuse me.' He made a show of moving his hands away from the table. 'I seem to be bleeding into the sugar.'

'No, really though. I was maybe a little nasty. I can be, I know.'

'Such self-knowledge is overwhelming.'

'All right. But it's just that I don't usually talk to strange men in restaurants. You never know just how strange they might be.'

There was a pause while Cameron examined the remark. She was finishing off the haddock. He had half an inch of cigarette to kill.

'You're right about me, though,' he said. 'I may as well confess it. I'm a white slaver. I go around the country talking to girls in restaurants and cafés. Buy them a meal. Drug the tea. Just a simple matter of switching the Tetley tea-bags. By the time they're in my car, their lids are heavy with unnatural sleep. Drive them to one of our depots. And that's it. Flown out to Casbahs all over the world. Fifty quid a time. Not a bad return for the price of a haddie and chips.'

She smiled, which should have been a formality. But somehow with her it wasn't. You felt that this was no mere social convenience, something she used to facilitate the passing of a bread-plate or to wrap politeness in. Her whole face went on holiday with it. Cameron felt like a busker who finds a £100 note in his hat. His hammy burlesque hadn't earned such a reward. He sensed immediately that this was the sort of expression he could become addicted to and set himself deliberately to satirize his own reaction, like mentally pulling her teeth. It's not my stomach this time, Dr Culley. I want you to put me on the official list of ivory addicts. I'm a junky for smiles.

'You were right about me too,' she confessed. 'I *was* embarrassed. That's why I was a bit narky. I fluster so easily in front of strangers. Do the wrong thing. Like ordering this.' She put down her knife and fork. 'Haddock. I don't even like it very much.'

'You're not so bad.' He caught himself striving for the remark that would evoke another smile. 'I've a friend who once drank the fingerbowl. No, that's true. In a big snazzy hotel. Same bloke, same hotel. He spread the Cranberry on his bread. This is honest.' He made mental acknowledgment to Jim Forbes.

The smile suggested itself again. Behind his eyes flippancy worked hard to neutralise his fascination, mocked him mercilessly, made him imagine himself devoting his life to a deeper appreciation of that smile, like a Japanese artist painting one flower endlessly till he died. Cameron in grand old age, the world's foremost authority on smiles, giving one of his rare television interviews: I think some of the best smiles I ever inspired were in the sixties. . . .

'Well, that makes me feel a lot better, I must admit.'

'Mind you, he's in an institution now. Under observation. Menuphobia, they call it. Obsessed. Sees everything in terms of menus. If someone dies, he says they've been "taken off"'.

'I'm sorry to hear that.'

Having been present at their introduction, whimsy remained a basic ingredient of their relationship. It had a leavening effect on the spasmodic depressions which tended to deaden their times together, and it came to be introduced automatically in greater or lesser proportions as the need demanded. Margaret learned the technique quickly and together they evolved mild fantasies that they would run through in duet from time to time.

Pretence was to some extent their necessary climate since their relationship had its origins in a caprice and everything that had followed occurred in a vacuum kept separate from the real issues of their lives. He seemed to have acted on a reflex which progressed into a habit and from a habit enlarged into a pattern of behaviour. All the result of one spontaneous, almost accidental moment.

'Where are you headed tonight?' he had asked.

She did not answer at once and in the pause they both appreciated the implications of his question, which faced them like a crossroads. They could leave things like this, a casual chat between strangers in a restaurant, or they could follow this incident further in one way or another.

'Night school. I take a literature class. As a student, I mean. Scottish poets just now. Tonight it's William Soutar.'

'You don't fancy doing something else?' Cameron wasn't sure that he did. The question just seemed to emerge naturally from his previous one. She said nothing. 'We could have a seminar on Soutar.' He managed to quote a couple of lines, and found that he was out of business. Closed. Owing to sudden clearance of stock. But his two-line erudition had its effect. He was grateful for the time spent reading and getting paid by Stan Gilbertson. Manifold are the uses of literacy.

'Don't you have anything to do?'

'If I have I can't remember.'

'Where would we go?'

'Pictures. Play. For a drink. Swimming in the moonlit waters of the Clyde. Guided tour of the Gorbals.' She appeared still to be waiting. 'Sorry I don't have my brochures with me. I do give Greenshield stamps, though.'

The game palled on him. His cigarette was finished. He stubbed it out. At least he had managed to exercise verbal muscles long atrophied. Time to grow up again and leave.

'All right.'

Her words broke the rules of the game, were real currency

given in exchange for toy money. Her voice was nervous. She had her head turned away, the eyes lowered, leaving her voice to negotiate with him while she sat submissively apart from it. What kind of pressures could make her undersell herself so far as to go for a corny old song? He sat nonplussed, like a man who carelessly scratches his head at an auction and finds he has bought something very valuable he knows he can't afford. He stared at her. She wasn't being coy or winsome or knowing. She simply waited, wrapped in her own expectation, a parcel of private mysteries waiting to be collected. He understood with some embarrassment that she had no attitudes, only reactions. She could only respond to situations as herself. He glanced uneasily round the room, as if everyone here knew what was happening except her.

'I'll get the bills,' he said.

'No. Please. I'll pay my own. I don't want you feeling you didn't get your money's worth later on.'

Her fears weren't unfounded. They went to a cinema and were glad to have an excuse for ignoring each other. The enforced silence left the things they had said receding into pointlessness and unreality. While the characters in the film agonised to themselves incomprehensibly, the two of them appraised each other furtively in the dark, fidgeting over a wasted evening. They were such total strangers still that Cameron wondered if she would get up and go out on her own at the end of the film. But driving her home afterwards he felt in touch with her again. When he dropped her at her flat, they both indicated that they would probably be in the restaurant at the same time the following week, and left it at that.

Cameron remembered that he had felt more guilty about lying to Allison the next week than about going out for Margaret, because nothing was going to happen. Margaret might not even be there. But she was. And the next week. And the week after that. Scottish poetry, Margaret said, seems to get boring after Soutar.

The fifth week he went to pick her up at the flat but they

didn't go out. They stayed talking, trying to rationalise what was happening. That was when he told her he was married. She declared that the whole thing was finished three times and rescinded the decision three times before she admitted to herself that somehow it didn't make any difference. Having lost one of her moral bulwarks, she found that the rest collapsed. That evening their affair was consummated. Whatever implicit compulsion had sent them in search of each other for four successive weeks had finally revealed itself to them, and it held them, establishing itself more and more strongly in their respective lives, interweaving one with the other in countless small ways, so that separation would be a tearing in many places. Unseen tissues breaking for how long into the future?

'Eddie! The sweet. Which one do you want?'

'Sorry, Margaret?'

'Swiss tart as usual, is it?'

'That'll be fine. Yes.'

'I'll have the peach melba, please.'

The waitress smiled understandingly at Margaret.

'Swiss tart again, Eddie. Every time. You're not the most adventurous.'

'I'm sometimes called the Marco Polo of the trencher.'

There it was again. Presenting Mr Whimsy. The world's foremost exponent of emotional ventriloquism. Inside yourself you could be screaming, but if you knew how to throw your voice it came out funny. He had become so expert at it that he didn't know his real voice from the imitations. He had to find it soon because he was going to need it. All the conversational diversions he had created in the past weren't any use to him now. They never had been, when he thought of it. This cold and comfortless necessity had always been the place where they met each other. It had been decorated with talk, furnished with dreams. But it was still as they had found it, a cellar of themselves, where they harboured their fugitive affair, sustaining it with scraps of their lives, whispering freedom to it. It couldn't last. Either you let it grow strong enough to break out into the open and rampage the rest to wreckage. Or you turned the key on it quietly and forgot to go back. Love can't inhabit stasis.

He lit a cigarette and watched her finish off her sweet. The motions of her eating, all the gestures they had made together, the walkings, the furtive arm-links, the grapplings of flesh, the smiles, the becks, the surprising understandings mined from the abstruse reaches of buried conversations, all were part of the same enjoyable but sinister ceremony, intricately devised for the evocation of the inevitable. He had sometimes wondered at the tenacity of their first meetings, surprised at how they persisted through long empty occasions when they were no more than guests of the same evening, waiting in vain for their host to arrive. At those times it had all seemed so accidental what they were doing, biological roulette. Now he understood their persistence, was amazed that he could ever have countenanced believing in the innocence of accident in what had happened. They had fumblingly perfected a process which, as if by sympathetic magic, must evoke an inevitable outcome. That outcome was pain, for themselves and for others. Their orderly behaviour in this room was conjuring imminent chaos out of others. The luxury of their enjoyment was likely to be charged to his family. His hands moving quickly across Margaret's flesh could leave permanent bruises on Alice and Helen. He was assaulted by the complexity of things: the inveterate interdependence of lives whose proximities defied time and space; small actions enlarged to enormity when reflected in certain eyes; pleasure that bloomed innocently from the compost of other people's hurt. He saw Margaret's smile of that first night as a ravening after other people's happiness. He withdrew from the callousness of his own past thoughts of leaving Allison. All the connotations of 'love' became in the instant euphemistic. What it meant in essence was the exchange of blood. The possibility of birth began in the issue of it. Virginity died in it. Faced with the inevitability of pain, caught in a nightmare of the multiplying contusions of daily contact, he knew of only one sanity he could live with: cause as little hurt as possible. For him that meant sparing especially Alice and Helen, who were innocent anyway. Their precariousness terrified him. Children were so vulnerable, open to every specious argument, their determinations diverted from one direction by the throwing of a vague adult promise in another, at the mercy of one another's malice. Every decision they attempted seemed to totter on spindly intentions against a hurrying crowd of determined conceptions and prejudices, brushed aside heedlessly, only recovering from the impact of one thoughtless collision in time to be knocked down by the next. Bumped and bruised, they fell and were left to rise again and again. The wonder of it was that their natures weren't broken in every bone or permanently maimed. Life would make them casualties soon enough. He wasn't going to help it. Unable to decide for himself, all he could do was ask the circumstances for a show of hands. Even just numerically, Margaret had to be the loser.

'What about coffee?' he asked.

'Wouldn't you rather come back to the flat and we could have a cup of tea there?'

He nodded. She smiled and that brief jaw-swell of muscles stirred an undertow of feeling in him. It was a bitter irony that in the perspective of renunciation he saw her most clearly. Loss is an expert auditor. What he used to think was her plainness had been merely a reflection of his own indifference. Beauty, he understood, is the product of our involvement in the lives of others, a grace it is the prerogative of each one's love to bestow. But it still didn't amount to much of a parting gift.

'Always been a good place this, hasn't it,' she said.

'For us it has. Pity we couldn't just live here.'

'It would take an awful lot of furnishing, though. Could you afford it?'

'That's the trouble. Always the same with me. Money beats me every time. Did I ever tell you about the first time I was jilted? I would be about twelve. She left me for the boy round the corner. He had a milk-run. Able to keep her in the jube-jubes to which she was accustomed. I went round with a face like a sandwich-board for weeks.'

Even to elegies the only form he seemed able to give was whimsy. He was such a jocular fellow. They would carve a funny story on his headstone.

12

The room was reasonably tidy today but everything was scummed with stale light, as if it was still using last year's sunshine. Cameron stood in the middle of the floor, trying not to notice the veteran furniture, in the varnish and leather of which millions of small comings and goings had inscribed themselves. Margaret hung up her coat in the hall and switched on the electric heater. While she went through to the kitchen to put on a kettle, the two bars of the fire came up like weals into warmth.

Cameron sensed the machinery of their private custom whirring into motion like an invisible generator, self-regulating. He heard the water drumming into the kettle, statement of an assumption, and the gas going on popped complacently. He wasn't staying, he told himself, and he wasn't coming back. He had to explain it to Margaret. But her temporary preoccupation was prohibitive. He merely stood, passively opposing the progress of habit, patiently creating a hiatus in normalcy, until she noticed him still with his overcoat on and paused in her routine, laughing.

'Are you sure you're at the right bus-stop?' she said. 'Take your coat off, Eddie. Are you not waiting or something?'

'No. Actually I'm not.'

He hoped the words were to hand to effect their separation with the minimum of surgery.

'I'm packing it in, Margaret. I'm sorry.'

'What in?'

Sometimes you had to forsake the ambiguity of euphemism.

III

'This. Us'. Slow steps towards the truth. 'I don't think we should see each other again.'

He still couldn't bring himself to the statement of a fact but canvassed for agreement. Not yet comprehending, she abstained.

'It's no use, Margaret. We're kidding ourselves. We're down a dead-end. Where does this go? Nowhere. I'm not leaving my children or my wife. I thought I might. But I never will. I don't have the right to hurt them like that. Not for your sake or anybody else's. Least of all for mine. So it's better to stop it now. For you as well. I'm sorry.'

Oration to an absent audience. Margaret was still several sentences behind, trying to relate what was happening to the glow of the fire, the water heating pointlessly, the empty tea-cups in her hand, one of which had just become an irony. She set them down on the table, instant mementoes. Around them the city, insinuating sounds of traffic, nudged and niggled at their quietness with its idiot dread of silence.

'When did you decide this?' The words emerged tone-lessly, a question groping for something solid to attach to.

'Today. I suppose.'

'Just today?' She prolonged the moment until she could improvise a reaction. 'Nice of you to let me know so soon.' Having found sarcasm, she used it as a medium for her confusion. 'I must say you do it very well. Rather like a Roman orgy, isn't it? Feed the victim well. Then it's thumbs down for dessert. All very civilised.'

Helplessly, Cameron listened to her talk herself into an understanding of what was taking place, watched her turn this way and that to determine the dimensions of her hurt.

'Today! You asked me out today. For this? What did you do that for? If that was all you wanted, you could've written me a letter. Nice and formal. Your services are no longer re-quired. Why did you have to do it this way?' Then at once she abandoned her sense of affront, since it gave her no measurement of what it was a part of, like a thimbleful of ocean. 'You just decide like that. A year and a half erased in an afternoon. How can it be? How can it be? It's not possible. Or else you live on lies. They're what you breathe.' She paused, turning the statement into a question to which Cameron could give no answer. 'What does that make me? Why did you come near me in the first place? A superannuated whore. A dirty joke that lasted eighteen months. Didn't you have a family then? You just misplaced them for a wee while. And now it's my turn. Well, what if I don't want to be paid off? What if I decide to tell your wife? I could, you know.' Even as she said it, her head shook in denial of the possibility, her face grimacing as if she regretted her limitations. 'No. No. You can't do it. It's too late. Not now.' She stopped against the realisation that he *was* doing it. 'But I love you, Eddie.' Her voice planed out on the words. 'I love you.' Looking around her as if they contradicted the sullen persistence of the bleak room to which she was being abandoned. The words staked her to an inevitability and like an act of self-immolation she repeated them: 'I love you.'

The openness of her need was unbearable and Cameron wanted to meet it, to comfort her at any cost. But desperately he thought of his children's faces. If the pain Margaret and he had tutored themselves in assiduously for more than a year wasn't to be prematurely imparted to Alice and Helen, it had to be endured in this room now, not prolonged into further corrosions of mutual deception. He gritted under the necessity of his own silence like an armlock.

'You don't feel anything, do you, Eddie?'

The question was without self-pity, and answered itself by its own resigned conviction.

'Margaret,' Cameron said. 'I love you. If that's any use to you. But it doesn't make any difference. I love my wife and my children too. Maybe one love should cancel out the other. But it doesn't.'

There ought to have been more words with which to punish the patness of his reasoning, anger, recriminations, past promises brought out like IOUs. But she said nothing. There was no point. The protestations of passion are a species

of the moment, the present committing suicide with the
future to immortalise itself, epitaphs on transience. And
their vows had all been made under the compulsion of their
bodies. Besides, the suddenness and directness of his decision
caught her without more than a token resistance, hit almost
at once on the naked nerve at the centre of all her reactions:
she loved him. That concession paralysed all other responses.

'It's best for you too, doing this, Margaret. It really is. I
mean it. You'll find that out.'

'Please, Eddie. Don't tell me you're being good to me.
Next year you can give me cancer for my Christmas.'

'But it is. Really. I'm far too old for you in the first place.'

'Eddie.'

'You'll get somebody else. Easily. You'll easily get somebody else. You're still young. You're just a girl.'

'Do you have to talk like a women's magazine? You
haven't mentioned Mr Right yet. Eddie. I don't want anybody else.'

Words were separate from any meaning but they kept falling like dead leaves from his mouth. Anything to cover the
indecency of such a naked acknowledgment of need.

'That's not true. You do want someone. You will. And
you'll have someone. You're young and you're pretty. You're
intelligent. And you're a tremendous person.'

'Would you like to write me a reference? Mistress seeks
new employment.'

She made as if to say something else and stopped herself,
wishing neither to cry nor to demean her love by offering it to
his rejection, poised into a strained kind of dignity. She
stood in the middle of a drab room, caught in a shabby little
crisis that must have been about as commonplace as cough-
ing in many rooms of this hard city, and yet her intensity
made a uniqueness of it, a small but ferocious fire in which
she burned. Anything Cameron could say was merely another
faggot to the flames.

But he wanted to remain, as if he owed her something still,
ought at least to be bearing witness to her sadness. Or was it

just that he needed to undergo some redemptive suffering? The thought silenced any further consolation he could offer. He felt ashamed of standing here, masochistically appeasing his own guilt. Having deliberately engineered this moment of anguish for her, how could he pretend to be assuaging it? Every gesture rebounded into selfishness. He realised with a shock that he had separated himself from her, made himself redundant here. He had created the isolation in which she stood and all he could do now was to complete it.

The kettle began to whistle, a small geyser of noise burgeoning stridently in their silence. Margaret didn't move. As Cameron crossed towards the kitchen, he stirred their tableau into animation. There was a small sound in Margaret's throat, a rupture in constraint, and she was crying, not loudly, but with an immediate insistence. Cameron turned down the gas to a bracelet of small blue flames and came back through. That was what politeness meant: a code of behaviour in which small ciphers could be used to express the enormous incommunicable. People called for help from a cavern of need and you turned down the gas below their kettle for them.

'I think I'd better go now, Margaret,' he said.

Her head was lowered, her body still held in an unnatural stiffness, arthritic with suppressed sobs. He learned her posture like a commandment: thou shalt not wantonly invoke the love of another.

She said something that sounded like 'I love you'. But the words were rain on water, fading before they formed.

'I'm sorry, Margaret.'

'I don't know what to do.' She said it to the room, to the feeling in herself. He just happened to overhear.

'I'm sorry. I'm sorry.'

He turned away and into the hall. The closing door lopped the sound of her weeping. But the room pursued him. He tried to console himself with its counterpart: the prolonged security of his family. At least he had localised the infliction of pain. Wasn't the psychology of the slaughterhouse central to our lives? Hurt the few that many may survive.

Outside he regretted not having his car. Feeling a certain loss of identity without it, he took flight on foot through streets that jostled his concern into hiding with their callous activity. The transition from room to street had been so sudden that he had the sensation of being simultaneously involved in both, so that bluff faces, complacent voices, feet on familiar errands seemed all to encroach threateningly upon that luminous greyness where in his memory Margaret still stood quivering in her misery, vulnerable as a nerve-end. To escape from her image, he gave himself a purpose. He would go and collect the car. He had intended getting it out of the garage tomorrow but they had told him it would be fully serviced by the afternoon, unless a serious fault was found. Having found a direction, he became one of the purposeful many, merged protectively with them.

It was some time since he had travelled on the underground. It reminded him of mornings on his way to school. Memory casually dug up pieces of those mornings. Duffel-coated students. Strap-hanging somnambulists. An inspector tapping along the windows with a penny to get them to move up inside. Girls beautiful in their anonymity, to be abducted by the mind and seduced behind a textbook. Chance shards of a buried past that cut a little as he unearthed them. But most clear and still complete was the memory of the general feeling the underground had always given him. It hadn't been so much a means of transport to him as a place spinning in the darkness, where an endless ritual was performed. It was almost frightening to be forced daily to acknowledge the sheer numberless variegation of humanity, limitless permutations on the secrecy of mouths, exoticism of noses, infinity of eyes, hardly a face occurring more than one day. Even the modes of responding to the emptiness they circled in were ritualised, newspapers, glances that never settled as if mobility meant survival, eyes laid leadenly on the chart of stations overhead, to be left until called for – formal celebrations of futility. His juvenile romanticism had always been depressed by those whey Glaswegian faces whose pallid mysteries haunted his early morning journeys to the school, set in surrender. Now he sat as one of them, glad that the almost empty train contained no counterpart of his adolescence.

The car was ready. With it he regained routine, welcomed the safety of habit, as if the car could bring him home of its own accord. He drove quickly, still dogged by a feeling of somehow evading himself, of postponement. But what had he postponed? He had acted decisively, in the only way that enabled him to face the consequences of his action. The same sentence was recurring over and over in his mind with a persistence that obviated the possibility of answer. What else could I do? What else could I do? What else could I do?

He was glad when his suburb rose around him like camouflage, neat buildings presenting bland, polite faces, orderly gardens. His open garage took him in like a refuge.

Going in by the back door, he found Alice and Helen in the kitchen. They had finished their after-four glass of milk with a biscuit. Alice was doing her homework, her expression vague with concentration. Helen was using her empty glass like a tannoy, making experimental noises into it. Their attentions were protective as a fence around him.

'Daddy!' Helen's announcement was muffled in her glass. She liked the sound and set out on a programme of repetitions, varying pitch and tone.

'Hello, daddy,' Alice said from behind her problem. 'Can you give me some help?'

'She's stuck again, daddy.' Helen shook her head as if Alice was the family failure.

He helped Alice with a couple of opposites and watched her face clear like an eye from which a mote is lifted, looking out for the moment on a worryless world.

'Listen, daddy. Listen to this.'

Helen handed him her latest card and, as he bent down beside her, related its dull contents dramatically. After the first few words, she didn't look at the card at all but watched Cameron's face so as not to miss any of his elaborate admiration. Waiting till his praise had run its course, she casually put her achievement in perspective.

'These cards is easy,' she said, returning to the more challenging intricacies of tumbler-talk.

He set this scene against the one with Margaret, almost wishing that she could see it, as if it would appease her hurt. Didn't this one justify the other?

He savoured the moment like a vindication, conscious of precisely the same demand being made upon him by the completely contrasted stances of his daughters, Alice already moving out of her momentary halcyon into another minor worry, Helen innocent of everything but the glass in front of her. Both were utterly dependent on his protection. What he had done today was to give them it.

'Where's your mum?' he asked.

'The living-room,' Alice said. 'The workmen are in. With the new fire. I hope they're finished before the television comes on. Tell her to stop that, daddy.'

Helen's efforts were becoming more obstreperous.

'Helen! Alice is trying to do her homework.'

Helen became silent but went on making monstrous mouths inside the glass. As he went through, he heard her whispering to her tumbler, 'Alice Cameron can't do her home-work!' He hung up his coat before going into the living-room.

He was just in time for the unveiling ceremony. The two workmen were fiddling around the fire, bantering each other and engaging in the masonic exchange of a few technical terms. Allison was watching relentlessly as if determination could compensate for ignorance.

'Oh, hello, darling,' she said. The endearment was a little musty in her mouth. She was one of those who wear their intimacies most conspicuously in the company of strangers.

'Hello, everything all right?'

'Just finishing, sir. The main, Dan. Yer wife's a good gaffer, sir.'

His laugh didn't conceal from Cameron the fact that by coming into the room he had inherited a small tension. Allison had annoyed them with her supervision. While the other workman went out, Cameron felt a sudden resentment of their presences. They had somehow compromised the completeness of his homecoming, were a pointless intrusion into his privacy. What were they doing chaffing each other in his living-room and obliquely insulting his wife? He wanted to bring himself nearer in some way to Allison, to show himself that he had arrived not merely in his house but in a deeper place where others couldn't come.

'Did you get out to Elmpark today?' he asked her.

'Yes.' Her answer came so close upon his question it almost gagged it. She stepped back to let the workman who was coming back in separate them like a broken connection.

'Excuse me,' the workman said.

'It's all right,' Cameron answered. I'm a stranger here myself.

'There we are then!'

The fire was on.

'Now is it safe enough?' Allison asked.

'Safe as houses, missus,' the older one said. 'See. There's your switch. Right? Anti-clockwise for off. That's it off. Clockwise for on.'

'You couldn't gas yourself or anything?'

'No! Unless you work at it. There's only one way, really, Look.' He outlined it briefly with demonstrations.

They collected their tools and Cameron saw them to the door. He wasn't sure what the tip he gave them was for. Conscience money? When he came in, Allison shook her head at him.

'Why did you have to ask that question in front of them?'

He stared hopelessly into her question. It had grown naturally out of what had gone before and looked innocent as a flower, but its roots were poison and they ran everywhere.

Their relationship was choked with them. Deception and pretence were so prolific. Let them grow in one small area and they overran you. How could they nurture any honesty between them when they had so many strangling conventions that they fed with themselves? Things that they could tell to some people and not to others. Deliberate silences. Careful deceptions. Reciprocal lies. Parasites that killed the truth they lived off. Margaret came up before him like an indictment. Somehow she made their failure worse. Because of what she felt, their deceptions were the cheaper. We have to be more, he thought. We should be honest, he wanted to say. So let him begin by telling her about Margaret. He couldn't. Allison was right. They lived by evasions, bound to the maintenance of a delicate fabric of lies. What right did he have to be demanding honesty?

Instead, he confessed simply, 'Because I wanted to know the answer. What do you think of the fire then?'

And they talked about that, throwing up trivia like an earthwork.

13

Allison drained the cup and to her surprise found herself suffusing with a rare contentment, as if the night had slipped a Mickey Finn into her tea. Probing the feeling, she tried to distinguish its ingredients. Alice's party had been a great success. Paper hats, aggressive games and fractured eardrums. The pristine pleasures of childhood. They had squandered sufficient energy to build a couple of pyramids, or wreck a room. But nothing had gone wrong. Not one disappointment. Except for Bobby Mason, and it was a vocation with him. The way he gorged, as if eating was inhaling. You could almost see his freckles stretching. He was such a cliché of boyhood gluttony, he almost convinced you that all the other physical attributes were extensions of the stomach, eyes to see food with, legs to go towards it, hands to stuff it into the mouth. As if auditioning for Son of Billy Bunter. The rest of the evening had for her been haunted by the image of pyloric retribution. But his father had arrived in time to run his stomach home before it became a party piece. With that event the success of the party achieved accomplished fact. Yet it was hardly a fact big enough to justify the feeling which laved her mind in pleasure. Mrs Gilchrist's grand-niece had enjoyed herself. When Mrs Gilchrist came herself to collect her, she had complimented Allison on the house and said she would be asking her over just as soon as the redecoration was finished. That was something to look forward to. But Allison's enjoyment of the moment was present tense, not future. Was it just tiredness sluicing her of her worries?

Watching Alice undress, she knew it was more. It was involved somehow with Alice's vegetable progress in taking off her clothes. Her movements slow against the gentle tug of her tiredness. Muted to ceremonial in the half-light from the table-lamp that made a mezzotint of the room. In each eye a reflected fuse of the fire glowed, like kindling womanhood (though her voice was innocent of Allison's prophetic contemplation, 'Gas fires aren't as good for looking in as real ones'). The unhurried gestures of self-revelation seemed time's accomplices. The mechanical nightly disclosure found organic counterpoint in herself. The inevitable blossoming of the nature inplicit in the white stalk of a body. Breasts budding patiently. Uterine mysteries unwinding themselves within her. A life caught in the skein of its own growing. A body creating joys that the being inside would have to explore, discovering empty hungers that were for experience to colonise. The world is a single physiological event, each one of us is a ghost of. Allison wondered about the events Alice's body would create for her. Events completely predictable and utterly unforeseeable, age-old and new, typical and unique.

The maternal reflex to chivvy was made ineffectual by her absorption in her thoughts. ('Hurry up, Alice. You'll be meeting yourself getting up.') The occasion was licence for indulgence. Alice was ten. Another year nearer to herself. ('Oh, can't I wait up to see my dad?') For Allison the raw voices and relentless enjoyment of the party, which at the time of their occurrence had been no more than a cacophony of discordant demands and requests, were ordered by retrospect into an étude, herself as composer. It was only with the work done, dishes cleared and washed, room hoovered, the cup of tea looked forward to all evening brewed and enjoyed, that she could appreciate what she had been doing. Memorialising a mode of pleasure which they would all outgrow. That was the hub of her contentment. She reflected that she wouldn't have many years longer in which the small things that she did would matter so much to Alice. Tonight she had the certainty of her importance to another person frozen for a moment, enshrined in an evening. The sudden comprehension of her sense of well-being surprised her with its simplicity: she was happy.

With the realisation came another like a twin: happiness was by nature fugitive, established its identity by flight, was the foundling all our more proper concerns and sophisticated commitments disowned. Recognising it for this moment, she hugged it to herself, knowing with a pang that their reunion was temporary, since it was too embarrassing, too idiotic, too unimpressive to be admitted to the serious business of her life. Other things were too important, too pressing to let her spend much of her time with this inane, instinctive feeling which took a complete, unquestioning pleasure in working through each day as it came and losing itself in the concerns of others. But it was hers, unchallenged, for tonight.

As if his entrance had been rehearsed by her mood, Cameron came in smiling, standing in the living-room by the time the outside door shut like a mistimed cue.

'I've done it,' he announced. 'Eureka. Hallelujah. And other restrained expressions of joy. How's my girl? Ten and still not married. Many happy returns. How much are the presents worth? How many times did Bobby Mason puke? Sid Morton phoned yet, Allison?' His mood was a Guy Fawkes night. The effigy was logic.

'No,' Allison following the last flare.

'He will, he will. Who's the best salesman you ever saw?'

'Have you been drinking?'

'Deep. Of success. I'll probably get a knighthood. I can just hear her now. With that Martian accent. Arise, Sir Eddie. Or maybe I should expect something a bit more modest. Can you get nameplates with 'MBE' on them? Try Woolworth's tomorrow morning.'

'What is it?'

'Auld has finally succumbed to my winsome charm.'

'You got the contract. That's marvellous, Eddie.'

'Fifteen thousand quidsworth of marvellous. Two whole new plants they're lighting. And I'm the learie.'

'Terrific. What will it mean? For you.'

'I'm still not exactly sure. Promotion? With Sid Morton leaving. Assassination by petty rivals on the steps of the office. I'm a bit too near it yet to tell. I've got the negatives.' Tapping his head for darkroom. 'But they're not developed yet.'

She wanted to hear more but it was his show, and he wasn't saying yet. Remembering this was mainly Alice's night, he gave himself over to her eager account of the party. It was good to watch him. Everything Alice said he took and gave her back at double its value. His reactions enlarged her trivia into importance. Only Allison was aware that a part of his attention was reserved, so that when the 'phone rang he was ready for it, knew who it was.

'What's the news, Eddie?'

'As good as you can imagine.'

'Bloody great. You hooked him. How did you manage to win over his holiness?'

'I just told him you get a free bible with every fifteen thousand quidsworth of stuff you buy.'

Allison had gravitated towards the phone, magnetised by Cameron's laughter.

'That's great. This gives you so many feathers in your cap, you could make an eiderdown. You should go down big with the London men after this. Your timing couldn't be better.'

'Mind you, I'm claiming boredom money for this one. I've spent a night listening to what's wrong with the world. And hearing his patent remedies. Chapter and verse. He talks enough hot air to float a zeppelin. But I agreed with everything he said. Fifteen thousand times over.'

Cameron enjoyed bringing in the figure itself as often as possible. It was so definite, clear-cut, a shape for his satisfaction. Morton was talking about the trip to London: 'Okay to use your car then? Ted Dewar and Bob Beattie want to travel down with us. Bob can regale us on the way down with his prophetic conquests. You'd better get the roof of your car raised a bit. Some of the stories will be tall ones.' Cameron was laughing. He had his arm round Allison now and he could feel her body duplicating his own enjoyment. Through the open door he could see Alice come out in sympathy, laughing just to see them laugh, and he winked to her. The moment stilled to a bright crystal with himself inside it. It was one of those instants when our small successes inform us with a vast confidence. Like a skilled trainer he held the ferocious complexity of things tamed to his mood. It didn't seem to matter that the thing between himself and that ferocity was an accidental irrelevance, a fifteen thousand pound contract, a chair of balsa.

14

Margaret stared at the brightness of her lips, impulsively wiped off the lipstick, and just as impulsively applied it again. She might as well let her mother and father see her as she really was, in all her scarlet glory. Her face was convalescent white, even with the make-up. A sign that would have meaning for her father. Jezebel beneath the wrath of the Lord. She shuddered at the prospect. Why was she going at all? Why not? When John had arrived at the flat in pious Christian charity to arrange this confrontation, she had agreed, or rather had failed to refuse. It had occurred to her that he must still be spying on her, to know already that Eddie had broken with her. ('Spurned' would have been her father's word.) Or perhaps her father had received a sign. Presumably they foresaw a reconciliation. What did she foresee? Nothing. They would fetch her and she would go. What would happen there could be no less pointless than everything else that had happened since that day with Eddie.

She turned from the mirror and was assailed by the untidiness of the room. The bed was unmade, the covers whorled with last night's restlessness, her night-dress languishing across them. A library book lay open on the floor beside the bed. Had she been reading it? She could remember taking it out of the library two days ago. But the title escaped her. The bedside chair was festooned with a brassiere. Like a Dali painting. The woman who was a chair. She crossed and made up the bed, not from any positive decision, but as if the crumpled covers had issued a command. The night-dress she put beneath her pillow.

She found herself in the living-room and, sitting down,

lifted a magazine. Bright faces riffled before her eyes, grinning, pouting, staring, models sinewy in woollens, celebrities in casually precise poses. 'Success can come too soon.' 'Go gay this summer.' 'Is the pill safe?' She let the magazine close between her fingers and gazed emptily towards the light.

Grey Sunday pressed up to the window like granite. She felt trapped in this room and was seized with a claustrophobic panic. She was never, never going to escape from it. This was where she belonged, this was her room and it would hold her. She wished for John to hurry up but she felt powerless to rise herself and go out. The bleak articles of furniture, that had been here long before she had, seemed to rise up like jailers, overpowering her presence, crushing her identity. The squat armchair opposite her sat witnessing to the presences of so many others previous to her, so many strange lives that had had to be lived. A cigarette-hole burned in the arm-rest, a scar on the side, a dull stain, seemed implicit with the drabness, the swamping futility of so many pasts. And her own present feeble in the face of them. The table, shining malevolently in the grey light, the legs scuffed and chipped and marked. Children? Meals, voices, arguments. People. Coming and going. So many. A sea of grey lives. Absorbing hers. Overwhelming her in their aimlessness. Till she was drowning. In unheard words and useless actions and the need to do constantly things that had no purpose.

Desperately she clutched for something that would anchor her to herself, fix her to safety. Her eyes searched the anonymity of the room for something of her own, one of the objects with which she had tried to superimpose herself on the fifth, sixth, seventh hand furnishings. The poster of Paris. Nothing of hers here. No recognition. Blankness everywhere. Faces in a crowd.

Signs of someone here, though. Strange signs. Traces of half-completed things. A folded newspaper, some crossword clues filled in with red pen. Not to be finished. Earrings on the mantelpiece. Not to be worn. Shoes discarded on the carpet. No one to put them away. No one. Like a room come to in an empty house. Far from anywhere. Abandoned by whoever lived there. You can only guess who it might have been.

Jotters beside the chair. Uncorrected. Accusing names, demanding attention from someone. James Anderson. Elaine Evans. Thomas Campbell. Ciphers demanding interpretation. An army of strangers, identified only by their special stigmata. Bad syntax. Wrong spellings. Glottal stops. A changing mass of faces. Snub noses. Pimples. Fringes. Spectacles. Pushing up stairs. Whistling in corridors. Passing notes. Scuffling feet. Sniggering behind desks. Writing. Smiling. Hands raised. Please miss, he's got my rubber. Please Miss, I've no pencil. Please miss, I'm feeling sick. Please miss. Please miss. Please. Everywhere faces craning. Eyes like blowtorches. Voices jabbering. Noise. Endless spirals of noise. Vistas of voices down which you reel. Mr Carson standing in the doorway. 'I'm sorry, Miss Sutton. I had assumed there was no teacher in the room.' Lips pursed in distate. Billowing back to his orderly declensions. Paradigms in strict phalanxes. The sanity of Cicero. Smiles caught in cupped hands. Always eyes feeding on her. Faces trapping her. Miss Fox. 'Have you a moment?' Hair shadowing her upper lip. 'Very pleased with your work in the past, Miss Sutton.' A muscle humping like a mole beneath the skin of her jaw. 'And your discipline has always been excellent. But now.' Brow wreathing with sympathy. Crueller than unkindness. 'Appreciate I'm responsible for what happens in my department.' People tall as trees around her. Her father. Mr Carson. The man in the park. 'Hello, darling.' His breath like something dead. 'Where are you headed?' Smiling. 'Come on, now. Come on. Take it easy.' His fingers shiny with sweat on her hand. 'Don't panic. You're all right.' Running. Pursued by faces. Trailing voices. Miss Fox and her father staring into her like a tunnel. Where all their voices reverberated endlessly. 'My department.' 'No daughter of of mine.' 'Please miss.' 'I'm sorry, Margaret.' 'Hello, darling.' 'It's a sin you're committing.' 'Please miss.'

The sound of the bell sent her thoughts scurrying into cover, startled her mind into a void in which the room congealed slowly. A shapeless fear hung for a second before crystallizing into a commonplace on the second buzz of the bell. It was John.

She rose, checked in the mirror, and straightened her dress. She had to be self-possessed to meet her family, must cover her panic from their eyes. By the time she opened the door to John, she was as unruffled as her clothes. John was buttoned into a tight suit and his hair had its Sabbath slick. The sight of him surprised her back into the past. She thought for a second he had come to take her to the Sunday School. Neither of them was anxious to wait long in the flat (John seemed to enter warily, as if not wanting to disturb whoever else might be there), so they wasted no time.

John drove rather quickly, perhaps to get home before Margaret changed her mind. He spoke little. It was the car he had this time, not the van. She wondered if his father gave him the use of it more often now. It was a new one. Very plush. Pleasant how trivial actions could sometimes let you hide behind their normalcy. Sitting beside her brother, being driven home to see her parents on a dull Sunday afternoon: what could be more normal? As they pulled up outside the house, her mother drew back from the window, trying not to be seen. So much for normalcy.

Her first impression was that the house was not as she remembered it. New wallpapers in the hall and in the living-room obtruded their strangeness. But gradually as she settled herself in the living-room, familiar things pushed through the alien pattern of flowers on the wall. The convex mirror. The ducks that had been flying across the wall in unchanging formation as long as she could remember. The small shiny placard beside the fireplace. A rustic cottage. Trellis and plume of pure smoke from the chimney. Hens pecking beatifically in the foreground. All painted in various shades of sugar. And beneath the picture, the rather irrelevant caption, in ornate letters, 'God couldn't be everywhere so he made mothers'. She had bought that herself, as a present for her mother from a holiday in Arran. Aged nine. It looked back at her now like an accusation of lost innocence.

'And how are you yourself, mother?' she was asking. 'Is your back any better?'

'I'm fine, Margaret. Fine.'

But the answer was lost in Margaret's contemplation of her mother. She hadn't changed, only faded further. The hair greyer. The eyes more diffident behind her glasses. The features less clearly defined. Instead of age, as it frequently does, giving a sharper edge of character to the plainest of features, in Margaret's mother it seemed to have instituted a process of regression so that Margaret could imagine her mother's face ending as a featureless blank, all personality having absented itself. Her movements too were even narrower than Margaret remembered them, spiralling in on themselves, as if they didn't like to take up too much room. Her hands were habitually clasped on her lap. Doing perpetual penance. Forgive me myself. As she sat, she seemed to be listening uncertainly for something. John, sitting with them, was the same. Margaret suddenly realised what it was. Her father's absence was more powerful than their own presences. You could almost believe he was in the room. Behind the curtains? In the sideboard taking notes? Was his absence at the moment part of some family plan?

'Your father'll see you in a wee while, Margaret,' her mother said, intercepting her thoughts. 'He's resting just now. In his study. He has a chess long in there now. For lying down on. Doctor says he really must rest. Thinks there's a wee murmur at the heart.' Margaret noticed that her mother still liked to preface things with 'wee', especially if they were threatening, like a household charm with the power to domesticate misfortune. 'You know your father, though. Work, work, work. Drives himself as much as he does anybody else.'

130

'Which is plenty,' John said, gilding the implied criticism with a filial smile.

'And at his age you can't take any chances. So we get him to take a wee rest when we can. He won't be long.'

Margaret wondered what he was thinking at the moment in his 'study', the small room down the hall. She used to call it the 'tabernacle' to herself in her first irreverent flush of intellectual emancipation. Her father would withdraw into it fairly frequently, and nobody ever disturbed him. She had often speculated what exactly he did in there. Once when she was still very young, she had found the door ajar and gone in. She still remembered the strange, furtive feeling that would have amounted to desecration in an adult. There had been a bureau and a high-backed chair with a cushion on it. Invoices and bills, a couple of ledgers, and a bible lying open. She had left hurriedly because the smell of tobacco imbued the room with a mysterious presence for her, like incense in an empty church. Now she thought of him lying there. With a murmur at his heart. It savoured almost of medieval mysticism. The comparison had a certain aptness. Saint Sutton heard celestial murmurings in his heart. The callous flippancy of her thinking shocked her suddenly into guilt. He was her father, after all. How could she make such shabby mental jokes at the expense of his illness?

'You're far too pale, Margaret.' Her mother was shaking her head, oblivious of her own pallor. 'Are you taking care of yourself well enough? And thin! You're so thin.'

Margaret reassured her mother and changed the subject. They all steered round anything that could connect even indirectly with what was most in their minds, Margaret's alienation. It wasn't easy to avoid the subject because they tended to come upon it suddenly, round the corner of an accidental remark. John mentioned a man who had once worked with them, and then they all remembered suddenly that he had left because he had been involved with one of the girls, and they backed away from the topic. They helped each other to cover tracks with fresh questions whenever they

131

seemed to be leading to anything dangerous. It was very successful. Anyone sitting in would have assumed that Margaret had returned home after an extended holiday at some place that nobody else was interested in.

After a time her mother brewed tea and brought out cakes that she knew Margaret liked. When Margaret was finished, her mother noticed crumbs on her lips and gave her a tissue to wipe them off. It was only after Margaret had done it that she realised that she had wiped off her lipstick as well. Her mother was obviously anxious to make Margaret's appearance as inoffensive as possible before her father saw her. Margaret's first reaction was to put on fresh make-up. But she curbed it as being childish. Perhaps already the family reflex of submissiveness was reasserting itself in this familiar atmosphere. If so, she couldn't find the energy to oppose it. Her mother and John were being very nice to her and the very banality of the things they were all talking about was almost a luxury. Margaret was enjoying a feeling of sheer physical well-being that she didn't want to probe too far into, to dissipate under examination.

'Would you like to see your room?' her mother asked suddenly.

The question startled Margaret, made her wary. Its softness gloved an urgency as tight as a clenched fist. She could sense her mother's impatience, like that of a landlady determined to fix terms soon. They couldn't be expecting her to live here again?

'Just take a look at it,' John said. 'It's all been done up too.'

'Show her, John,' her mother said. 'See if you like it, Margaret.'

'This way, madam. As if you didn't know.'

She was aware of her mother and John exchanging secret looks, but she let him take her along to the room. He opened the door with a flourish, as if it led to a revelation, and she went inside. When she turned to make a perfunctory comment, the door was swinging shut by itself and John was gone. She wanted to shout after him not to be silly. She was too old to play this game of hide-and-seek with the past. They were conducting their little conspiracy as unobtrusively as a parade. What did they hope to achieve by leaving her alone in her room for a few minutes? It was ridiculous.

But the peacefulness of the room nullified the stridency of her first thoughts. It was a pleasant place. In spite of herself, she stayed. Away from the pressures of other people, her mind surrendered its defensive position, ceased to bristle with ready-made reactions. Bit by bit the room reclaimed its hold on her memory. She sat down on the bed tentatively, half-afraid that the frenetic terrors which had harangued her loneliness in the flat would return. But this room, unlike the flat, belonged in some sense inseparably to herself. How often her thoughts had come stealthily back to this room like a thief in search of solace. For though she had fought to be free of it and had been glad to leave it behind her, her loneliness had often craved the companionship of physical objects that had been long acquainted with her past. They were here. The bed she sat on, that had carried her through the furtive fears of childhood, dynamic dreams of sex, adolescent brooding on death. The low scratched desk across which her pen had pursued problems of grammar, understanding, personal belief. Its surface still showed faint doodles in ink, frozen whims of boredom. The small book-rack, empty now, which had registered the development of her taste from fairy tales to Rimbaud.

She crossed and opened the wardrobe door. It smelled of disuse in spite of her mother's duster. A couple of metal hangers rattled sadly and her memory fleshed their skeletons immediately with dresses. A bright skirt flared in her mind, evoking a day spent at Ayr with a girl-friend. Two boys had bought them coffees and they had made a date which they never kept. She recalled a red sheath dress which her father threatened to burn the first time he saw her with it on. She had wept her way to victory and gone out of the house with the rims of her eyes like matching accessories. The ridiculousness of it seemed to typify so much of her life. So often she had had to go to war to establish her right to what was no more than a reflex in other girls. Her father's habitual opposition had made her rationalise every urge, gut it with questions until the living impulse had become an anatomical specimen. Deprived of naturalness, she had been forced to build up attitudes on the mechanical foundation of intellectual conviction, made up largely of the spare parts of other people's thoughts pilfered from books. She realised for the thousandth time that she was the least spontaneous of people, and the knowledge was infinitely enervating. Every instinct had to be fought for against doubts and misgivings. Except with Eddie. With him for the first time she had experienced a relationship the intensity of which had created an area burned bare of complexity, had annihilated doubt and inhibition in its heat. At least for one of them. But that lay lost behind her and the future stretched impossibly ahead. She couldn't face the prospect of humping the complicated and fitful machinery she had made of herself alone through years where every day was tangled with decisions. As she closed the wardrobe door, the hangers clashed faintly.

She went to the small dresser and opened the bottom drawer. The notebook was all it contained, looking scruffy against the smooth lining of green paper. She was surprised that her mother hadn't thrown it out. Taking it out, she sat on the bed and flicked through it. Her personal archives. Diary of a small rebellion. Like a lot of diaries, it was in a sort of code. When she was making notes in it, for a year or two before she left the house, she had been afraid some of the family might read it, so that the entries had a cryptic objectivity about them that denied an outsider access to herself. But even yet she recognised immediately the significance of each of these secret markings along her route to independence. Many were quotations: a poem called 'Jenny kissed me when we met'; an extract from D. H. Lawrence beginning 'That I am part of the earth my feet know perfectly'; an epigram from Robert Frost: 'We love the things we love for what they are'. Some were brief records of casual incidents: an old man sitting in the underground, wearing senility like a sandwich-board; a mother reprimanding a child for dirtying her dress. Some were small thoughts that had occurred to her, like: 'Either salvation is open to everyone or to no one. But a person can be born by chronological or geographical accident outside of a Christian context'. They had all seemed important to her at the time, small nuggets of certainty won from confusion and put towards the purchasing of her freedom. Now the desperate industry that had gleaned them mocked her present lethargy. The strongest expression of her individuality at the moment was a desire to lie down and sleep on this bed. She was simply exhausted with her struggle to be herself. She put the book away.

As she came back into the living-room, her mother and John were watching her closely for signs of surrender. Perhaps the signs were there. She only knew that if they asked her to stay she wasn't sure what her answer would be. But before they could do more than elicit her impressions of the new wallpaper, there were sounds from her father's room. Silence rolled across the living-room like a boulder. The presence would soon be present. As they waited, his footsteps came sonorously along the hall. Margaret wondered if that was why he preferred parquet to carpeting, as something on which to measure out the dignity of his progress, a means of announcing himself to his subjects. She deliberately began to talk against the solemnity of his footsteps, trying to neutralise the impact of his arrival.

'I see you've still got my old desk in the room, mother. You should sell it to an art gallery as a genuine example of primitive art.'

But the footsteps won. Neither her mother nor John heard what she was saying. As the door opened, her mother offered Margaret a blank furtive smile into which she was left to read what she wanted – encouragement, a plea for restraint, abdication of responsibility for what was to follow, nervousness.

The moment of the Grand Confrontation had arrived. Her father stood in the doorway. He was heavier than her mental image of him. His face had in her thoughts always had the quality of those faces of American presidents that are hewn out of the cliffs of Mount Rushmore. Now it was as if the rock had been crumbling in her absence. Flesh had eroded into pouches below the eyes. The jowls sagged. The cumbersome bulk of his body all but filled the doorway. His expression was one of Tired Stoicism. With him every expression had capital letters. His face was no casual edifice on which he allowed mere whims to scribble their graffiti. He reserved it for the expression of the momentous, and on it his limited range of moods was sculpted slowly and unveiled with formal dignity. The text for today was evidently: 'Why Persecutest Thou Me?'

'Oh hullo,' Margaret said. 'It's daddy.'

The remark was deliberately fatuous, an attempt to sabotage his moment, like laughter in the stalls as Hamlet broods. But the quiet persistence of his seriousness silenced her impertinence. He came slowly into the room.

'Margaret,' he said simply, making the word sound like a Scots translation of 'De profundis clamavi'.

And again Margaret bridled instantly, and then felt instantly ashamed. What right did she have to assume that every attitude of his was false? Perhaps before, when he had sermonised against everything from modern morality to lipstick, there had been some justification in the assumption. But since then she had surely done enough to teach his poses honesty. She had committed adultery. She wasn't sure what horrible images that word would conjure up in the bleak and secret recesses of his mind, but she could guess that they would be very harrowing. He was a man who hugged his principles to him before all else and what she had done must have made a hairshirt of them. The suffering she had caused him was a kind of compensation for her own. Perhaps better to leave it at that.

'How are you, father?' she asked.

136

'I'm fine. Fine,' he said, sitting down. 'And yourself?'

'I'm all right.'

The formalities were a declaration of peace. It only remained to establish terms. He wasted no time.

'We think you should come back to us, Margaret.'

'We've just been showing Margaret her room again,' her mother said.

She wanted them to exchange more inanities, knowing that small talk compromises our ability to meet one another on more dangerous ground. But Margaret's father's talk was never small. Precepts were his stock-in-trade.

'Blood's thicker than water,' he said. 'We've all had a long time to think about this. What's happened is over with. This is your home, after all. It's where you belong.'

'We've missed you such a lot, Margaret. All of us.' Her mother was discreetly mitigating her father's solemnity by including him in her admission.

'I've certainly missed having to queue for the bathroom in the morning.' John added his feather of flippancy to try to balance the scales of the moment, which were already tilting with the weight of coming dicta.

'The past few years haven't been easy on any of us. But we can get over them. This wouldn't be a Christian house if we couldn't practise forgiveness in it.'

Margaret wished desperately that she didn't know him quite so well. It meant she hadn't missed the swift displeasure his face expressed at the interruptions of her mother and John. It made her feel that she could interpret that displeasure exactly: he had several sonorities to deliver; this was not a time to be ad-libbing. That one perception set up inevitably a multitude of echoes of itself out of the past. He had always been so overbearing. Did he still see God as a cosmic bully and himself made in His image? Flippancy had no part in his world. Had it never occurred to him that any God who had been responsible for life must have had a very active, if frequently opaque, sense of humour? He had always had the gift of oracular ambiguity. Who was to be bestowing the forgiveness and who receiving? Regretting that knowledge of another which corrupts the innocence of our reactions, she tried to come to her father openly, in a small act of faith. Perhaps she was wrong. She hoped so. Any offer of refuge from her loneliness wasn't something she felt inclined to turn down lightly.

'I never deliberately set out to cause any of you any pain, father,' she said.

'No, Margaret, no. But what matters isn't the past. What matters is will you come back to us?'

In spite of herself, the moment overwhelmed Margaret. It was the unexpected directness of the question, her father in an unfamiliar attitude of appeal, showing a vulnerability which was somehow all the more moving for his long-standing edifice of impregnable rectitude, as if she had glimpsed him for a moment skulking in the clangorous emptiness of his own myth. It was her mother's attendant anxiety, casting her once again in that role that expressed her life, liver by other people's decisions. It was John encouraging her with his silence. It was most of all how her father's question touched suddenly on the raw of what had happened to them. How did a family reach the point where such a question had to be asked? How could you answer such a question?

'I suppose I could, father.'

Her quiet reply seemed all they wanted. The tension relaxed into smiles. Even her father looked benign. Margaret's participation in their pleasure was a bit laggard, caught up uncertainly. Was one sentence all it took to heal so many breaches?

'That's great, Margaret,' John reassured her.

'Then you definitely will come back?' her mother pressed.

'Of course, she will!' her father answered for her. 'You can stay here from tonight, Margaret. John'll get the van and bring anything you want back to the house for you. There's no point in going back to that place again.'

The novelty of being swept away on other people's concern for her made Margaret happily helpless for a moment. She could only laugh.

'You'll soon have forgotten all about *him*,' her mother said, made daring by success.

'Hannah!' Her father's reprimand was gentle in honour of the occasion. 'There'll be no mention of that. Ever again. Margaret's gone through enough. She knows her mistake now. She's aware of what *he* is, well enough. We won't be ramming it down her throat. It'll be as if it had never been.'

The smile he offered to her as he said it made her lose faith in everything. Did he understand nothing? She felt her momentary happiness receding, and clutched at it despairingly.

'Wait a minute, father,' she said. 'I want to come back. But I can only come back as myself. Please, now. That's what I have to do, isn't it? And I don't think you realise what I feel about Eddie. That's the same person as 'he' and 'him'. In case you're wondering.'

'Margaret. That kind of talk'll get us nowhere.'

'It'll get us to the truth. Which is quite important. But I don't suppose you're interested. You never were.'

The brief charade of carnival homecoming was over. They were themselves again, entrenched in their old positions as if the past few years had never been. A few sentences had been enough to dispel the mirage. Yet she mourned for it very deeply and felt bitter that they should have fooled her into believing in it at all. It would have been so good to come home to somewhere. She wouldn't have been asking for much, only for the run of her own convictions.

'Margaret. Listen to me. Can I do any more than what I'm doing? I'm prepared to take you back. I want to take you back. You can come here and we'll go on from where we left off. As if nothing had happened. It'll be all right, Margaret. I know it will. You'll forget all that . . . unfortunate experience. We'll help you to do that. A few years from now it'll be forgotten. Gone. It's better like that. Time heals. But you can't ask me to condone what you did. That's all I'm asking from you.'

Now she understood the offer he had been making. The future was to be a return to the Authorised Version of her life, making a palimpsest of the past few years. All adulterous daughters will be made welcome, provided they are virgins.

'I'm not asking you to condone what I did, father. I don't need you to condone it. All I would ask is that you allow it to mean what it means to me. That's all. And don't do me the favour of acting as if nothing has happened. An awful lot has happened. And what has happened matters to me. What would you want me to do? Leave my past in the flat for the next tenant?'

'Correct me if I'm wrong. But are you trying to impose conditions on *me*?'

'Father. For God's sake –'

'Don't take the Lord's name in vain in this house!'

She had forgotten just how preposterous he could be. Why had he allowed John to bring her back in the first place? It was the same, everything was the same. What he wanted wasn't her. He wanted the daughter she should have been. She couldn't come back. In spite of his earlier generous protestation, she didn't belong here. She stood up, trapped hopelessly between the loneliness of this house and the loneliness of the flat. Refusing to cry, she had only anger to escape into.

'Did you bring me here just to let me know what you thought of what I've done? I could've guessed. Why didn't you leave me alone? You've never understood anything. Have you? I love Eddie. That's all. And if he left his wife, I would live with him. Tomorrow.'

'Don't say these things. They aren't true.'

'Oh yes, father. They're true. Be very brave. And face up to seeing just what a monster you have spawned. I've made love to a man. You'll have to try to live with the shame of it.'

'You're sick, Margaret,' he said pityingly.

She was nearer now to crying. The room seemed so cosy, so secure, a place she would have liked to stay in. But she knew that, with every word, she made the possibility of ever living here again more remote. She was saying things that had never been uttered in this house before, shocking the very furnishings, it seemed, with ideas whose existence had never been openly acknowledged here. Yet she couldn't stop herself, pushed herself helplessly further and further away from them even as she needed them to be nearer her. Her voice rose hysterically, defying tears. Too often her father had reduced her to that state of surrender. This time he wouldn't.

'Yes, I'm sick, father. And you're the one who made me sick. Crippled me with your own prejudices. So that I've come to doubt just about everything I do. What were you so afraid of, father? What was it? That I'd turn out to be a whore? I'm not. But even if I had been going to be one, you could have let me at least be a competent one. This way, I don't know who I am. Or what I am. You never had enough respect for me to let me just become myself. But what little I am, I'll keep. It's not for sale for a nice bed and my meals made for me.'

His face read, 'Father, forgive her.' Shock accused her from every corner of the room. She had talked herself inside out and her family could only offer her embarrassment. She turned to her mother and touched her shoulder.

'I'm sorry,' she said.

'Oh, Margaret.' Her mother made one of her small ambiguous movements towards her, hobbled with diffidence.

'Poor mother,' Margaret said, as if it conveyed the unnecessary sadness of what they had all become. 'Poor mother'.

'Don't presume to pity anyone in this house,' her father said. 'You can get your coat and go.'

John fetched it for her and helped her into it.

'I'll run you home, Margaret,' he said.

Where was home?

'You'll let her walk.'

'It's all right, John. I'll walk.'

'I'm running you home.'

'The car is mine. I said you'll let her walk.'

'You can take the petrol money off my wages. And the wear and tear shouldn't amount to much really.'

'What's happening in this house? John. You will let her walk.'

'Go to hell,' John said evenly.

He escorted Margaret into the car. He tried to console her on the way back to the flat but she didn't speak. Coming in with her, he waited around vaguely, looking for things to say that would help. But she was alone long before he left.

Going out, he said, 'I'll be along to see you, Margaret. Next Sunday. And every Sunday after that. Any time you need me, just let me know. Any time at all. Even if you just want to talk about things. I'm no philosopher. But I've good big ears for listening. That might help. You'll do that if you're feeling bad. All right?'

She nodded. At the door he said with sudden anger, 'Damn him!'

She sat remembering the words when he had gone. They were so unlike John, they constituted a minor insurrection in his nature. They reminded her of herself, a long time ago. A very long time ago. But the comfortable simplicity they expressed was a long way behind her. Nothing was simple any more. Even now she was ashamedly searching what she had said for injustices. It came to her more clearly than ever that her father had won. His real arguments antedated her ability to defend herself, were planted in her too secretly for her ever to be able to locate them, remove the fuses. They went off time after time, triggered by some unsuspecting action or thought, wounding endlessly. For how long? The cold anonymity of the room encroached on her again, bringing jotters, untidiness, bleak furniture, reclaiming her slowly, slowly.

15

'For they are jolly good fellows, fellows, fellows. And so say all of me.'

Bob Beattie sang, a forty-year-old boy-soprano, his voice an accidental innocence that was mocked by his satyr's face. As he bowed towards Morton and Cameron, the whisky tumbler he held up magnified the right half of his face so that it swam out of proportion to the rest, projected on the striations of the glass. His right eye bulged out at Cameron like a tumour, grown ludicrously into the middle of their evening where he sat beside Morton, with Ted Dewar opposite, and through the open door of the residents' lounge the receptionist was bent over her desk, looking up from time to time to have a buckshee share of the fun. Everybody laughed, laughter that emerged not from the humour of anything Bob had done but from the benevolence of the moment.

'Remember me when you come into your kingdom,' Bob said and sashayed out to talk to the receptionist.

He wasn't missed. The evening had pretty well played itself out and each was improvising his own conclusion. Cameron and Morton chatted fitfully about the past. Ted Dewar had drunk himself into a private nirvana where his usual pleasantness amplified into a cosmic benevolence and his natural deliberateness of speech, scar of an old impediment, took on undertones of profundity. Dip a platitude in drink and it comes out wisdom.

Only Bob still fretted after some other unrealised evening which the banality of the present one was somehow hiding from them. The three of them had allowed him to conduct them through the evening in search of the Big Night he believed in, had followed in the geisha steps of his small, jerky body while, like an Ali Baba who has forgotten the formula, he brought them up against one blank wall after another. Beginning with the confidence of a magician who knows the strange things he is keeping up his sleeves, he set out to show them some of the 'real places'. One of these turned out to be a pub whose only distinction was the number of homosexuals in it. Another place was a club where some tatty girls coaxed themselves out of their clothes. By the time each had dismantled herself to the chassis all that was left was a goose-pimpled anti-climax, rather touching in its standard-issue anonymity. The effect of the most flamboyant display of eroticism on Ted was to bring forth the remark: 'Wee soul! She'll catch her death'.

Some locales later, it was becoming obvious that Bob had no more up his sleeves than a couple of arms. Desperation set in. As the others talked among themselves, they were fleetingly conscious of the number of varied *decors* they were seeing. Bob would sit for twenty minutes or so in a new place before saying, 'Dead, isn't it?' And the caravan pressed on. Before it the city unwound like a mummy-cloth. Nothing was relentlessly happening. The only thing that approximated to an event occurred late on. Going up for more drinks, Bob referred to a lady at the bar as 'kiddo', suggesting that she 'Shuffle the beam a bit' to let him in. The man she was with came round from the other side of her and told Bob to apologise. He didn't ask for an apology in so many words but since he said, 'You're very impolite for a pygmy,' the implication was present. Looking him straight in the tie-pin, Bob said nothing. The metallic glitter worked on him like hypnosis. Whatever gangster film had inspired his request, he found himself out of script. Only the intervention of the other three discouraged the big man. It proved to be the only offer of excitement the evening made them. Afterwards, on the pavement outside, Bob stood like Cortez on the kerb, gazing up and down the ordinary street, muttering, 'This is London, boys. Must be a helluva lot going on somewhere. If only we knew the places. I know a spot we haven't tried.' They took him back to the hotel under protest.

Since coming back to the hotel, Bob had been roaming round the lounge, drinking, looking out of windows, throwing the odd irrelevance into the conversation, still absently trying to invoke the Spirit of the Big Night. Now he was consoling himself with the receptionist, a woman who looked around forty and whose professional niceness had innocently ignited Bob's combustible imagination.

'It's you two's night sure enough.' Ted often compressed remarks to syntactical capsules that were easier to get over without stammering. Sometimes difficult words were omitted, imparting a certain telegrammatic urgency to the most mundane sentences. 'You moving to London, Sid. Eddie taking over Glasgow.'

'You make it sound ominous, Ted,' Cameron said. 'Ticker-tape and jackboots. The Fasces in George Square.'

'Might not be a bad idea, Eddie.' Morton had been giving Cameron jocular advice all night, discreetly passing on his mantle of know-how. 'It's up to you to get results. You've got to push people a bit. Unpleasant sometimes, but it has to be done. I'll leave you a couple of my rhino-whips in the cupboard.'

'First thing I'll do is buy a manual on flogging.'

'Sid's right though,' Ted announced and gagged momentarily on the follow-up. 'Me. I couldn't. Couldn't be hard enough. Used to think I might. But no. Some have, some haven't. I'm no boss. By the time you're reaching fifty, you're what you are. I'm a seller. An average seller.'

He raised his glass and swallowed as if drinking to it. It was like Ted hanging his future on a hook, having no further use for it. And he was smiling as he put down his glass with a click of finality.

'I leave ambition to the boys,' Ted laughed.

He had a married daughter, a son at university. His future lay in becoming a grandfather, father to a graduate. Tomorrow would come by proxy. It was chilling to witness such an admission made so happily. Ted seemed to erode before Cameron's eyes into one frozen reflex of pleasantness, a skull condemned to grin forever.

'That's fair enough, Ted.' Morton recharged their three glasses, prelude to philosophy. 'Up to a point. It's what I used to tell Eddie. Even at school. Nobody ever gets what he wants. You have to learn to want what you can get. Eddie here used to have some helluva ideals. Remember, Eddie?'

Cameron remembered. From the beginning Morton had been the Octavius to his Anthony. Coming on a scholarship to their school, which was mainly fee-paying, Morton had gravitated almost at once to Cameron. It wasn't so much friendship as that strange rivalry which schoolboys express by proximity. Their closeness hung ambivalently between an arm-link and an arm-lock. The wrestling matches of boyhood were sublimated into the arguments of adolescence. But though the cockpit changed from bodies to ideologies, the terms of conflict remained more or less constant, Cameron eager always to move beyond himself and striking poses from which he hoped to realise positions, Morton pinning everything to the limits of his own reach and hitting Cameron's pretensions remorselessly with small, hard facts. Their relationship had never really altered. Cameron remembered.

'Same with all kids, I suppose.' Morton was running smoothly on the whisky. 'The more's the pity. The other night there, Eddie. Elspeth's cleaning out a cupboard. Hauls out this old photograph. Us. The whole class. Christ, what a bunch. We were a ghastly crew. You wouldn't believe it. I mean, were we ever as young as that? Eyes like open wounds. Apply salt here. It's funny. With all their science, they haven't managed to find any way of by-passing adolescence. You would think they could do something about it. Have people getting born about twenty-two or so. Relegate all their illusions and crummy ideals to a kind of post-natal waste. Something disposable. Like placenta.'

To Cameron it almost seemed that that had been the case with Morton. From as early as Cameron could remember,

Morton had been a compendium of various ages bound up temporarily in a boy's body. The blue eyes showed fleeting depths of knowingness the others couldn't fathom, the wide mouth issued adult and unquestionable dicta between phrases of fourth-form jargon, and the whole mechanism steered itself through classroom crises with awesome impunity. It was as if he had come into the world with all his teeth and clutching his private book of rules.

'Take Jim Forbes as an example. What about Jim, then? I mean, don't get me wrong. I like him.' Morton's smile expanded into the largesse of a laugh. 'But what a bloke! No idea of what it's all about. The man from Mars. A hotchpotch of this, that and yon. Never be anything because he wants to be everything. What did he want to be at school? Remember? A missionary. Right? So what is he doing now? Working with the electricity board. It figures. One of God's metaphorical jokes. 'Let there be light'.' Morton laughed along with God. 'No I think they broke the mould *before* they made old Jim.'

'He's a good bloke,' Cameron countered feebly.

'Of course, he is. Amen. So put that in the bank. No, Eddie. He's one of the lotus-eating many. That craphouse we went to was full of them. It fed them on fancies. Fattened them for the world to make a meal on. Kitted them out with toy ideals and marched them into the lion's mouth. And they went. Idealistic to the end. And what are they now? Failure-addicts, every one. Remember Ralph Simpson? The writing man. A hot tip for high places. Brooding in corners. Dreaming Utopia. Now he's a civil servant. Grade B. And what's he written? A couple of constipated poems in the *Glasgow Herald*. The kind of doodles you would put in the margin of the margin. Think of the straining and stressing he went through to produce a few cold droppings. Break your heart. That man just dreamed himself to death. Count yourself lucky you didn't go that road, Eddie. The list is endless. Don Walker. Lawson Emmerson. Remember them? The young pretenders. Where are they now?'

Cameron drank from his glass of aloes to evade an answer. Morton had recited the names effortlessly as if he had learned them by heart, like the books of his personal bible. Certainly Cameron could think of nothing to refute Morton's testament. His own sense of failure found a kind of bitter solace in the sermon, like a dying man hearing Armageddon preached. Perhaps it was only a habit of antipathy that made his mouth withhold the agreement his heart was yielding bleakly.

'You've got to see what's there for you to take and take it. The rest can go to hell. Right, Eddie? Lucky for you, you're working a good seam now. Stay with it. You can see your road ahead to something definite.'

Morton's book of words was closed. His last sentence remained in Cameron's mind like a minister's parting precept, portable wisdom for taking home and pondering. Whatever motives Morton had for delivering his homily (to win the final skirmish of a conflict that had begun in a distant, clamorous playground?), the moment was well chosen. Taking Cameron at his weakest, he had pinned both shoulders to the mat. The last submission.

Cameron could see that road ahead, too. The night was a small crossroads. By agreeing to take over Morton's job, he had chosen a route. From it there stretched an undeviating future he would follow. In every sense that mattered, what he was now was all he would ever be. With the slow coming of the thought Cameron felt a coldness small as a grain revolve in him, an ice age in embryo. He was apprenticed to the condition of which Ted was a master.

'Aye. It's only when you get older you find out who you are. I was a different person every day when I was young. Never came in the same person I went out. One minute wanted to be a surgeon. Five minutes later, writing away to the army. Once had a strong ambition to be a sailor. For a while.' Ted laughed at himself. 'Now I get sea-sick going to Arran.'

That was one of the basic skills you had to learn: how to make irony compensate for the loss of faith in yourself. You imitated the economy of nature, feeding new qualities from the carcass of the old. Yesterday's romance is today's satire. 'Why not?' Cameron thought. The harvest was home. At least you could get some heat from burning the husks.

'If you're going to be a hero, you must die young,' Ted reported from his cosmic vantage.

'Rule number one,' Cameron agreed. 'From Dewar's Handbook for Heroes. Twelve easy steps to heroism. Tell you another thing.' He slid over the remainder of his whisky in one smooth gulp as if it was something solid, like a jellied eel. Take that, you ulcer. Morton was refilling the glass as it touched the table. 'It's the small things cut you down to size. Other week I was one day without my car. Running for a bus. Five years ago I would've caught it. Just to realise that gave me wrinkles. I'm telling you. I aged five years in ten yards. You could kid yourself on all right if it wasn't for the wee fifth-columns. Thinning hair and rotting teeth. Paunches and varicose veins. They're the real killers. Eh? Your ideals've got to be cast-iron to survive them. They get through to you eventually. I mean, who ever heard of a hero with halitosis?'

They had all been drinking enough to share in the perception of the moment.

'That's right,' Ted confirmed. 'Or rheumatics.'

Morton downed his drink and poised on the thought, closer to toppling into drunkenness than Cameron had ever seen him before.

'In-growing toenails,' he said.

They started to laugh, suddenly realising that they had discovered a new form of conversational snap. The quickening tempo had spun into instant vortex the drunkenness that had been whirling slowly for some time below the surface of their remarks, gathering a gradual momentum.

'Short-sightedness,' Ted adjusted his glasses.

'Housemaid's knee.' Morton wondered if the introduction of a feminine complaint would disqualify him.

'Ulcers,' Cameron said, and drank some whisky.

Their laughter rang out again, a decibel nearer inanity.

'Eddie thinks he's got an ulcer,' Morton said and it seemed funny.

'Welcome to the sacred brotherhood of ulcermen,' Bob Beattie announced from the doorway.

His presence precipitated all sense from the scene. They looked at him and he brought the earlier part of the evening back in with him. What had at the time been only a meaningless succession of places now cohered into a unified satire on Bob. He made a comedian's entrance, getting an advance of laughter on reputation alone.

'You're one of us, Eddie,' he said. 'Come round to my house some night and I'll put you through the inauguration ceremony. Compare duodenums. Duodena? Some sod's been drinking my share of the whisky.' He filled his glass. 'You better leave the rest of this to me, Eddie. Not good for you. Good thing for you I've just been chatting up the receptionist. She's bringing in a tray for us. Sandwiches and milk. Just what you need.'

'Sandwiches and milk!' Morton's expression archly involved Cameron and Ted in a conspiracy. 'That's quite a come-down for a *bon viveur* like you.'

'Ah, but you don't know what I'm getting for afters.'

'Don't give us that,' Morton said. 'Judging by your performance earlier, it's probably an electric blanket. What a sodding night! We'd have got more fun doing a tour of the wayside pulpits.'

'You hit these off nights. Last year was different. A bunch of us went to this wee place . . . You boys weren't with me last year, were you?'

His answer was a chorus of derision.

'Well, I'll show you a trick,' Bob said.

The scene took off completely for Cameron, shored away from any relation to anything at all. The room was a corner of nowhere, a lighted patch in a void, peopled impossibly with their bodies, loud with their braying voices. He felt an iconoclastic urge to compound its chaos, to clown himself out of commitment to anything, to be a part of the aimlessness, a fragment in the vortex, to say or do something, anything, that would merge him with the happy pointlessness of the moment.

'Make it a vanishing one,' Morton was advising Bob.

The receptionist came in with the tray as if cued by Bob's embarrassment.

Cameron got up and crossed to her. The sandwiches were cut into dainty triangles. He seized three, putting one into his mouth like a sweet.

'Excuse me while I salivate,' he said. 'Sometimes I get really vicious about food. Like an animal. I get this terrible hunger. It suddenly hits me. Maybe I come in late some night. And I'm desperate for food. Anything. I *shake* with hunger. Anybody gets in my way, I'm liable to chew their arm off. It's weird.' The rest of them left the tray on the table where the receptionist put it, untouched for the moment. They sensed Cameron's words developing into a performance. Morton was shaking his head and smiling. 'It must be an ulcer. That must be what it is. Where we work, all the most successful men have ulcers.' He gestured at Bob, who bowed. 'Sid there must have two or three he doesn't talk about. Ted, that's where you made your mistake. You didn't get an ulcer.' They were laughing, had become an audience. 'It's a kind of status symbol. The sign that you've arrived. That's the key to their success. That hole in their gut to which they consecrate all their worry and frenetic energy. They feed the ulcer with themselves. The pearl in the oyster.' Cameron made a pause out of taking another sandwich. 'Bob's right. They're a sacred brotherhood. The ulcer men. You can't really make it till you're one of them. They lack something you don't lack. And they've got you. Because, what is it? You don't know. And who can ever be sure he's going to have an ulcer? You can't. It's something mystical. You can work late and cut down on your sleep. But that's not to say you'll ever earn your ulcer. Unless you're one of the chosen. Unless you can make the final act of faith. Endure the ultimate agony of perforation.' The phone rang on the hotel desk and the receptionist went out. 'The ulcer men. That's the new spiritual élite. You can recognise them by the halo of personal suffering, the twinge of quiet communion. They've got the sacred marks. The stigmata of Mammon.' He touched his stomach reverentially. 'Maybe this is a sign. That I'm to be one of them. If it is, I've got to endure it. Unworthy as I am. Mammon's will be done.'

Their applause was interrupted by the receptionist.

'It's for you, Mr Cameron,' she said. 'A woman's voice. She didn't say who she was.'

'For me?' Cameron said vacantly as if he wasn't sure who that was.

'Good for you!' Bob's altruism became sullied at once. 'Rally round, boys. She might have some mates for us.'

'Could be Eddie's wife,' Ted explained.

'Wives never phone at this time. Come on.'

Ted was far enough gone to see amusement in the situation. While Morton and the receptionist tactfully remained behind in the lounge, the other two followed Cameron to the phone. It barely occurred to Cameron who it might be. This was just another senseless ramification of the night. The receptionist might as well have said anybody else's name as his. The receiver lay abandoned on the desk. Why should it be his hand that had to pick it up? As it did so, he protested laughingly against the encroachments of Bob and Ted.

'Hullo.'

'Eddie?'

The voice came fraught with an immediacy which the distance it travelled mocked to irrelevance.

'Who is this?'

'Margaret. Eddie, I had to phone you. I'm sorry if it's awkward for you. But I just had to. Eddie?'

Bob nudged Cameron's elbow.

'Who is it?' he giggled.

Cameron couldn't get his attention focused on the shape of what was happening, slewed dizzily from fragment to fragment. Ted stood a little back, uneasy chaperone, Bob tried to catch the echo of what was going on from Cameron's face.

Margaret waited for some reaction. Cameron offered nothing, a hollow where the centre of the whole thing should have been.

'Eddie. Listen to me. I'm phoning from a public box. And I don't have any more change. I've got to see you again, Eddie. When you get back. When do you get back? You're leaving tomorrow, aren't you? Well, I must see you when you get back. Please. Eddie! For God's sake, speak to me. Will you come and see me when you get back?'

'Well. I don't know.'

Bob had a sudden inspiration and leaned as close as he could to the mouthpiece.

'Put down the phone, darling,' he said in a woman's voice encased in a home-made London accent, 'and come back to bed.'

Then he retracted, buckling in a laugh.

'Even a eunuch has his uses,' Ted observed.

'What's going on, Eddie? What's wrong? It doesn't matter. Look. I've got to see you again. To speak to you. I don't know what I'm going to do if I don't. I just don't know.'

Cameron wished he had never lifted up the phone, had never involved himself in the hearing of those words, because they made him share in the pain of a despair in which he couldn't help. He was like a radio ham tuned in by accident to the distress signals of a ship far out to sea, awed at the broken phrases of desperation which he caught, and riveted to his own incapacity. What could he do from several hundred miles away? And even if he were home, what could he do?

'Come on,' Ted told Bob. 'You've had your fun. Let's go back through and let Eddie get on with it.'

Bob let himself be ordered back to the lounge.

'Margaret,' Cameron said. 'What's happened?'

'Everything's happened. I don't know. I can't stand much more of this.' The pips started and Cameron could hear the click of the operator coming in. 'I don't know what's going to happen. I just don't know.'

'I'm sorry. Your time's up. Do you wish to pay for more time?'

'Eddie. You will come, won't you? Say you will.'

Cameron said nothing because he didn't know. Helplessly, he listened to Margaret's voice talking against that of the operator. The operator spoke to him and he didn't answer.

'I'm sorry, madam. Your party's off the line.'

The clinical voice calmly overruled her desperate objections.

'Eddie. You will come? Eddie. Eddie . . .' and the voice was locked away to rage in privacy.

Still pressing the receiver to his ear, he heard it sough with silence, eternity in a sea-shell. The mouthpiece was beaded with his breath, like substitute tears, as he set it down and turned back towards the lounge.

He saw Morton with a sandwich, laughing, pleasantly drunk. Even when he was drunk, there was a sense of deliberateness about it, like a man consciously making himself a concession in return for something accomplished. But what was it exactly he had accomplished? What had they both accomplished?

As Cameron went back into the lounge, he held his mouth strained into a smile that blistered his lips.

16

With the curtains unclosed, a window of moonlight was in
the room, broken across the different levels of floor and bed,
making a glacier of the coverlet that their bodies humped
into arbitrary contours. Her breathing was the only sound
but it seemed to confirm the silence rather than negate it,
was the small, steady pulse of the peacefulness which filled
the room.

The alarm at the bedside had stopped ticking a few minutes ago. Its sudden silence had summoned him back from
the exploration of his thoughts. He had made to get up and
rewind it when he remembered that tomorrow was Saturday.
Holding his wrist close to his eyes, he stared patiently until
the dial kindled slowly to a glow. Twenty-five past one. Today was Saturday. Shopping with the family in the morning.
Lunch in the city. An afternoon that offered a pleasantly
limited range of choices: to wash the car, read something,
make a few ritual gestures in the garden, referee the children's
squabbles? To be or not to be. A Hamlet of the suburbs. An
evening of television, and too many cigarettes.

He decided to have a cigarette now, to cash in on his sleep-
lessness. Learn to enjoy your insomnia. Carefully he extri-
cated himself from Allison's looping arm and eased himself
out of the uniform mass of their flesh. Emergence from
protoplasm. The coolness of the carpet below his feet was a
sensual windfall, the dressing-gown thawed to the warmth
of his shoulders, lagging the heat. The match revved to a
wooden candle in his hand. As he stood at the window, the
cigarette glowed and dimmed like an esoteric signal.

No one was there to see it. Outside, dark, still houses

colonised the moonlight, and fenced its acres of mystery into neat order. Within each darkness, people bedded as carefully as planted seeds, imbibing their dreams, sap of tomorrow. All growing in salubrious separation, protected from entanglements with others, drawing sustenance from the roots of their own privacy, the tubers of certainty. Like Cameron himself.

Allison stirred on the bed. Sleep and abandon seemed to bloat her body a little. He smiled, a confession of affection made to the darkness. His private burial mound. Temporary monument in whose recesses all his wealth had been stored away over the years, hopes, pleasures, frustrations, despairs, all smelted down into the only currency that life always honoured, raw energy. She looked ageless, mummified by the moon.

The curtains should have been drawn. But they had come to bed too quickly. Lust didn't take stock of irrelevancies, though the irrelevancies returned. Frightened off by motion, they resettled in stillness, feeding quietly. Big and small, migrant and resident, they fouled the purity of each moment with their droppings, the harpies born of habit. Curtains to be drawn. Appointments to be kept. Margaret.

Margaret. The name ambushed his conscience. For most of a week, since his return from London, he had successfully evaded her image. Escape routes had been numerous. Laurelled with promotion, he had come home to a house festive with smiles. Allison's manner had declared a holiday from the usual daily business of trying to out-negotiate each other's ambitions. Under the new dispensation bed had lost its inhibitive atmosphere of an endless case being heard in camera, and had reverted to being a place where bodies could be bartered without complications. Enjoying an immediate pleasure, he had postponed looking beyond it, except insofar as he could distribute without discomfort the surplus of his goodwill beyond the walls of his house. That meant in practice doing such innocuously nice things as taking more of the administrative load off Morton than could have been expected of him at this stage (he had been in and out of Morton's office so often in the past few days that he had almost established a joint tenancy), making complete preparations for his trip to Dumfries the following week (with as few demands on the office staff as possible), indulging a Croesus reflex to the whip-round for the two girls who were being married, taking upon himself the organisation of the office-party (although it was almost certain that he wouldn't be there to enjoy it), making out a mock invitation to Jim Forbes and having it delivered to his office. His altruism had been thorough, almost professional, as if he was driving a hard bargain with events. I'll be good to you, world, if you'll be good to me. Now a single image proved it rotten. The effect on him was to face him with his own absurdity, as if someone who had been giving generously towards the upkeep of historic buildings in Outer Mongolia should turn a sunny corner and see a famine poster bearing the face of a friend.

The face was Margaret's. He had to meet it. Until he did, he could never lay the ghost they had both helped to conjure out of restless dissatisfactions of the past, formless hopes for the future. If it could haunt him still, as it had done, in the company of each day's brisk mundanities, what must it be doing to Margaret in her flat, where everything gave it access to the memory? Whatever havoc it caused was at least partly his responsibility. He had to go and see her. He didn't want to face it again, to try to disprove its existence with logic, to make it vanish before a few practicalities. After all, was he quite sure himself that he didn't believe in it any more? Afraid or not, he had to go. As soon as possible.

He left it at that. As soon as possible. Not fixing a time, in case his mind should take advantage of the interim to work out excuses for making it later. He stubbed out his cigarette. Reaching up to close the curtains, he paused. The street stunned him. Drowned in moonlight, it seemed asleep in its own fable, remote, unchangeable, a new Atlantis fathoms beyond the possibility of stirring. It was like the coloured pictures he used to stare at as a boy and wish he could walk into, imaginary places, where reality was *persona non grata*. He drew the curtains, extraditing himself from Avalon. The room compressed to the darkness of his own skull. He created the room in handfuls until he found the bed. As he crawled in, Allison's arms took him in torpidly, adhesive with sweat.

As he drove, Saturday morning's forest of shoppers thinned to a scrub of occasional walkers. He pictured Allison still in the thick of it, Alice and Helen playing a duet on her nerves, improvising demand to suit supply as they passed sweet-counters, record shops, toy departments. She hadn't been very pleased at his desertion. 'Something I want to check up at the office.' An unchallengeable necessity. It was only with lies you could get that authentic ring. They had argued at a corner for a few minutes, fixing the duration of his furlough. An hour at the outside. That was one hour longer than he wanted. The prospect numbed him slightly. What was Margaret going to be like? If her behaviour fitted the voice he had heard over the phone, it would be some meeting.

It wasn't until he was locking the car that he realised he had automatically detoured to one of his secret parking places. Deceit had become a reflex that forbade direct responses even to innocent situations. He wondered wearily if this was a moral tic too late to cure. He decided to walk directly to the flat as an elementary exercise in honesty. Cripples must rehabilitate themselves by stages.

The brief walk helped. The houses he passed were fortresses of the commonplace, dull tiers of windows defying entrance to all but the most banal activities. How could one of these rooms contain the sort of anguished scene he feared? Three boys went past him in an argument about football, blessing him accidentally with ordinariness. The familiar potted plant was emblem of the street: growth stunted into practical proportions.

His feet on the stone of the entry drummed to a battalion in his head, evoking ironic echoes of the past. All those other times were with him now, countless furtive comings and hurried goings, secret instalments paid on a future that would some time be theirs. A hundred lost and wistful evenings lobbied his purpose, all sharing the anonymity of the past, yet poignant with distinctive memories, the newsagent's lighted window, the mustiness in the hall of the flat, roads on which lights ran molten in the rain; all of them haunted by something, the same unseen presence, a wandering hunger incarcerated somewhere, communicating still through these small apertures on the past, something as mournful and persistent as the foghorns on the Clyde, something he was welshing on. I've come to tell you to take your love back. I can't afford it.

One of the downstairs doors he passed was slightly open and a hanging coat was visible. In all his visits here this was the first visual sign of habitation he had had. He walked more quietly until he reached the bottom of the stairs. The entry door leading to the backyard was also open. He could hear two women talking. On the second floor a radio was blaring. Saturday morning certainly made a difference to the mortuary of the building. Compared with those past evenings, the place was pulsing with life. The thought teased him into a private smile that died at Margaret's door.

The etiquette of entering halted him. Did he knock or use his key? It seemed a choice of insults. One was the calculated irony of formality, like calling her Miss Sutton. The other was an infringement of the privacy he had himself imposed on her. The small complication epitomised their problem: the only way out of love is through hurt. The problem was simplified into expediency by the sudden increase in the volume of the radio. A door was open on the next floor. He couldn't let himself be seen standing here. He opened the door with his key and went in.

Inside, his embarrassment stopped him like a second door. The living-room door was just ajar. He listened. Only the

160

radio downstairs, dance-music filtered to a whisper. Perhaps she was asleep. He tapped at the living-room door.

'Margaret,' he said, pushing open the door. 'It's me – Eddie.'

The room was empty. He took in the flotsam of jotters, magazines, cardigan, which her untidiness had left temporarily stranded about the room. Crossing to the kitchen, he called again.

'Mar-'

His voice abandoned the syllable to silence. The teapot trembled on the cooker, registering his arrival. The nylons on the pulley swayed. She was either out or in bed. He hoped she was out. A bedroom scene was too much. The awkwardness of meeting was enough without further refinement. Lounge-suit versus negligée. With the demon of tumescence threatening to impose his anarchy on reason. He went hesitantly towards the bedroom, knocked and pushed. The door swung slowly, hinged on his uncertainty.

She was out. He savoured his relief and was surprised to find it adulterated with a recalcitrant trace of disappointment at the empty hollow where her body had been. He went back to the living-room at once, feeling more secure in the suburbs of temptation.

He wondered about leaving a note before he went. Saying he had been and perhaps trying to give her some advice. But it seemed a bit like a salesman for solace. Our representative called today but found you not at home. You are invited to try our free sample of philosophy. We have precepts to fit every household contingency. Besides, wouldn't that encourage her to get in touch with him again? Better to let her sort things out for herself, leave this visit as a gesture made to his own conscience. She was probably out shopping at this minute. A new hat or dress maybe. The great feminine therapy, advocated in old songs and women's magazines.

He felt absolved, for the moment anyway. What more could he do? Should he wait? The objective depressingness of the room was made the more subjectively unbearable for him because of its implications. Few judges wish to watch the hanging. He reminded himself that Allison was coping single-handed with the children. He couldn't wait.

About to go, he remembered the key. While he had it, he was still involved, if only because Margaret could justifiably entertain some hope of his using it. To leave it without a word, some scrap of paper, was brutal. But brutality was sometimes a necessary discipline for kindness. Wasn't a slap on the face the kindest gesture you could make towards hysteria? He took out the key and placed it carefully on the table. It stood out against its dark background with heraldic simplicity, representing rejection. He was finished at last with that part of his life.

In the hall he was conscious of the bathroom door rattling on the jamb. As he put out his hand to close it, he created a small locus of silence within which a minute sound betrayed itself, persistent, secretive. Like water lapping the piles of a pier. He pushed open the door. The swinging door widened from fissure into earthquake. The room broke before his eyes into a debris of images.

He stepped forward and then went back a little, advanced and withdrew in shuffling uncertainty, until comprehension had coaxed him to the edge of the bath.

'No,' he said. 'Oh no. No. No. No,' his voice whined pleadingly.

Margaret lay clumsily, her legs caught under her, pushing her body upwards. The nightdress drifted and trailed, an illusion of movement moored to her stillness. Her head was twisted back, hair teased into tendrils by the water, and her eyes stared to the surface, cold as shells. Most terrible of all was the face. The mouth was a fossilised scream.

'It's not. It's not.'

He was kneeling. His hand was in the water, trying to raise her head, patting her forehead, an instinct that played at normalcy like a child unaware of the death of its parent. Her head rolled, stirring the hair into Medusa writhings, making waves that chafed against the subsided flesh. Just

162

below his eyes the water lapped endlessly, like an inland sea, where his hand trailed uselessly. The cuffs of shirt and jacket were wet but he didn't notice.

What he noticed, mounted like trophies on the blankness of his perception, were objects the triviality of which was almost obscene. Sponge. Bathbrush. Medicine-cabinet with a mirror on the door. Talcum. Bath-salts. Toothbrushes, one still in the cellophane. Toothpaste. Images of normalcy. Believe in us, and life is very simple. Something measurable in a tube of toothpaste. But Margaret still lay wallowing in the filmed water, grotesquely sprawled, a cumbersome contradiction of all the amulets of uniformity that could be bought in multiple stores.

It hasn't happened, he told himself. Things like this didn't happen. No. He crouched beside the bath as if he was trying to hide, his breath a muted keening trapped inside him. He felt very close to being sick, a physical nausea, as if the bath was giving off a stench, was an open sewer rolling with his own filth. The radio still sounded distantly, remote as yesterday. He could imagine the women in the backyard still acting out their Saturday morning parts. The shape of a bird alighted beyond the frosted glass, preened, paraded, and went, leaving him huddled in hoplessness.

'Oh, Margaret, Margaret, Margaret.' He was whispering as if he could keep what had happened a secret between them.

But it couldn't be kept a secret. Margaret was dead. Out of his hedging, subtlety, pretence, ambivalence had come something utterly uncomprising. Margaret was dead. This was final, irrevocable, something you couldn't gloss with words, reshape with thinking. This room led beyond sophistry and equivocation, closed on comfort and complacency, opened on a bleak place where no pretence could survive, private lives were skinned to the marrow, and his mind surrendered every assurance to shiver in awe. While the pleasant day went on around him, he was lost in this desert at its centre, finding no way that would take him from one to the other, unable to imagine being part of such a Saturday again. He could neither do anything here nor bring himself to leave.

Rising painfully, he wandered into the hall and from there into the living-room. He touched a cardigan that was over a chair, some jotters, a magazine. They were nothing, belonged to no one. He went through to the bedroom, came back to the living-room. The whole house yielded nothing of Margaret or of anyone. It was a triumph of anonymity. All the lives that had gnawed themselves to nothing in these rooms left not a trace.

It wasn't my fault, he told himself. What else could I do? But the empty room that for him enshrined the frightening mystery of her going made an impertinence of excuses. There were a lot of small things he could have done. Like coming to see her a day or two sooner. Like having the dignity to talk to her on the phone. Instead of being ashamed for her in the presence of Bob Beattie and Ted Dewar. The memory curled him with disgust for himself. Who has the right to turn away from the suffering of anybody else? And most of all there was one big thing he could have done. He could have been honest from the start. He could have been enough of a person to know who he was, so that he didn't have to improvise an identity from minute to minute, run through a repertory of imitation men in the course of a day. He had played so many substitute roles, salesman, philanderer, promotion-seeker, that the assumed blurred with the real and none of them could be taken seriously. He was an itinerant Thespian, in residence at home, appearing a few times weekly at Margaret's flat, making impersonal appearances at fixed times in various places. Now an unforeseen development had made one of his illusions a reality, and the rest of them were revealed as empty fictions, composed of mechanical gestures and unreal attitudes, incapable of coping with the truth of this situation. For how could he ever acknowledge this to Allison? Or admit it to any part of the life he lived every day? It wasn't possible. The delicate fabric of the rest would have fallen apart.

So he stood immobile in the hall. All that seemed left of him was a faint, fluttering pulse of honesty. Not strong enough to stir him into doing anything positive. Not strong enough to take him to the door, to throw it open, and shout for Saturday to come and see what lay in the middle of it. Though that was what he felt he should be doing. Committing himself to Margaret's death. The feeble pulse was just strong enough to make him look at himself honestly, to commit a small kind of cerebral suicide. To acknowledge the worthlessness of what he had been, was and would be. You bastard, he informed himself bitterly. You're going to do nothing about it. You rotten, miserable, gutless bastard. And he stood there, paralysed by his own admission.

How long he waited he had no idea. But the sound of feet on the stairs outside, meaningless at first, then defining themselves into the menace of approach, instantaneously recreated the hall with himself standing in it. The moment quickened him into a living reflex: save yourself. Footsteps outside. You're in danger here. Mustn't be found. Voices.

'Morning.'

'Nothing for me, then?'

'Not today.'

'Terrible life, this. Only letters Ah ever get are from the *Reader's Digest* folk.'

The letter-box lifting. Envelope fluttering to the floor. Footsteps receding. Door closing. An electricity bill. No one need ever feel forgotten.

Must leave without being seen. What about Margaret? Impossible just to leave her. She looks strange, hybrid. A mermaid. Never quite one thing nor the other. Nobody should ever love without reserve. Against the rules. It calls too many bluffs. Phone the police? Anonymously. Muffled with a handkerchief. Too dangerous. Enquiries. Phone her brother? He would know. Might suspect something, tell the police. Where you conceal the truth, people will invent it.

The most self-righteous imaginations are the most fertile in spawning monsters. Nobody to be told. Nobody. Nobody.

Leave her, leave. Her brother may be coming. Soon. To-day or tomorrow. Margaret wouldn't be caring. Are police called in in a case like this? Fingerprints. Rub door-handles with a handkerchief. Not too thoroughly. Natural. Like something out of a film. A tenth-rate actor. Stop it. Stop it. What does it matter? Her brother can tell them everything, anyway. It's hopeless. It's hopeless.

The key. A give-away. Throw it away outside. Everything as it was before. Cuffs damp. No one will notice. Water on the floor. Dry it. Handkerchief smeared. Allison will notice. Used for wiping the windscreen. Lying becomes a vocation.

If the door is unbolted before being closed, her brother will be able to get in. He will knock and get no answer. Turn the handle. Find her. Or a neighbour may do it. Someone. Lucky it's a tenement door, with an outside handle. One of fate's small concessions. Our parcels of private suffering come with ribbons.

The door closes, deft as a conspirator. No one hears. Let the beginning foretell the end. Eternity in a staircase. So very long, so very long. Like creeping down an upward escalator. What if someone sees, speaks, remembers? Every step an irrevocable risk. This floor is empty. Wireless very faint. Let them listen well. Let them all have their radios on. And bless Marconi. A corpse is making jokes.

The entry looms, dangerous with sunlight, mined with possibilities of meeting. The back door is menacingly open. Voices awesome in their complacency. 'On shifts just now.' 'Week about? Our Alec says he couldn't do that now.' Crumbs from an inaccessible comfort. Augmenting the hunger that feeds on them. A measured escape, with fear leashed to a straining walk by caution.

Into the sunlight. An ordinary street. Nothing is happening. Be anyone. A man going to meet up with his wife on a Saturday morning. Indistinguishable from any other. Can't they tell? Does nothing show? No canker spreading on the forehead? Nothing is happening. People are walking. Passing. A girl shouts to a friend. A man stops to light a cigarette. Nothing is ever happening. Saturday sends out the unalterable message to whatever may be interested: situation normal. The situation is always normal.

The cards in the Newsagent's window. Rooms to let. One of them will be Margaret's epitaph. Neat, clinical summations of untidy lives. Appearances are expensive things. Nothing is happening. How many sacrifices to conformity take place behind these curtained windows in unseen rooms? Lucky to have parked the car well away from the flat. Careful with the traffic, no accidents now. Dumfries on Monday morning. Safer there. Out of the way. Let the whole thing blow over. Will it be a neighbour that finds her? Handy parking space. Allison looking around hopefully. Aged since an hour ago. A Saturday morning older. They don't notice anything. Nothing is happening. Restaurant not a comfortable place. Too many people. Cardboard steak. Feeding between Allison's haranging of Helen. 'Don't eat your chips with a spoon.' Helen is a determined improviser of uses for cutlery. A fork for her soup. Margaret is dead. Hurry up, hurry up. Home, and hide till Monday. Office-party on Wednesday. Jim Forbes's date with debauchery. 'We're not stopping at any toilets, Helen. You can wait till we get home.' How long does it take for a body to rot in water? The car is going fine now. Lock the garage. Going nowhere today. A weekend hibernation. Nothing is happening. 'Get the 'phone, Eddie. Will you?' Who? The police? Her brother? The doctor. 'Happy to tell you . . . all right . . . no trace of an ulcer . . .' The voice of sanity. Giving simple, easy-to-follow instructions on how to remain fit and normal. It's all a matter of diet. 'You'll find it sorting itself out. All right? So there you are. Nothing to worry about. There is absolutely nothing wrong with you.'

Thanking the doctor, he put down the 'phone. He felt as if he had just been pronounced the healthiest leper in the country.

18

Fear honed him down to a single impulse that cut through all other considerations: he mustn't be found out. Nothing could blunt that purpose, not shame, not concern for the others involved, not the thought of Margaret mouldering in her bath. Through the rest of Saturday and all of Sunday he treated each hour like an enemy, deluded the time into passing harmlessly with small tasks like weeding a part of the garden, meticulously reading the Sunday papers, amusing the children. The routine phases of the weekend, which were usually at best tolerable, boredom worked up into a certain style by habit, were made almost poignant by the imminence of their disruption. Every little domestic ritual which their common lives had instituted and sanctified with custom was overhung by a danger of which only he was aware. Helen laughing at her television programme brought him close to tears. Locking the door at night became a primitive gesture of more than practical significance. When Allison summoned his support in chastising Alice, he took both sides, harbouring some barely formed belief that the more idyllic their microcosm was, the greater was its right to survival. Perhaps the fates weren't above falling for a confidence trick or two. And lying hidden beneath it all was the unexploded bomb that could blow it all apart. He didn't want to think of how Allison would react, what it would mean to their lives if she found out. He only knew that knowledge would maim. They would all carry scars that he had no right to inflict, and he would have to live with them for the rest of his life. Any second, as Allison baked or Alice cut out scraps or Helen chatted to an unearthed worm, they might stumble on the detonator. A knock at the door could announce a cataclysm, a ringing 'phone rattle their mindless security into fragments.

'Give me till Monday' repeated itself in his thoughts like a prayer. Monday was the border across which lay a greater safety. He felt that by going to Dumfries he was putting himself out of reach of the immediate repercussions of Margaret's death. It wasn't a rational conclusion, merely an article of faith spontaneously generated from his need to have one. Going to Dumfries took on for him the significance of a profane pilgrimage, the act of indifference to the facts which would deny them, the irrelevance which resolved a dilemma by contravening it. That he couldn't see how this was possible was the very ground of his faith. The forces of chance into whose care he committed himself gave him till Monday. When Monday came, they further demonstrated their benevolence with a gift of comparative quiescence to take with him.

He had to drive into Glasgow for samples and literature, the bacilli of persuasion. At the entrance to the office Margaret's brother was waiting for him.

'Good morning, scum,' he said quietly.

It was a fair beginning. Cameron read the nervous crackle in his voice as a warning: danger – high voltage. He decided to insulate himself with silence.

'I've just come to invite you to a funeral. As guest of honour.'

Cameron saw at once how the Procrustean pressures of the situation had worked in reverse for the two of them. Whereas Cameron had had to become small enough to crawl through the hole of his own evasion, Margaret's brother had grown to meet his grief. Necessity had added its cubit. Margaret's death had purged him of many confusions and distilled him to a bitterness which his tongue could tap at will. The dross burned off by the intensity of his recent experience, he had survived into himself, hard round the edges. Margaret's description of him to Cameron as a dinky model of her father seemed like a bad joke now. Perhaps this was a temporary stature, assumed to fit the heavy role the weekend had forced on him, but it was enough to overwhelm Cameron. Margaret's brother held the moment in the vice of his own exactly gauged contempt, capable of twisting it into any shape he chose. Was he here to create a public scene? To inform Cameron that he was going to tell Allison? Or that he had spoken to the police? To find out if Cameron knew? Cameron, stalwart as a reed, sensed instinctively that his one strength lay in bending. Prostration was his only weapon. His mind was rehearsing surprise.

'My sister's dead.'

The avoidance of her Christian name excluded Cameron from intimacy with her. His pretended surprise gave way to an expression of utter dejection which he didn't have to simulate.

'My God! I'm sorry to –'

'Save it! You haven't heard the good bits yet. I found her yesterday. In her bath. 'Death by drowning', they're calling it. But it should read 'Cameron', shouldn't it? You killed her.'

Cameron wondered for a giddy moment if he meant it literally.

'It was because of you she died. She must've been hard stuck for a reason if she picked you. You're nothing. Nobody. It must be your jacket that's holding you together. What are you made of? You kidded her on all this time and then just dropped her.'

Cameron remembered that Margaret's brother had been one of the advocates of such a separation. But he said nothing. In this abrasive mood any friction was bound to lead to fire, and Cameron's security was as thin as paper.

'Morning, Mr Cameron.'

One of the typists edged past him, giving Margaret's brother an appraising glance as she went. Watching her go, he was aware momentarily of the street outside providing their confrontation with a changing cast of indifferent extras.

'I've thought of several things. Like involving you with

the police. Just so that they would come to your house. Maybe they will yet. It depends what they decide about Margaret's death. If they get suspicious, I'll have to tell them about you. Or I thought of telling your wife. Or just having it out with you myself.'

The thought came to Cameron that he should be pretty well able to handle Margaret's brother, but he dismissed it. If he was hit, he wouldn't even be defending himself. He couldn't think of anything about himself that was worth defending.

'But I'm not doing any of them.'

The returning typist smiled her way between them this time, a self-conscious parade of perfumed nubility that passed unnoticed across their tension. Only the smell from the paper bag of warm doughnuts that she carried affected Cameron with nostalgia for the safety of actions too small to matter.

'For the sake of my mother and father. They've had enough without another scandal. That's the only reason. So I thought I'd like at least to give you share of it. She gets cremated on Wednesday. Woodside. Two-thirty. Why don't you come along? If anybody has a right to be there, it's you. After all, it's all your own work. Then you can put it in your diary. Something to look back on. You really are the crummiest human being I've ever met.'

He walked away. Cameron leaned against the wall for a moment. He felt invertebrate. All that seemed left of him was the ignition key, a mechanical impulse for flight. He would go to Dumfries now. He would be travelling light, a body unencumbered by principles, purpose, or heart.

Upstairs he collected his material and was on the way out when Morton came into the main office and called him over. Cameron felt as if he had left his small talk in his other suit, but Morton had enough for both of them.

'Well, do your stuff down there,' he wound up. 'Take Dumfries by storm. Pity you'll probably miss the office-party. I thought you might be able to chaperone Jim Forbes. See that he only rapes consenting adults. Still, if you manage to establish a monopoly by Wednesday, you can hare back up. I'll tell them to keep you a nymphomaniac on ice. Just in case you make it. Do you wish your fornication blonde or brunette, sir?'

His parting laughter carilloned coldly for a long time in the wastes of Cameron's mind as he drove. His windscreen shucked off towns like rind. His destination was nowhere, called Dumfries, and his progress peeled every place to nothing. His car crawled deadly, bacterial, across the countryside, annihilating everything as it went. There was only Cameron, keeping himself alive by denying everything else. I was lucky, he kept telling himself, I was very lucky to get off so lightly, but the constant application of the thought couldn't thaw the glacier of his desolation into a trickle of submission. Desperately he kept alive his sense of danger, since it was only through it that he could feel himself still living. While it persisted, the emptiness he had made of himself had a compensatory purpose, could seem a necessity. Margaret's brother might still do something. Try to get at him. He had to keep completely out of it. So Cameron preserved an illusion of conflict between himself and the corpse of his fear, afraid of the silence, the hollowness, the realisation of nothingness that lay beyond his victory, once acknowledged. Already he dimly dreaded the knowledge towards which he was going, that the decorum of a nice and pleasant private life becomes increasingly expensive to maintain in a world of public suffering. In the end everybody else is the price that has to be paid.

At Dumfries he checked into his hotel and went straight to his room. Lying on the bed, he looked over the list of people he would be calling on. He would have lunch first. After lunch, he went back to his room and re-read the list. There were three men in particular he had to see. It would be better to start with them. He would have to get things moving right away. But he sat staring at the wallpaper, moved around the room, freshened himself up with a wash and a shave, looked out of the window at the mathematical precision of the white lines in the car-park, wondered how many more cigarette stubs he could get into the minute ashtray which had begun to drift ash across the dressing-table every time he used it, emptied the ashtray into the wastebasket, started to refill it, filled in a few clues of a crossword from the page of a newspaper he had found lining a drawer. He spent the entire afternoon holed up there like a wanted man waiting for the delivery of the currency that would make him viable outside this room. It never came. He was out of enthusiasm, energy, everything.

After tea, he phoned Allison. He dramatised it into a crisis for himself, waiting at first for her recriminations, and then, when she spoke quite naturally, listening for some hint of concealed agitation in her voice. There was nothing more significant than a muted annoyance at the time he had picked for phoning and a few perfunctory comments on the behaviour of Alice and Helen, who could be heard as noises off. Helen insisted on speaking to him and started to work up the day's happenings into an epic of trivia. He was sorry when Allison cut her short and rang off to put her to bed.

The evening grew ominously around him. In the public lounge a couple of voices were having a practice tune-up preliminary to the imminent orchestrations of the evening. Cameron sadly imagined larynxes being cleared in bars and lounges all over the country, vocal chords thrumming responsively against familiar dicta, old scores about to be gone over, all preparing for the nightly assault on silence. He couldn't face it. Yet the thought of his room was worse. There came over him a chill that was almost malarial in its suddenness and intensity. He couldn't identify it. Perhaps it was just depression at the evening that lay ahead. Perhaps he was still afraid of discovery. He only knew that he couldn't go back and sit in that room. He had to do something, move, get out. Collecting his travelling-bag, still not unpacked, from the room, he paid his bill to the manageress and left with a feeling that she would have the linen counted before he was out of the car-park.

Once he was sure he was moving in the opposite way to that in which he had come, he gave himself up to the road. Movement generated the illusion of direction. He would find some place where he couldn't be contacted. He still needed time to let everything settle. It was impossible to conduct any business from his present confusion. He had to be certain of his safety. He wasn't in the clear yet.

He drove for a long time, just following his headlights, waiting for instructions from an impulse, until a sign read "Gatehouse of Fleet". In the middle of the village he turned into a hotel car-park, got out his travelling-bag, locked the car. The name was auspicious – 'The Angel'. Guardian, Cameron for the use of. He booked a room, dumped his bag, refused a meal, and took refuge in the bar.

Recrimination was his drinking companion. As soon as he sat down, it started to feed scrag-ends of doubt into his mind, which was starved of certainty. What was happening now? Perhaps it would have been wiser to keep in touch. If Allison found out, there was nothing he could do from here to influence her reaction. He drank a couple of slow whiskies that merely stimulated the panic which was raging inside him. So many conjectures were spawning in his head that their fertility overran every other thought. Having immunised himself by distance against reality, he was down with a fever of imagination. Every fact he did not know bred half-a-dozen possibilities. The guilt he had refused to treat with honesty rotted to a swarm of fantasies. He saw Margaret's family in a dozen ramifications of their grief. He devised several ingenious uses to which her brother could put his hate. Allison stormed in his thoughts through a repertory season of Grand Guignol *dénouements*.

After a few casually skilful probings, the pleasant barman had diagnosed morbidity, and left the therapy to whisky. When later some locals came in for the ritual pint, Cameron bought a half-bottle and went up to his room. He drank the whisky conscientiously, like a course of medicine. But nothing helped. Ravaged by imagination, he paced shoeless in the room until the rest of the hotel had soothed itself to silence. Eventually he lay, still in shirt and trousers, on the bed and gradually let his chaotic fears order themselves into the formal discipline of dreams.

He woke quite suddenly into clarity, the room revolving into instant fixity. The light still burned. The whisky bottle stood half-empty on the bedside cabinet. His tie across a chair memorialised the accidental, an instant sloughed. He was quite calm. The fever was over. It was half-past three in the morning.

He got up. Taking a mouthful from the bottle, he rolled it around to scald away the fungus of old breath and drooled into the sink, flushing it with the tap. The whisky cauterised his mouth. He lit a cigarette. Smoke was inhaled ceremonially.

It was finished. He was safe. If Margaret's brother had been going to do anything, he would have done it yesterday. The thought came to him as an absolute conviction and put him beyond the capacity for doubt. Miraculously, Margaret's death wasn't going to disrupt the established pattern of his life. Nobody was going to make him acknowledge his part in what had happened, nothing would ever force his public life to come to terms with his private one. The fears that had bayed him to this room were kennelled for good. He had succeeded.

He exhaled into a certain future, a little surprised that the realisation evoked only a limitless depression. His luck seemed as anonymous as the room, belonging to no one in particular. For a second he forgot where the room was. Dumfries? Gatehouse of Fleet? There had been so many, indistinguishable from one another. There would be more. He understood for the first time the sad fraternity of those men he had often sat with in residents' lounges, mumbling towards midnight. Their aimless conversations became meaningful, as if he had suddenly cracked a code, their gatherings took on the significance of ceremonies. He was initiated into the quiet futility of those whose friends are strangers, the hoarders of anecdotes, 'Have you heard the one about?', the ones whose lives are always elsewhere. He lit a fresh cigarette from the butt by way of celebration, shivering. The room was as cold as eternity.

19

Later the same day he decided that he would go back to
Glasgow without seeing anyone in Dumfries.

Now that he had decided that, it seemed as if it was an
inevitable conclusion, a certainty dubious only in the time it
took to come to pass, like the descent to ground of a thrown
ball. It had taken most of the day for his resolve to come to
earth. In the morning he had driven out of Gatehouse in the
general direction of Creetown, parked in a lay-by, and
scrambled down through trees that seemed transplanted
from the summer holidays of boyhood, out through a rock-
cleft that was open sesame to a bay, where the wind was
farming empty acres of dun sea.

Finding a sheltered space among the rocks, littered lightly
with a shard of driftwood and the bones of a couple of
branches that the sea had made a meal on, he sat down on the
sand like a reluctant Crusoe to inventory what was salvaged
from his shipwreck. There wasn't much, and what there was
was scarcely usable now that the crisis was over. So desperate had he been to save himself that he had clung to the
naked fact of flight like a lifebelt, incapable in his haste of
judging the extent of what was being left behind him. It was
only now in the calm of survival that he could think clearly
of what his panic had lost him and gather the broken bits of
what might have been together and set them out as measurement of his failure.

His safety had already become irksome in its limits. His
secrecy had left him marooned in a future barren of everything but the present, the limits of which were final. (He
walked up and down the beach as if enacting them physic-

ally, coming back to his haven.) The price of his security was its relentless perpetuity. He had trapped himself for good inside the lie to which he had escaped. There could be no development, no cultivation of new directions, only futile comings and goings within the narrow routine of his life. Having posed so successfully as what he wasn't, faithful husband, innocent salesman, he found he had come into an identity that burdened him with responsibilities like an unwanted inheritance. The future had already taken place.

He saw the life to which his oath of dishonesty had committed him as being impersonal as a ceremony, in which the individual participant was unimportant, since the externals would persist more or less unchanged regardless of who was animating them. There would be the same intermittent truces between Allison and himself, times in which compassion or self-pity would stand as temporary substitutes for honesty, grey mealtimes when concession and demand would deploy themselves cunningly among the cruet-stands and sugar bowls, visitors, laughter, prearranged pleasures, Alice and Helen providing justification by proxy, while the mileometers of successive cars patiently recorded his stationary progress.

His self-pitying wonder at the bleakness of the place he'd come to was short-lived. What else could he have expected? The lonely atoll of self-sufficiency on which he found himself stranded was a secretion of himself, formed from how many lost chances, dead choices, growing invisibly out of the heaped skeletons of past moments, irreclaimable, inseparable, having knit patiently into more than the sum of themselves, until they emerged as one out of unfathomable possibilities into a defined fact, waiting to be discovered. Now he had done that, had let events carry him to the point where he had to acknowledge himself. It would have helped him to be able to convince himself that it was all a sad chance, that he was a victim of the aimless currents of other people's lives. But he couldn't believe it. He had brought himself here. His last action of leaving Margaret to drown in her own despair seemed to him now definitive. No matter how often he told himself that it was all he could have done, that his life couldn't contain her, he knew he would never believe it. His act of evasion was not a single instance, explicable by specific reasons. It had been prophesied in countless actions and attitudes, was implicit in the apathy of his marriage, in the ambivalence of his relationship with Margaret, in his refusal to break with either her or Allison, in his subsequent denial of her existence. What he had come upon in Margaret's bathroom was the apotheosis of his way of life, a credo not of his own devising but one to which he had subscribed. Every day the mystery of things was being denied, another part of each one's potential was sacrificed to the sacred trinity of habit, routine and complacency. Every day to the dark thought, the inadmissible urge, the untenable ambition, the unrealisable hope, the inconvenient suffering, the unshakeable order was saying: you are not. As Cameron had said, to Margaret, to a part of himself. By her death Margaret had made his denial final, unretractable. With her went the possibility of something in himself and the possibility of pretence. He would be what he had become, was trapped in the past.

The honesty of the admission was a liberation, gave him courage. All his complexities resolved themselves into a simple choice. He could either live with what he was or try to construct from the flotsam of his failed past the means of escaping from it. The first was intolerable. If he chose the second, what means did he have? There wasn't much of him left. He was Margaret's ex-lover, Allison's husband, the children's father, a salesman who didn't want to be a salesman. The permutations of what he could be had narrowed themselves to these. Somehow from them he had to devise a combination that would admit him to whatever was still unrealised in himself. He suddenly remembered Stan Gilbertson's oblique offer through his father. He would accept it. The simplicity of it was encouraging. He would stop pretending to be what he wasn't. He would go back to the bookshop. He would attend Margaret's cremation. He would tell

Allison the truth. His course was set: Woodside, the office, home. What was waiting at the end of it, he didn't know. No marvellous Newfoundland, no fabled Eldorado. But perhaps a habitable life.

A shape coming nearer on the vanishing foreshore had identified itself as a family, man and woman, a boy and a girl. The boy was running, throwing a ball that was being tirelessly retrieved by a dog. As they approached, Cameron felt his decisions clarify themselves into immediacy. He would leave tomorrow morning. In time to get to Woodside for half-past two. Afterwards he would go to the office and then home, so that by the time he came to Allison he would be no longer a salesman. Tonight he would phone Stan Gilbertson. Just now he would eat. He was ravenous, having forgotten about lunch today. Carcasses don't eat.

When he stood up and brushed himself down, the girl suddenly saw him.

'Oh, there's a man,' she gasped as they came up to him.

'Thanks for the vote of confidence,' Cameron said.

20

By taking a wrong turn at Pinwherry he found himself with a good twenty miles added to his route. He couldn't think why he didn't turn back, unless it was that he had plenty of time. When he gained the coast road, his mistake was revealed as a blessing. The road rewarded him lavishly. Climbing and dipping, it juggled bright fragments of the day before his windscreen, past his windows. For seconds the sea would plane into running furrows on his left, flick into invisibility, reappear over a rise, tilt recklessly at the sky. The sky itself changed focus on his windscreen, rushing at him through a defile, soaring away on the levels, trailing its kiting clouds. Driving became an assault on the banal stability of things, a mechanised version of the childhood game of whirling, while sudden perceptions exploded on him like fireworks.

Exhilaration intensified the determination which burned quietly inside him, bellowed it to a brightness. On that small flame he would forge a vague dream into a hard reality. The final shape he was unsure of. It would be nothing very impressive, but it would be himself, and nothing was going to stop him. Not anything. He had found sufficient self-knowledge to make him hammer away at his life until it had assumed a form that was recognisably himself. Meanwhile, the day endorsed his hopefulness and every mile stoked decision higher.

He had switched off the radio some time ago. Usually on a long journey the radio would be on almost incessantly. But today with a flick of the wrist he staunched that running sore of sound which had dripped for years into his privacy, bleeding unrequited love, synthetic jokes, canned laughter, police messages about accidents in unknown places or girls who had disappeared from one anonymity into another, news bulletins about recurrent crises whose muffled reverberations were caught on television programmes or in newspaper headlines before dying as mysteriously as they had risen. He had suddenly realised how much he resented the massive accumulation of irrelevant pressures to which he was daily subjected. The amount of useless information you had on tap was overwhelming. The number of injustices that shoved their worthy causes in your face like collecting-cans was so vast that no sane and balanced response was possible. You strove desperately to give everything its due and finished up emotionally bankrupt, or you arbitrarily aligned yourself with one cause or another like a favourite charity, thus merely compounding the confusion, or you bestowed on all alike the same hollow gesture of counterfeit sympathy. All the time the individual was being badgered to make decisions that no one could honestly make and, once made, that the individual was powerless to augment.

Cameron could not afford to minimise the urgency of his purpose with irrelevances from the radio. He had defined his personal area of corruption and that was all that could concern him for the moment. One worthy cause at a time. You have to be your own man before you can be anybody else's. For a while it had to be only himself against himself. It was as if his progress, like that of an invading army, scorched through the day a path for itself that excluded everything else. He had no sense of places or objects existing in their own right but merely as the means to sustain his determination. The only images his mind acknowledged and retained were those that could be adapted to the expression of his feelings, afforded fodder for his thoughts. A man working in a field he read as a parable of the essential simplicity of things, an old man hirpling on the pavement had the force of an epigram on transience, so that he wanted to go faster. His mood subjugated everything relentlessly to its own purpose, reduced everything till it was no more than a context for his confrontation with himself. Like a military map, the day was stylised into an emptiness with only three clear objectives marked on it: Margaret's cremation, Morton's office, his home. At each of them was a part of himself he had to win back. The road he travelled ran direct to the first.

Glasgow happened by the way. The feeling he commonly had on entering Glasgow after a day's driving was that of surrendering his own motivations to those of the city. Streets passed you from one to another like conveyor-belts that led to successive processes all of which were prearranged, meals, meetings, obligations, entertainments, while around you the city duplicated your condition more than a million times like a machine of incredible complexity which no one knew how to stop. But today his purposefulness protected him. The frenetic urgency of the city was no more than a background noise, something from which he was separate.

Having made good time in getting here, he drove around for a while, not wishing to dissipate himself in aimlessness, as if casualness would compromise the small mission he had set himself. He knew exactly how he was going to go about making his own hybrid offering of sorrow and contrition to Margaret. Because he didn't want to foul the simple act of going to the service by causing hurt to anyone in the process, he would try to make sure that he went in last and could sit at the back. With any luck, he could get out at the end before any of the family saw him. He didn't want to add any more pain to a situation that would already have reached saturation point for them.

Immediately after half-past two he left the car just inside the gates of the crematorium grounds and walked up slowly past the long line of parked cars. The doors of the chapel had been left open. From a grey gloom the minister's voice boomed rhythmically out into the brittle sunshine and died among the well tended bushes and clipped grass.

Cameron found a seat at the back. A few heads turned momentarily towards him, eyes blank, before resuming the

183

contemplation of a death. The little building was a delicate, perennial twilight set in the middle of the day, a mood in architecture. His eyes worked the motionless rows of heads into gradual relief. The coffin was on an elevation at the front, covered in some sort of silk drape which set an incongruously military tone.

He was conscious of the woman beside him furtively checking over his face, perhaps in search of a genealogical hint. When they started to sing a hymn which he obviously didn't know, she obligingly shared her hymn-sheet with him, camouflaging her curiosity with a sad smile. In deference to her he tried to sing, but after a few bars had to resort to the esperanto mouth-music he had perfected as a boy in church. The quiet chicanery of all those distant Sundays came back to him now, the imitative mouthings, the deliberate lengthening of one note to prove that he was singing, words slurred into ambiguity. Hymns had always defied him, seemed to be sung in some celestial key outside his range. He envied the others their practised participation, wondered if perhaps it was just the absence of a simple mechanical skill which left his grief struggling inside him like a bird with broken wings, while that of the others soared on their voices into some imagined empyrean.

He noticed Margaret's brother quite suddenly, and deduced that the woman next to him in the very front row was Margaret's mother and that beyond her was Margaret's father. From the back her father looked very powerful, tall and erect. Her mother was a sliver of endurance, bending under her grief. The fussy little hat was a poignant mockery. For him those three became all that was happening here. When they all sat back down, he didn't even hear the minister. He stared at her family, mutely telling them his sorrow and his pity and his shame. It was nothing, he knew, but it was everything he could do. In return they took the enormity of his negligence and his cowardice upon themselves and gave it flesh, measuring it for him, which was more than he had any right to ask for. This place showed him what he had been.

It was for him to come to terms with it, redeem what he could of himself. He had no way of judging how big a part they themselves had played in destroying Margaret, and it was an impertinence for him to try. You can't shrive yourself by accusing others. Whatever they had done, their grief perhaps forgave them. Even as it indicted him.

When they stood up to sing the last hymn, the woman beside him edged her hymn-sheet towards him again, but he ignored it. He had the feeling that they were a roomful of compromises, hypocritically lamenting the waste of Margaret's life while upholding the gentility which had caused it. He at least was one whose compromise had helped to kill her as surely as a knife-wound. He wouldn't make the same mistake again. It was all he could offer by way of atonement.

During the hymn there was a whirring sound. By the time Cameron had identified it he couldn't believe what was happening. The Barnum and Bailey mechanics of the thing astonished him. The coffin was slowly disappearing, lowering automatically into what? The furnace-room? As the drape fluttered mysteriously empty like a magician's silk, Margaret's father broke, his body buckling into a sob. Her brother sustained him while the hymn was carried to an uncertain conclusion by fewer voices. At the end of it Margaret's father regained his stature.

Cameron was out first to avoid the hand-shaking with the immediate family. But before he reached the bottom of the slope where his car was, he was being overtaken by cars driving slowly out. He had to stop to let some of them pass. His hand was on the door of his car when someone shouted.

'Just a minute!'

Margaret's brother was coming towards him down the hill, half-running, half-walking. Perhaps he felt it was irreverent to run, under the circumstances. He stopped beside Cameron.

'So you came,' he said.

Cameron nodded. They stood exchanging silences for a moment. The honesty of the instant seemed to have taken

Margaret's brother by surprise. Cameron felt he had intended to exact some further penance. Instead, they found themselves tacitly sharing the same sorrow. Their emotional proximity was so intense that both sensed strangely how they might have liked each other if the only bond hadn't been a dead person. They watched a car going past.

'This was what she wanted,' Margaret's brother said at last. 'Cremation. My mother and father would have preferred a burial. But she said cremation a long time ago. Maybe it didn't mean anything. We were just talking around it once. And she said cremation. We thought maybe she meant it. At least we could give her that.'

It was a strange thing to say, as if he were trying to justify his family to Cameron. There was pathos in imagining how they must have combed their memories for that scrap of solace, like attempting to make up for the past with a bigger wreath. Margaret's brother looked up the hill and Cameron's eyes followed his gaze. The minister stood with Margaret's mother and father and two other people. Against the sky, the minister's robes stirring feebly around him as he gestured, they had dignity imparted by distance, were etched into small, universal ciphers. Most of the cars had left. There was nothing to say.

'I'm sorry,' Cameron said.

Margaret's brother looked at him with an earnestness which was conveying something Cameron couldn't understand.

'So am I,' he said; and then repeated inexplicably, 'So am I. Remember that.'

He walked back up the hill.

21

The office was full of the heightened atmosphere that comes from a sense of lives in transit, a distant and less robust relation of that found on quays from which troopships are departing. Arranged originally as a farewell to two of the girls who were getting married (one stopping work, the other moving to England), the occasion had acquired added piquancy from the imminence of Morton's moving south and of Cameron's supposed withdrawal to the base-camp of bureaucracy. None of these events was all that significant taken in isolation, but together they fused mysteriously into a feeling of minor exodus. Although what was being drunk was negligible, the situation induced a kind of nostalgic double-vision by which those who were staying saw a part of themselves leaving with their colleagues, remembered that these offices were a place where their lives were passing away. Conversations with the two girls tended to improvise themselves into speeches. Eunice, the one who was going to England, usually a remorselessly happy person who wore her naïveté like a chastity belt, was steadily rising to the drama of departure. It had been obvious for some time that she was going to cry. Perhaps other associations moved her as well. Her father had worked with the firm until his death. Already, having drunk deep of a babycham, she had engaged twice in preliminary sniffings. People were waiting ambiguously for the finale, liking her too much to want her to cry, yet sensing a vague rightness in it if she should, a means of crystallising their own sentimentality, which it would have been self-indulgent to express. In the meantime, as she fluttered brightly among them, laughter was loud, words outran one another, the afternoon was for enjoying. An urgent gaiety prevailed.

Cameron met an advance party of it before he entered the main office. As he reached the door, Jen Adams came out. In her early forties, Jen had been widowed after a few years of marriage and, lacking the involvement of children, had developed an almost maternal solicitude for the efficiency of the office. Normally she had the austere practicality of someone who, having nothing on which to spend the residue of affection left over from her work, salts it away rather than waste it without the possibility of return, until thrift becomes an indulgence. But today she seemed to have broken the piggybank. Her slightly bemused eyes had a funny, windfall look, as if she had just discovered a day left over from her teens she had still to spend.

'Oh, excuse me, Eddie.' Her outstretched hand absorbed the shock of their collision. The enthusiasm of her inhalation suggested someone who had just become hooked on air. 'Just arriving? It's hectic in there. Don't go too near Eunice without your waterproof. You've got good shoulders for crying on.'

She pressed on towards the cloakroom, laughing as if everything was a clever joke she had only just seen, trailing a wake of mild surprise across Cameron's mind. At the door of the cloakroom she turned and said, 'I suppose I'll have to start calling you Mr Cameron soon.'

Her smile was a brief Indian summer of coyness.

The office baulked Cameron's purpose for a moment with its strangeness. The substitution of voices for typewriter keys, the unfamiliar occupation of this functional room by casual laughter made it appear that he had come to the wrong place. The presence of Jim Forbes made it even more alien. He was standing by the door.

'You're too late,' he winked. 'Casanova was here. Thanks for the invite, Eddie. I'm glad I came. You can have what's left. I'm just giving her time to get her coat. Seeing her outside. After a suitable pause. We make the sweet music, no?'

Cameron understood with difficulty the reason for Jen's friskiness. The improbability of such a duet was modified by what was going on around him. Routine was on holiday. Bob Beattie was chatting with a couple of juniors. From across the room he toasted Cameron in lager. Even Ted Dewar had found his way in from his rounds. He was talking earnestly to Eunice, substitute father giving her away to the world.

'Have you seen Sid Morton, Jim?' Cameron asked.

'Through in his office. Finishing off some work he has to do. Gave a wee speech at the beginning. And all who sail in her kind of thing. But says he's got a lot of clearing up to do before he hands over to you. He's hoping to join in before it dies.'

'I have to talk to him. I'll see you later, Jim.'

'Right. Oh here, Eddie. Mind if I look in for a blether tonight? If you're not doing anything, anyway. Eileen's got a couple of friends coming in.'

'Aye. Fair enough, Jim.'

Cameron hoped it wasn't an excuse for recounting the memoirs of the day. Easing his way among the conversational quadrilles, he closed the door of Annette's small office, crossed, knocked at Morton's door and opened it. Sound and sight mingled in a miniature snow-storm: Annette was saying, 'No, Mr Morton,' she was sitting on the desk, her back to Cameron, Morton's arms were round her, someone was breathing like a grampus, Annette's head was turning towards him, Morton's face surfaced over her shoulder, his eyes blank with pre-occupation, not yet focussed on the present.

Morton said, 'What the hell –'

Cameron closed the door. But the face remained stamped on it, Morton with his mask off, an anonymous faceful of raw hunger. In that instant Cameron lost his resentment of him, saw Morton's unshakeable tenets as being quarried from the hollowness of his own need, felt sorry for him. The voices coming more faintly now from the room beyond the partition

189

seemed no more than infinite refinements of primeval grunts, all melodious glosses on 'I want.'

Annette brushed past him with her head averted through to the main office. Cameron waited a minute or so, knocked again and went in. Morton was walking back and forth as if learning his lines. He let Cameron close the door before he spoke.

'I hope you don't mind me being here. I'll try to be moved out by the morning. What the hell are you on? Pussyfooting in on people. You had no bloody right to come into this room like that. You wait till it's yours before you walk in and out.'

'Sorry. I didn't realise.'

'No. Don't apologise. Next time I'll sell you tickets and you can bring all your mates. When I think of it! I don't want this mentioned to anybody, by the way. Not anybody.'

'I've got more to bother me. Look, Sid. I came to tell you I'm packing it up. I thought I'd better tell you first. In case it delays your promotion or something.'

Morton was taking a cigarette. His anger siphoned itself off on the desk-lighter, finally thumbed it into flame. Calmness emerged like a genie from a puff of smoke.

'What's this? How come you're here today anyway? You been to Dumfries all right? What goes on here?'

'I've been and back. I'm telling you I'm packing it in. As from now. I didn't see anybody in Dumfries. I just couldn't. You'd better get somebody else onto that. From now on I'm nobody's message-boy but my own.'

Morton took his amazement for a walk, up and down, up and down, till the room should settle back into its place. He turned towards Cameron again.

'What in hell's name are you trying to say?'

Having already said it, Cameron merely waited.

'You can't do that. Have some of the samples fallen on your head or something? What are you talking about? You're fixed up to take over from me. Remember? This is a real chance for you. Why would you want to chuck it away? Why?'

'It would be hard to explain to you.'

'Have you been applying elsewhere? That's it, isn't it? You've got yourself fixed up in a better number.'

'No, not really. I'm going back to work for Stan Gilbertson.'

'In the bookshop! That's where you were when you came here. And flush away fifteen years? You're kidding. You'd pay more in income tax here than you would *earn* in that place. What's it in aid of? Why?'

'Margaret Sutton's dead. She committed suicide.'

'How's that? Margaret who?'

'Margaret Sutton.'

Morton couldn't quite pin the name. It had been several weeks. Cameron watched recognition arrive in his face belatedly.

'Oh yes. Did she? But, well. How does it follow you should pack up your job? You're sorry about it. All right. So am I. I really mean that. Who wouldn't be sorry? It's a tragedy when you think of it. So young and that. It's her folks I'm sorry for. A girl with her whole life to live. But when you've said that. Well, that's it, isn't it? I mean, things've got to go on. Haven't they?'

'Look,' Cameron said. 'Just leave it, eh? Let's just say I'm leaving. Personal reasons. All right?'

'But it doesn't make sense, man. Eddie, Eddie. You're not blaming yourself, are you? Don't be such a mug. The girl's dead now, and God rest her. But listen, Eddie. She was a strange one. And that's putting it mildly. I could read beween the lines the way her brother talked. If it hadn't been you, it would've been somebody else. She would've had a fixation for, I mean. The girl was ripe for bother, Eddie. She would've made a mess of herself if she had never known you. Believe me. That's the truth.'

Cameron said nothing. He thought he would go now. Morton waited for a reaction, studying his cigarette.

'What's Allison going to say? Have you thought about that? She'll never wear it. She's got too much sense to let you do a thing like this. She won't have it.'

191

'She's going to have to. One way or another. I'm going to tell her the rest of it too.'

'You mean about you and the girl?'

'That's right.'

'Jesus, Eddie. You really have gone off your head. You can't do that. Do you realise what's going to happen? You'll blow the whole thing up. Please, Eddie. I'm asking you. At least don't tell Allison about that.' Morton seemed genuinely perturbed. That bothered him most of all. It was strange. 'Give me that assurance anyway. Do yourself a favour. Will you?'

Cameron smiled deprecatingly. Morton took a nervous mouthful of smoke and exhaled incredulously. He looked at Cameron carefully as if to reassure himself of who it was.

'I don't mind admitting you're putting me in a spot too. This is going to hold things up a bit. I'm more or less all fixed up for going down to London. Bit of a swine. Your timing could've been better.' He paused a moment to be interrupted, but wasn't. 'Not that that's much of a consideration. I know that. It's you I'm worried about. You just can't go through with this, Eddie.'

Cameron was impassive. Morton started to stub out his cigarette thoughtfully and was laughing before he had finished.

'Ach, Eddie. You're at it. You must be. This just isn't you. You've had a fit of the blues or something. Look. Forget Dumfries. I'll get somebody else onto it. You take a couple of days to think about this. I guarantee you'll be back on the rails by then. I'll have the throne-room ready for you. How's that? And for God's sake and yours don't mention any of that business to Allison. It's finished. Done with. She'll eat the head off you, if you do. Now come on. There's some free drink out here. You can stand me one. I'm not going to let you do it, Eddie. People like you have to be protected from themselves.'

'Be your age, Sid,' Cameron said quietly. 'Be your age.

Stop trying to manipulate folk. Go home and play with your tin soldiers.'

He turned to leave.

'Wait a minute!' Morton had him by the arm. 'Do you really intend to do this?'

Cameron nodded.

'That's it then! I know what's going to happen here. You're going to try to get back in. When your tender conscience heals. In a day or two. But you're finished. I mean, really finished. Not just here. Everywhere!' The words were flying in a froth from his mouth. 'I'll put the bar up for you in every company under the sun. They'll have you nowhere. Not Remington. Not Phillips. Not Crompton-Parkinson.'

He named them as if they were the tribes of Israel and he was banishing Cameron to some lonely waste, somewhere to the east of Eden. Cameron wondered how he could ever have felt at a disadvantage before when faced with the strength of Morton's convictions. It was the strength of an impermeable selfishness. There was no point in trying to talk to him about anything other than himself. Perhaps something would happen some time that would enlarge his emotional vocabulary until it could convey to him the feelings of others. But at the moment he reminded Cameron suddenly of something he had heard about the Eskimo language, that it contained no equivalent for 'I'. Morton was simply the reverse of that. It was the only word he had.

'Mug! Utter mug! You've thrown it all away. The lot. All of it. And for what? For a cow. For a stupid little cow.'

Cameron hit him. The blow surprised himself as much as it did Morton. It was a short, precise punch, flush on the mouth. Delivered on reflex, it seemed hardly a violence at all, was almost formal. What motivated it was simply that it was the most convenient convention available for putting a full-stop to Morton's mouth. Every word he said was debasing Margaret's death a little more. It had to be stopped.

Cameron's knuckles skinned painlessly on Morton's teeth. Surprise abetted the blow. Morton backed slightly in clumsy slow-motion, as if trying to get a better view of what was happening, until his legs got in each other's way and he sat down quite gently on the floor. His upper dentures slipped momentarily and his hand automatically replaced them. Cameron was irrelevantly surprised. He hadn't imagined that Morton's teeth were false. He was rather young. Morton sat ruminating on his own blood. Cameron crossed to help him.

'All right, Sid,' he said. 'Get up.'

Morton dismissed his hand angrily. He made to talk and spoke a little blood, like an augury.

Cameron managed to avoid getting waylaid by a conversation on his way through the office. On the street he remembered that he was hungry and that this was Allison's day for going to Elmpark. He might as well use the time until she came home by having something to eat. He left the car parked where it was and went into a café.

In his washroom Morton rinsed out his mouth and checked in the mirror. When he flapped back his upper lip with his forefinger, a knob of purpled flesh showed round a hairline cut. Apart from that there was no visible sign other than an infinitesimal hint of more sensuousness about the mouth. A lot less damage than Cameron would come out of it with. Revenge was a soothing ointment. Hearing Annette come back into his office, he tried a quick smile in the mirror. It hardly hurt at all.

By the time Cameron's poached egg on toast, without chips, had been brought to him, he calculated that he had somewhat less than half-an-hour before Allison was home. But then he wanted to allow a little time for the depression that always followed a visit to Elmpark to wear off a bit, and to let the children have their milk and get out to play. He could afford to take his time. Paying, he found himself trying to bribe his luck by tipping the waitress overgenerously, as if she might be some minor deity in disguise, patron saint of small but vivid dreams.

22

The big tree just inside the gates was beginning to bloom, discreetly deployed the bunting of the coming spring, still furled in the bud. Familiarity had made Allison conscious of the subtle gradations of its growing. Her attention habitually touched on it in the passing so that she had learned to read it like a living chronometer upon which the seasons measured their progress from bareness to buds to a prolixity of leaves that aged in a muted complex of tints, dappling towards dismissal. That image, multiplied in the trees throughout the grounds, had always seemed to her a harsh reminder of time unhurriedly but remorselessly running out on the pale lives that were lived here. She had often wondered if the trees were elms. Was that how the place got its name?

There were a few people out walking in the grounds, mainly with that taut precision she had noticed before, as if they were leashed to something invisible. They always struck her as being somehow unsubstantial, little more than their own shadows. It would be several weeks yet before Anna was brought out in her wheelchair and she could expect to see her sitting in the verandah, her face stunned by the sunlight into that defensive smile she wore like protective clothing against the hazards of the outdoors.

The café wasn't very busy. As she waited in the short queue at the counter, Allison noticed the perpetual in-growing conversations taking place here and there. A worried-looking couple were talking earnestly into the face of a young man who sat staring into the table. A grey-haired woman who was chatting with a friend held her head cocked, smiling secretly now and again, as if tuned in to a commentary which was inaudible to everyone else. A middle-aged man drummed incessantly and elaborately on a table. Buying the usual box of chocolates, Allison went along to the ward.

Anna was propped up in bed, wearing the pink open-work bedjacket. Her uncomplicated smile reassured Allison. This should be a reasonably unstrained visit. She had probably the pleasant day to thank for it. She had frequently noted how barometric Anna's moods were, wavering on a delicate pivot that seemed governed by the weather. On a bad day she could huff for a whole hour, only breaking silence to tell involved stories of the spite shown her by the other residents of the ward.

Today she thanked Allison pleasantly for the chocolates and opened the box at once. Allison automatically refused the offer of a sweet, knowing that Anna made the gesture as part of a game, and to accept was cheating. The chocolates were for Anna probably the most important part of the visit. She ate systematically through them while they talked, keeping her favourites till the end.

'Any more word of daddy then?' Anna asked through her first sweet.

The question cued Allison into the role she would have to play today, established the context in which they were conversing. The time was to be the past. Anna had several distinct frames of reference and you had to move cautiously among them, determining which one she was employing before you committed yourself to a positive answer. For weeks she appeared to have forgotten major facts about their lives and then to remember them without warning. Allison tended to suspect that it was merely another game to Anna, a means of enlivening the dullness of their exchanges. They had a variety of conversational routines to which they could switch as Anna dictated. The resurrection of their father was the one that seemed to have least basis to Allison. She wondered how Anna could have any very clear image of him at all. Allison's own memory of him was uncertain, his earlier homeliness having metamorphosed into a mystery, so that she recalled

him mainly as an immense khaki stranger who emerged inter-
mittently from the darkness to hoist her out of her bed and
make a gentle fuss of Anna, distributing unseasonal gifts from
a bag like a Santa Claus who has lost track of the time, only
to disappear almost at once, leaving a residual impression of
himself in their mother's absentmindedness, until he finally
vanished down a street in which she was skipping rope, to
exist thereafter merely as an influence on their mother's
moods, especially in the evenings, before he resolved himself
at last into a telegram that unexpectedly reduced their
mother to terrifying tears.

'Nothing much new. Just the usual.' Allison was deliberately non-commital, concerned to maintain ambiguity as
long as possible. It wasn't unknown for Anna to lure her into
a pretence and then strand her on it with a glib return to the
truth. The fact, for example, that she talked as if their father
was still alive didn't mean that their mother was included in
the fiction. She seemed to arrange unrelated fragments of the
past into apparently wilful patterns.

'I hope he's doing all right. In the pink.' It was a phrase
their mother had quoted from his letters. 'I hate a war if I
hate anything.'

Remarks like that made when she was young had made
people laugh good-naturedly, suggested a kind of paradoxical
precocity. Now that she was over thirty they merely provided glimpses of the endless nursery in which her mind
wandered locked, playing with words, doodling out half-
shaped ideas that had no unified perspective.

'Tell me what Alice and Helen have been doing,' she said,
taking another sweet.

Allison dredged her memory for every trivial event of the
past few weeks while Anna responded delightedly, becoming
mobile by proxy in the escapades of the children. She asked
questions which would have suggested to a stranger that she
knew them well, although in fact she had never seen them.
That was Allison's decision. Eddie had often wanted to bring
them along. He thought that she exaggerated the effect it

might have on the children and that it would please Anna. But Allison had so far refused to tell them about Anna. She didn't even encourage Eddie to come along here, nor did she ever mention Anna to anyone else.

It was the basic dichotomy of her life, a fissure cracked by circumstances and widened by years, separating her from a part of herself. The break had completed itself in successive crises. Anna had been from the start a part of their lives isolated from everyday things. Allison didn't know when she had first become aware of Anna's difference. She had learned it by hard experience, which is a brutal dominie, simply teaching us facts by rote and letting us try to understand them for ourselves. So Allison for a time constantly found her forgetfulness chastised by happenings, Anna hurting herself with a toy Allison should never have given her, children shouting about her 'glaikit' sister, her mother and father overheard talking sadly, her mother caught occasionally indulging in tears like a secret vice. Allison learned it all thoroughly before she could comprehend it, so that by the time adult understanding arrived, dispensing its logical explanations like an amnesty from pain ('irreparable brain damage'; 'will never be able to walk'; 'will never mature beyond the mind of a child'), it was too late. Allison had already assimilated the message at an inarticulate level beyond the power of reason to mollify with words. It was a simple, bitter lesson: there are those who emerge from the womb as casualties. Time had added its riders to that thesis. The difficulty of coping with Anna had increased when their father was conscripted. It was only in retrospect that Allison had realised how much pressure there must have been on her mother from circumstances and friends to put Anna into an institution. But even after their father was dead, her mother had persisted in looking after Anna herself. Allison remembered the minor penalties of being just a little poor, jumpers washed from bright colours to a luminous greyness, the embarrassment of scuffed shoes, outings paid for by weeks of dull economy that made them seem unfairly short, her mother sewing incessantly through long evenings at other people's clothes. It was a sufficient training in deprivation to enable her to graduate successfully to a greater loss when the time came. Her mother died, quite suddenly in the street. 'Heart attack': another visitation from the pantheon of adult mysteries, no more incomprehensible than the rest, bringing about by its own inscrutable logic a few weeks of dislocated existence among relatives. Neither then nor now had she felt any particular malice about what followed. It seemed an acceptable progression that it wasn't 'suitable', not even 'possible', for them to remain where they were. Allison went into an orphanage; Anna came eventually to Elmpark. Nor had the orphanage been a bad place. They were very kind to her. Because she did so well, they had even given her the benefit of a special arrangement they had with an elderly lady who ran privately what she had liked to call a 'finishing school': etiquette and anecdotes of vanished graciousness. But what Allison was really gleaning from it all was simply herself. From the refugee lives she lived among, she learned what was expendable and what wasn't, what mattered and what didn't. One bulwark had been missing from the past lives of everybody here: money. There was in the orphanage no one who had come from a very impressive social station. There might be many whose families had loved them well enough. It hadn't helped. Life wasn't playing at happy families. Love had proved not to be negotiable currency. When the crises came (and they would come; that was one of the things you could depend upon), you needed to belong somewhere strongly enough to be there still when they passed, to have a dyke round your position. The mortar was money. You had to know what mattered to survive. By the time Allison left the orphanage, she knew. The suitcase she carried with her when she went to her approved lodgings was small. There was no room in it for luxuries. But it contained the nucleus of everything she was after: material possessions. Whatever else she might have would grow from that. In all other respects she was to be an ascetic. Courtship and early marriage were a brief self-indulgence in emotion for its own sake. But shortly after the birth of Alice she found herself involved emotionally in the one uncalculated and careless situation of her adult life. The reprehensible folly of it, the dangerous consequences it could have led to, restored her more determinedly than ever to her former single-mindedness. It had been an attempted substitute for the dissatisfaction of her relationship with Eddie; now that dissatisfaction was sublimated into the furtherance of their social position, the endeavour to cement their partnership with a status that would be the very validity of their relationship. Their efforts hadn't proven ineffectual, and were about to be officially received onto a higher echelon. Nothing was going to stop that. No matter what might happen between Eddie and her, their advancement mustn't be halted. The position they were creating for themselves compensated for anything they might lack. All along she had known instinctively how much she was prepared to forego to reach as far as they could get. Any scruples that encumbered them would have to be discarded.

Anna was the one remaining anomaly. Listening to her talk now about old Mrs Everett's latest naughtiness, Allison employed a practised patience. She had never lost touch with Anna, had throughout the years submitted herself to these empty conversations. She knew that as long as Anna lived, she would continue to come here. Yet at the same time she also knew that every other aspect of her life would proceed as if Anna didn't exist. There would be no talk of her, no acknowledgment of her. Anna was like a localised illness in her life, a self-contained, malformed past, that her conscience acknowledged therapeutically once a week, but something that was not going to infect any other part of her life.

'The nurse says it's just bad nature,' Anna was saying. 'There's no need for it, she says.'

'You haven't finished your sweets,' Allison said. 'It's time for me to go.'

It was part of the ritual for Allison to take the empty box out to a litter-bin when she went. Anna sometimes seemed to think that she could slow time down to the pace of her eating.

'These two's strawberry,' she said.

'But you always eat them any other time.'

'I don't like strawberry.'

Allison said nothing, afraid that Anna was trying to engineer a parting scene. But her next remark showed her innocence.

'You can give them to old Everett if you want.'

Allison glanced round. The ward was peaceful. The few visitors who had come today were nearly all gone. She went along to the third bed from Anna's. Mrs Everett emerged demurely from her magazine when Allison spoke. A magpie glint flashed for a mere second in her eyes as she took the sweets and stashed them hurriedly behind her pillow. Then she inclined her head in gentle thanks, using her magazine like a dowager's fan.

Anna accepted Allison's goodbye without complaint. Outside the gates, Allison tried to dismiss Elmpark. She resented the way the place always seemed, in spite of her, to embitter the hour or so that followed her departure, as if she had tasted the rotten core of her own security. All those rejects from normalcy were no concern of hers. She was healthy. She had other things to worry about.

23

The noise of the engine died into a silence out of which there welled a few random sounds: a distant motorbike, a door shutting, children's voices. Cameron sat on in the car, obscure in the shadows of the garage. To get out of the car would be the beginning of something long and difficult, and he didn't even know how to start it. He tried to think of what to say, but nothing came. There were no words to tell it that he could imagine himself saying. But the difficulty of it did not for a second mitigate determination in any way. He remembered the blood on Morton's mouth and was glad of it, for it meant that he couldn't turn back. His course was irrevocable. He was headed towards himself, and nothing could stop him. He only delayed for a moment because there was a feeling of wanton brutality in throwing his bomb into the middle of Allison's neat living-room. The necessity for more wounds appalled him. Yet somehow the pain he was about to invoke increased his resolution, made him vow to himself that it would be redeemed by the honesty of their futures. It would force them to meet it with whatever they were. Once begun, it must put them beyond compromise, give them themselves. And only that could externalise the dream that burned inside him. Words would have to be found.

He heard footsteps running in the path and came out of the garage to collide with Alice. Helen was still running up the path, two years slower. 'Daddy, daddy, daddy,' she was calling, making an advance booking on his attention. When she got up to him, she claimed his hand like a consolation prize.

'We were playing and we saw you,' Alice said.

'We were playing,' Helen said and added competitively, 'on the swings.'

'Good for you,' Cameron said.

It still surprised him a little how they rallied to his presence. Now they stood beside him aimlessly. He put his hands on their shoulders like a benediction. Was that what they wanted? But Helen's demands were more practical.

'What have you brought us?' she asked.

He felt guilty at having nothing.

'I've been very busy, love,' he said. 'But look. Go up to the shop and buy yourselves some sweets.'

He gave Alice a two-shilling piece and, taking Helen's hand, she went off with a whoop of thanks. Allison had muffled them well, so that there was no excuse for an early termination of their banishment to the swings at the end of the street.

'And then play some more,' he shouted after them.

Helen turned round to wave at him and Alice pulled her on. The scene was almost preternaturally bright. The afternoon had shot its last flare that froze above the street before it should disintegrate gradually into dusk. He went into the house.

Allison was sitting at the table in the livingroom, writing.

'The wanderer's return,' she said. 'How did it go?'

'It didn't.'

She was at the window for the light and the sun edged her hair with a delicate aureole. The room gave an impression of domestic peace which his presence made illusory. Even the furniture seemed to militate against the utterance of what he had to say. Table, sideboard, and chairs echoed light in polished whispers. On the Chinese cushion, the dragon drowsed across the settee. The magazine-rack proffered normalcy in a daily paper. In another place it might have been easier. They should have met in a bare room with no distracting comforts. They were too expert at hiding from each other here. Allison was hiding now. The moving pen channelled all of her attention onto that piece of paper, from which Cameron was excluded.

'Who is it you're writing to?' he asked.

His question had to await the pleasure of her syntax.

'Mrs Gilchrist. She wrote asking us out to her place.'

'You're turning it down?'

'Of course not.'

'I think you should. What's the point of it?'

'Oh for heaven's sake. Don't start already. If *you* want to be a hermit, fair enough. I'm going.'

She wrote on relentlessly.

'There's something I have to tell you.'

Words seemed at once such raw and jagged things, broken edges of intent with which we bruise each other. Her preoccupation made her look more vulnerable.

'What is it?'

Some years of mutual loneliness. Numberless sweaty betrayals of something in a dingy room. A hand in manufacturing another person's despair. A kind of hope. Not anything I can tell you.

'I'm finished with Rocklight.'

Hit anywhere first. The numbness of a smaller pain might help to anaesthetise the larger. Her face turned towards him slowly away from the light and into the pallor of tin, the irises hard as sequins. He wondered for a second why he should have to tell this stranger about himself.

'You're not serious.'

'I'm finished with them.'

'I don't believe you.'

'I'm finished with them.'

She sat for a moment as if the silence would erase his words. But the words remained, ushering in images of removal vans and Mrs Gilchrist shaking her head and the children crying. She looked at him sitting with fifteen years of Rocklight on his shoulders and she stood up, the light behind her head crowning her into a Valkyrie.

'They can't do that to you,' she said. 'No, no. You gave them fifteen years. They can't do it to you.'

'I did it to them.'

The anger she had gathered to throw at them landed on him.

'You must've gone mad.'

'No, I've gone sane. Which is more awkward.'

She started to cross the room.

'I'll phone,' she said.

'Leave it!'

'I'm going to phone Sid Morton. Does he know?'

'I had a fight with him. Left him on the floor.'

She looked automatically at the letter lying on the table and then slowly back at him, as if retracing the last few moments to see what it was she had missed.

'What have you done?'

'Broken my pinky by the feel of it. Not much else. Maybe fractured his dentures.'

The levity was meant to be placative, but lay like vinegar on his tongue, a habit gone sour.

'Why? Why did you do it?'

'He said some things.'

It seemed to him that Allison had forgotten to breathe, as if what he had just said had a secret meaning for her. What? The silence drew an invisible line between them. Who was going to cross first? The room absorbed the sunlight, which was watery here, into its shadows.

'What exactly did he say?'

'It's a complicated story.'

'Then tell it. For God's sake! What happened?'

Cameron crossed to the middle of the room, turned, and nailed himself to the necessity to speak. It had to be now.

'Maybe you'd better sit down, Allison.'

The remark seemed fatuous, even to himself. It was a cliché from somewhere which he had plucked out of thin air because he needed a convention. It didn't fit, but nothing he could think of did. There were formulae for everything except telling each other the truth. She stood implacable, watching him.

'He said some things about a girl. This girl –' He forced himself to look at her face in the whiteness of which her eyes burned like acid. Incredibly, she was nodding gently. 'I knew her.' Carnal knowledge. Dank, dirty words to lap the hotness of life in. 'It was a short time ago. When we knew each other. Well, I've known her for a while. She's dead now.' He had said it as if it was an excuse. Expiation by proxy. The realisation sickened him. 'We had an affair.' The very term was an insult, a spittle on her death. But every other word his mind summoned reverberated hollow, echoing with trite associations – 'mistress', 'love', 'passion', 'I mean –'

'Margaret Sutton?'

It was Cameron who sat down, slowly. He nodded several times in answer to her question, senile with shock.

'If it's her you're talking about,' Allison said, 'you can spare yourself the embarrassment.'

'You knew.'

The situation redefined itself in the silence. Cameron sat awestruck and penitent before Allison's omniscience. He became aware with a shock of how little he knew about Allison, how little anyone knows of anybody else. Eleven years had taught him what she liked to eat, the stock phrases with which she met stock contingencies, the ways she did her hair, how she laughed, walked, gasped in coitus. But beyond each knowledge gained she had merely receded further into darker recesses. Who was she? Now with a few words she had reimposed her mystery, created another threshold. Hesitant to penetrate its dimness, Cameron could only offer his confusion to it as to an oracle.

'How did you know?'

'Does it matter?'

The words pushed him even further from her, seemed to make her utterly untouchable. He had committed adultery and his wife, knowing, had spoken to him evenly, asking how

206

his business trip had gone. Did it matter? Did anything matter?

'But you didn't say anything.'

'I might have got round to it.'

'How long have you known?' he asked hopelessly.

'Only since yesterday. Her brother was here.'

Of course. The mystery degenerated into a gimmick. The dark threshold led to the tawdriness of a fortune-teller's booth where all the cards were marked. Cameron felt somehow relieved. This was something he understood, the manipulation of injury for effect. It belonged in this house. They had both served a long apprenticeship in the deployment of pain against each other until suffering had been perfected to a game, self-contained, incapable of extending into any action which might effect a cure. That was what he was here for today, to break the rules and play the game to its limit, to try to make them grow up into reality. Allison's silence no longer surprised him. He doubted if she would have faced him with his adultery at all until she found an advantageous moment. That was another rule of the game: betrayal meant nothing in itself but only insofar as you could use it to achieve some end of your own. All that surprised him now was that Margaret's brother should have succumbed to sabotage. Not that he blamed him, he rather blamed himself. Cameron understood that expression on his face as they had parted. He had done something he was ashamed of, and Cameron's deception had driven him to it. Deceit infected everybody who came into contact with it. It had to be stopped.

'What are you going to do?' he asked.

'What can I do? Exhume the body and scratch her eyes out? Oh, it was cremation, wasn't it? That makes it even harder then. Throw refuse on her ashes?'

'I'm sorry this should happen.'

'God, how impersonal you make it. As if it was an accident.'

'No. Whatever it was, it wasn't that. Except for what it led to, I'm glad I knew her. What I meant was I'm sorry this should have to happen to you.'

207

'Have you a handkerchief? Your concern is so touching. She must have been an accomplished tart.'

She seemed content to strike sarcastic stances over what had happened, use it as a pedestal for a few careful poses. There was no way of knowing what she felt, or if she felt anything at all beyond a certain chagrin. Cameron stood up.

'Allison,' he said quietly. 'We've got to stop talking this way. A girl is dead. I'm involved in it. You've got the right to a lot of reactions. But burlesque in the face of her death isn't one of them. Don't talk about her like that.'

The blankness of her face filled slowly with incredulity.

'My God! You're marvellous. You really are! Now that your fornication's over, you want me to revere your – partner. Maybe I should be wearing black. Let's sing a few funeral hymns. We'll have her picture above the mantelpiece. Teach the children to call her Auntie Margaret. God! I'm not even to get speaking about it now.'

She was making to go out of the room but Cameron moved in a small hurricane of anger in front of her and shut the door with a slam that shivered it in the jambs. She backed slightly, staring at him quizzically. It was as if he had suddenly gone mad just as she was going through to make a nice cup of tea. Her expression swore that nothing more serious had been happening as far as she knew.

'No!' he shouted.

How often had they dodged each other down small actions like that, hidden behind chores, staunched honesty with a triviality, gelded pain with a huff? Not this time. Their relationship stood precariously upon minutiae, a narrow bridge across a darkness, woven of a million straws. If necessary, he would take that prop apart, strand by strand, to find what lay beneath it.

'Please, Allison.' His voice came tautly out of his loneliness. 'Not this time. Don't you see? It's too late for that. This is it, Allison. That door. Nobody opens that door until we talk. I mean, talk. By the time I walk out of this place, I'm going to know who I am. And so are you. We're going to introduce ourselves. These are our lives. We might as well know who we're sharing them with. Now take your time. To me what I've done is terrible. And I have to know what it means to us. To you. And if you're going to go through the usual repertoire from sarcasm to haughty silence. Fair enough. But it won't do. We use that for everything, don't we? From forgotten birthdays to adultery. It's a permanent run. But fair enough. Go on. I'll wait. When your performance is finished, you can take off the make-up. And we'll talk. Because we're going to have to talk. There are things that have to be said.' His words had sculpted her face to the hardness of stone. 'But what we're not going to do is hide behind the paper and the telly. Salve ourselves with the children. Have two days' commemorative silence. I've left a life lying round here somewhere. And when I find it again, it's me that's going to live it. You're not going to harness this lot to a huff. Too much has happened. A good cry isn't enough. So if that's what you were away to do there, get it over with now. And we'll go on from there.'

'Cry? You really *don't* know who I am, do you? I'm not going to cry. Laugh, maybe. What's the too much that has happened? Two or three dirty nights with a frustrated girl. And you talk as if the world had shifted course. That's too much for you? You must be a lusty liver, right enough. If there's been some sort of earthquake, I must have missed it. No. I don't think I'll cry.'

'All right. The tears are optional. So it means nothing to you?'

'I didn't say that. It means exactly what it is. Biological gymnastics. The beast with two backs.'

The primness of her face was denied by the cynicism of her words, a puritan with pox. Cameron's mind suddenly swarmed with images that were like animations of Hieronymus Bosch. Slit the underbelly of respectability and this was what it discharged. A world of peripatetic sexual organs. People formalised into obscenities. Its ethos was negative, no more than a libel on life, informing the world with its own rottenness.

209

'You don't feel anything more than that?' he asked.

'If I do, what does it matter?'

'It matters! It matters, Allison. I want to know if we can go on. If you want to go on. Do you?'

It seemed the first time the question had occurred to her.

'Yes. I do. Of course I do.'

'Thank God. I'm glad, Allison.'

He moved towards her and she retracted.

'Wait a minute, Eddie. It's a bit late for romance. You'd better know why I want to go on. I've ploughed eleven years into this and I'm not throwing them away now. And I'm not doing anything to hurt my children if I can help it. They need a father. You're the only one available. And that's about it.'

It would have to do to begin with again. The quality of a gift was that you couldn't specify its nature. Something had been achieved, though not in the terms he had envisaged. A partial compromise was perhaps necessary as a temporary scaffolding.

'All right, Allison. It's going to be all right. I'll be getting in touch with Stan Gilbertson again. I phoned him already. I'm going back to work for him.'

'No, you're not.' Her voice was a verbal echo of his act of closing the door, held them in a confinement that closed within his earlier one like the compartment of a Chinese box. Nothing was to be deferred. Her tone precluded compromise. 'You see, I know who I am, Eddie. I'm the wife of the future area-manager of Rocklight. And that's what I intend to stay. If we're to go on, you'll have to qualify.'

'Allison. This means something to me. For about as long as I can remember, I've been doing something that's got nothing to do with me. I'm finished with it. I'm going to start with this and just go on from there. I don't care what I finish doing, so long as it fits me. Carrying the hod. I don't care.'

'But I do. Oh, I do. Do you expect me and the children to suffer in silence for the rest of our lives because you're feeling like hiding? To do without to suit your stupid ideals?'

'That's ridiculous. Nobody's going to have to do without. We'll still have the house, if you want. How can the children suffer? They may have to forego a chocolate biscuit once a year. That's about all.'

'There is no question of you leaving Rocklight. Not the slightest possibility.' Her anger bypassed his levity, which receded irrecoverably like a diversion they might have taken. 'You're going to have to stay with them, Eddie.'

'But I've already left them. Can't you understand that? For God's sake! Does nothing matter to you? All you're worried about is the drop in status, isn't it? What does that matter in the face of what's happened? I don't know where I am and I want to find out. Look what's happened to us, Allison. Don't you care? I helped to write off a life! And I've been committing adultery for a year and a half!'

'Oh, don't be such a bloody boy-scout.'

'Allison! Listen to me –'

'Stop it! Stop it! You're not the only one, you know.'

Her eyes grew round, staring into her own remark as if it was someone else's. He let it engrave itself irrevocably on the silence.

'What does that mean?' he asked.

'Oh, forget it.'

'What does it mean?'

Her eyes assessed him, weighed loss with gain, made a decision. Another door was closing.

'Since this seems to be the day for revelations. I've cheated on you as well. Once. Though it wasn't the grand passion yours seems to have been. It was pretty tawdry. Not very successful. Not even very enjoyable. So you can stop chewing yourself to pieces about it. This only makes us even, I suppose.'

It was a game to Allison, entirely a game. She had even perfected the technique of using her failures to her own advantage. She had withheld this fact until he had compromised himself and she could apply it coolly as a counter. Checkmate. He was caught in the context he had himself created, forbidden to make a move. Anger, recrimination, disgust, contempt, hatred, reaction after reaction occurred and froze inside him, paralysed by the knowledge that they were as much her right as his. He sought desperately for a loophole that would let the feelings trapped in him escape into justification.

'When, when?' The words were distorted almost to incomprehensibility, scribbled onto the silence by a confused pain that could barely fix itself to the concentration of speech.

'A long time ago. A year or two after Alice was born.'

Her betrayal antedated his. But even as he tried to give himself some sort of superiority out of that, honesty forbade him. His failure was his own. Hurt was the only reaction he had a right to. Painfully he put its raw ignorance to school.

'Who was it?'

'What difference does it make now?'

'Bloody who?'

'It was Sid Morton.'

'Oh no. No.'

'The thing is it didn't mean anything. Really it didn't.'

'Shut up.'

While he surrendered himself to the realisation of it, a part of his mind was swiftly and dexterously rummaging the past, groping for screws to tighten on his own rack. Dr Culley's remarks. Had Allison been to see him because she thought she was pregnant? No, her visit had been too recent. The way she talked to Morton. Morton's concern for her when Margaret's brother went to see him. Morton's anxiety about his telling Allison. Truth was a multiple haemorrhage.

'It was one of our worst times then. Remember? We were quarrelling all the time. And nothing was going right. I don't know what made me do it. Sheer depression, I suppose. I had to do something.'

'Did he come here? To the house?' Why did that seem important?

'Well it was the other place, then, of course. That was another thing, that place. I hated that house. I wasn't myself there. It nearly drove me mad. He came there a few times. Neither of us really enjoyed it. Only two or three times it was.'

She spoke as if solace lay in continence. Imagination kept turning up images of coiled bodies that he had to force himself not to contemplate.

'It's something I could never do again,' she said.

The room was no longer real for him, became a narrowness between them, lit weirdly, garishly by their words, seemed foetid with their breathing. This was where they lived, this rank projection of their mutual failure, hemmed in by their own deceptions. These were who they were, these shadows that made two a crowd, multiplied every movement into a conspiracy. All of it, eleven years, the spoken and unspoken promises, the nurtured illusions, the giving and the taking, thousands of words of earnest conversation, love, hurt, and reconciliation, led to this instant in which they stared into each other, a mutuality of mirrors. Pleased to meet me.

'It's funny to think of it,' he said. 'We used to be people.'

He recalled an incident soon after their marriage when at a dance he had railed at her in savage undertones because he thought another man had been paying her too much attention. She had sat in a corner with him, crying, too upset to show herself on the dancefloor. That wasted evening was like a photograph, reminding him incredibly of what they had once been like. Now each stood like a monstrous mutation, measuring the other's deformity. Her matter-of-fact tones made adultery commensurate with having lost the laundry. He looked on in vegetable acquiescence, the dignity of anger lobotomised by his own guilt. That they had gone about for so long meeting people, walking streets, talking, laughing, living without their monstrosity being noticed surprised him a little. To continue with it once they had become aware of it was unthinkable. The only reaction he could have towards the ugliness of the past wasn't blame or recrimination. It was to transform it with the future. The only answer to today was the difference of tomorrow.

213

'I'll go and see Stan Gilbertson tomorrow,' he said. The trivial statement was made quietly and with desperate calmness, contained the ultimate irrelevance of all acts of faith, a man crossing himself in an earthquake.

'No, but you'll not.'

'Of course I will.' She didn't seem to realise where they were. Having come to this wasteland, she still wanted the old currency of established priorities to be operative. When would she realise that their hoard of attitudes was valueless here, must be committed into flux and reminted in new forms? 'Anyway, I doubt if Sid Morton would be likely to have me back.'

'He's going to have to. Isn't he?'

The meaning of Allison's words came to him in a slow sclerosis of comprehension. It was a new refined extension to the game. His move had given her freedom to apply what she had in reserve against Sid Morton, who would rescind what Cameron had done, and everything was back as it had been. It was the sort of neat manoeuvre that Morton himself would have appreciated.

'You bastard!' Cameron said sincerely.

'Possibly. But it's going to work. And you created the mess. Remember? I'm just putting it right. I think you'll find him more amenable after I've talked to him. Elspeth's a proud woman. A little bit naïve, maybe, but very proud. He can't afford to hold a grudge against you. I'll phone him. I'll try the office first.'

He found himself unable to move as Allison crossed the room, opened the door, and went into the hall. The incredibility of what was happening nullified any response. Every step seemed to take her further beyond anything he could do. It was as if he was waiting helplessly for her action to disprove itself. There were things that had to be impossible, and if they weren't there was nothing you could do about them, about anything. As he waited, hearing her lift the phone from its cradle, despair closed on him like a cage. If she could do this thing, it was hopeless. He had given her the means to

214

trap him and the trap was closing. He had only understood the corruption of their lives by becoming corrupt himself, and incapable of purifying himself. The door that opened on understanding had closed on practicality. Escape was only feasible in hindsight. He had learned the final rule of the game Allison played, which was 'no return'. The phone burred relentlessly as she dialled. When she talked, her mouth would consign the last of everything to the void. It couldn't happen.

The futility of eleven years swelled to an unbearable abscess and burst, discharging passion in a pus that overwhelmed his mind. On a reflex that threw him for twelve feet, he was in the hall. His hands on her shoulders dragged her back, with the velocity of falling, into the pit she had left him in. Their vertiginous progress dislodged a slender crystal vase from the sideboard and it shattered on the floor. The pieces flew like shrapnel from the explosion in his mind. The inhibiting physical gentility of the room, uncompromised for years, was suddenly broken, and violence came pouring through the breach. As he flung her down on the settee, her voice left the sketch of a scream on the air. Inside the phone that dangled from the table in the hall a casual voice was asking questions.

'No, no, no,' he was shouting. 'Christ! Who am I? Who do you think I am? Your bloody pander? You going to buy me a job back by going to bed with somebody? What makes you think you can do that? How did I get to be so small? Tell me how!'

While he raged above her, she lay half-crouched on the settee as she had fallen, a waxwork of fear, knowing herself inescapably at bay. At last she saw there was no way round this ultimate collision, only through it. But though her body cringed from making any movement that might conduct the lightning of his anger onto her, her eyes conceded nothing. They watched mercilessly as he struggled with himself, waiting for the subsidence of his wrath, hardened beyond yielding.

'No. You've got the wrong man. You're confusing me with

215

somebody else. That isn't me. It's not me. I'm going to see him, all right. I'm going to see Stan Gilbertson tomorrow. You'd better get used to that.'

When she answered, her voice matched the stillness of her posture, was carved out of inflexibility.

'And you'd better get used to doing without your children. Because if you do this, I'll divorce you. If you want to play at Puritans, you can do it on your own. I didn't come this far to start going backwards. Where I am is where I stay.'

'That's madness.' The wildness of his eyes gave his words an irony that wasn't funny. 'You can't divorce me. You're just talking.'

'No. I can make it happen. And I will. I think I could depend on Sid Morton for some evidence. And her brother. There's a lot of George Washington in him, isn't there? He'd just feel obliged to tell the truth. And nothing but. It would be very easy.'

'You wouldn't do it for the children's sake.'

'I'd do anything to keep what I have. Or to square the account if I lose it. If you're so worried about the children, you know what to do. But you'd better mean the next thing you do. Because I will.'

'I could cite Sid Morton against you.'

'Or the Duke of Wellington. One case would be about as strong as the other. Because nobody knows about it, do they? Or would you be wanting me as a witness?'

The scene had reversed itself in some slightly ludicrous but terrible way. The position his violence had forced on her she had adapted to a dominance. The way she reclined on the couch was almost queenly, a cliché of regality from which her words came with an absolutist authority. He had become by implication a pleader, someone being granted an audience with his destiny. His voice toned painfully into the role.

'Allison. Don't try to do this. Don't. This just can't go on on these terms. Don't you see that? There's been enough waste as it is. We've been playing at imitation people for years. Don't ask me to commit myself to it for the rest of my

216

life. All I want is enough room to be myself. That's all. But I've got to have it. I've got to. Please, Allison. Please. Don't try to prolong this. What we have is nothing. There's nothing here.'

'It's enough for me. And if you take one particle of it away from me, I'll teach you what nothing really is.'

She had passed judgment on him, and it was final. He knew there was no appeal, not now or afterwards. Once implemented, the sentence couldn't be revoked, because it was after all merely a choice of modes of execution. He wasn't fooled by the triviality of the point at issue. The decision to work one place or another was irrelevant, but the implications of his reasons for taking the decision were terminal. Now was the node of a future cancer. It was cut and survive as half a man, or leave it and perish wholly. Allison's recalcitrant cynicism had its hold on too many parts of his life, denying a total cure. He could either go on alone, leaving most of what was real to him behind, or he could submit to the gradual but utter suppression of himself.

Rationality disintegrated under the injustice of it. His thoughts broke into irreconcilable fragments of loss. He couldn't live without his children. No one had the right to make him, or to threaten him with the loss of them. They were more himself than anything else he had, and anything he could ever be was bound up with them. He had a small, bright dream of how they might have been, all of them, of the lives they had a right to, real selves suffocating behind the pretences imposed on them. But to keep his children, to hold onto what was real in him, he must perpetuate the pretences, and he couldn't. He couldn't any longer endorse the dishonesty of their lives, bury Margaret in lies. For the future to be more than an embalming of the present, something more was necessary. You became honest with the world or died. But he had no means of becoming honest. He could do neither one thing nor the other. Yet there was no further alternative.

Hopelessness made an Antarctica of his mind, a last place

217

bitter past endurance, lonely beyond comprehension, a cold and moaning desolation in which it seemed impossible that anything should survive. But something did. He was afraid of it, felt a welling terror as if he saw the tracks of something abominable, brute, too monstrous ever to be faced, that was coming remorselessly nearer. From the emptiness within him it enlarged, gross, misshapen, overwhelmingly strong, born of its own denial, nurtured in Margaret's death, fed to enormity by all their comfortable deceptions, until it came now to possess him, demanding existence. To everything but itself, it said simply, no.

Its presence overwhelmed him, seemed to fall across the room. Caught in its magnitude, he seemed to look upon the scene from a vast and helpless height. He saw Allison lying on her couch as if trapped, horribly vulnerable in her complacency, beyond the reach of warning. He saw himself standing above her like another person, coiled towards a foreseeable culmination. He heard his own voice, taut with hopelessness, try to talk them away from the overpowering imminence in himself, and Allison's flat rebuttals, a brief and fatalistic stichomythia.

'Please, Allison. Don't hold me to this.'

'Save your breath.'

'It was the only chance we had.'

'We used our chances up a long time ago.'

'At least we could try what I'm saying.'

'It's too late for experiments. I'll keep to the certainties.'

'It could've been good.'

'We'll never know. Will we?'

A slow groan broke from him like an exorcised spirit, and he seemed to be borne on it. The cushion was in his hands and he covered her face, falling across her. The dragon writhed in her struggles and he was saying over and over again, 'No. No. No. No. No.' His eyes behind closed lids glowed red with rage. She managed to free herself for a second and hissed for breath. The momentary sound created in him a lucid interval. With one last immense effort he took hold of his fury and flung himself off, the cushion still in his hands. For some seconds he thought she was dead. Then her lungs vomited on emptiness and took in air. On his knees, he whimpered, a noise barely human, evolving from a dog's whine into the self-terrifying reassurance of a child's voice in a darkened room, saying, 'It's all right. It's all right.'

The silence around them was a bland rebuttal of what had gone before it. The day slowly resumed solidity, re-establishing the whispered complacencies of the street outside, while in the middle of it Allison's breathing came back fitfully to evenness, registering their return to sanity. The smallness of things denied the enormity of what they had just felt. The dragon lay on Cameron's hands in garish quiescence. Turning over the cushion, he saw a smear of saliva, no bigger than the trail a snail would leave. Her death wouldn't have caused so much as a burp in time's gullet.

They said nothing for a long time. Immediate reactions were inadequate to the moment, would have been gadflies harnessed to a haywain. More had been said than mouths could answer. Something had addressed itself to them with the imperiousness of a divinity that charred every quibble which crossed its path. It left them listening humbly into the receding thunder of its proclamation. To each it had spoken in a different, private language. For Cameron it chastised the arrogance of his demands that would hold a life to ransom. To Allison it showed a gulf which both frightened and chastened her, as if her pretty carpet covered a chasm. Yet both were curiously united in their overwhelming awareness of being lost in a mutual mystery, a vastness in which the contrived limits of house and routine seemed suddenly a flimsy pretence, unable to conceal the trackless distances they lived in, too thin to keep out the winds which sometimes blew on comfort out of uninhabitable places in themselves. No matter how compact their house, no matter how well ordered their lives, there would be wherever they lived dim corridors down which strangers sought for someone, rooms no one had ever entered, unheard laughter, dreams abandoned to the silence, rusted locks that had never opened, closed doors behind which tomorrow aged to yesterday without ever knowing to-day. In the realisation of it all Allison's certainties dissolved. The house, which had been for her a finite measurement of what mattered, had become an irony, a museum of imper-manence and uncertainty. Every object in it connoted more than itself, from the embellished mirror, filmed with dusk, to the golf-clubs that were rusting in the cupboard underneath the attic stairs. Most of all, the husband she had calculatingly tried to manipulate had become something she could not measure. If she didn't know him, she didn't know herself. That meant beginning again. She rose aimlessly and wandered through the house like a stranger to it. She brought in an old newspaper and he helped her to put the pieces of the vase in it and she placed it ceremoniously in the dustbin, like an inter-ment. Cameron heard her put the phone back in its cradle. When she came back into the living-room, the cushion was once more in its place. They sat a little stiffly, as if this wasn't really where they belonged, like refugees whose only luggage was each other, waiting for life to reclaim them.

The 'phone rang. Lifting the receiver, Cameron heard an imitation of barking.

'Greetings from the dog-house,' Jim Forbes said. 'Eddie? Just wanted to check it's all right for tonight. For me to come over. You seemed a wee bit interstellar today. Wasn't sure you were receiving me.'

Cameron waited automatically for words to home from somewhere into the mouthpiece.

'That's all right, Jim. Of course.'

'Good then. I'll be glad to get out of Eileen's line of fire for an hour or two. Could'nt face my tea. And here. Wait till I tell you. Just a minute.' Cameron heard Jim crossing the hall, closing a door. The feet returned. 'I'm a failure. A natural one. I must have been born with a wooden spoon in my mouth. You know what happened, Eddie? I did nothing. Not a thing.' Jim was laughing. 'Can you imagine it? We went to her place. Everything was laid on. More drink. Soft music. Nice chat. But I just couldn't bring myself to push it. She was game too, I'm sure. But she seemed such a nice person. I felt nothing. That way, you know? What I did was I fed her tropical fish for her. Did you know she had tropical fish? Some beauties, too.' Why did Jim so determinedly reduce all experience to material for a funny script? Nothing could ever really change him. Was everyone like that, limited to a few stock reactions? 'I'm shot of all that, anyway. Retiring after one no-contest. I'm a loser before I start. The only thing I was ever first in was a slow cycle race.'

'Well, I'll see you tonight then, Jim.'

'Fine. I'll let those who have appetites enjoy them. See you, Eddie.'

Coming into the living-room, Cameron said, 'I'll phone Stan Gilbertson tomorrow,' and Allison nodded. They exchanged a quiet look, formal as a handshake. Intimacy would have to be relearned, but each was willing, if a little afraid of the strangeness of the other.

'Here are the children,' Allison said, her voice almost apprehensive.

They watched the girls come down the street, Alice wanting to run but Helen's reluctance impeding her like a ball-and-chain. Their uneven but relentless progress paralysed Cameron and Allison momentarily. Their life together was about to begin again. The letter-box started to rattle insistently, a little frenzy of noise that the house absorbed into its stillness. Afraid that they would get a row for being so late, Alice was busy proving their eagerness to be home. Helen, secure in the knowledge that elder sisters are a good buffer against the anger of parents, was unconcernedly counting her remaining sweets. At last Cameron moved and opened the door. As if his action was an understood signal, Allison went through to make the tea.

The house was at once caught up in gasping urgency and breathless messages. Coats were pulled off as if they were on fire, Helen's face glowed like a miniature brazier from the cold. Alice was saying, 'We would've been quicker, mum.

221

But a cheeky boy wouldn't let us pass. We had to go round another way.' Helen was announcing, 'I've got seven sweets and she's got none'. Allison was unconvincingly telling them that they shouldn't be eating sweets before their tea. Quite unexpectedly, he found himself moved by the endless benevolence of small things. How often a casual meeting with someone forgotten had redeemed a day in hawk to apathy, or Helen, touching his hand with questions, had come between him and an amorphous sadness that was closing on him. It was good how the idiot but benign persistence of such small things let you renew your innocence from theirs. Seeing the moment was a matriarchy, he went out into the front garden to be alone. He noticed Allison's letter to Mrs Gilchrist lying crumpled in the waste-bucket as he passed.

The salve of a gentle sunset drew tension from him, at the same time making him feel tired, and a little afraid. Now that he had earned some honesty, what did he do with it, how did he express it in his life? He didn't know. It was the same world he lived in as before. The same complexities, the same confusions, the same rules and routines deluding you out of yourself. Complacency was so well organised. Everything was being taken care of. Somewhere in all the bright assurances he was lost in a private darkness, led on by a recurrent dream of being more than he was. What means did he have to fulfil it? A family, a job, a house, a patch of garden. Suburban man's estate. With that he had somehow to contain and satisfy a hunger that seemed grotesquely out of keeping with its habitat – a brontosaurus in suburbia. He would try.

'Dad. That's your tea ready.'

Helen spoke through an enormous mouthful of food, her cheeks like panniers, and went back in.

'Right, Helen,' he called, and felt his eyes fill inexplicably with tears.

He cursed himself for it but couldn't stop. Unable to go into the house or face the street, he half-turned and pretended to be examining a rose-bush. He was shamefully conscious of what he was – a thirty-five-year-old man crying in his front garden. It just didn't happen. But it was happening, and with tears came pity for the waste the last few months had taught him, the mystery of being just each other sold for a dross of œrtitudes, the silences that rot inside us, the polite talk that kicks skulls and doesn't notice, the inner space in which Margaret had perished, the homicidal hardening of the heart. At least to know them was to fight them, although they were everywhere, affecting you from places you couldn't get at. To become whatever we are we need everybody's help. As he glanced up, the buildings around him elongated to hugeness, rainbowed on his tears. Across the street a woman closed her curtains.

CANON▌▌GATE.tv

CHANNELLING GREAT CONTENT

 WATCH INTERVIEWS, TRAILERS, ANIMATIONS, READINGS, GIGS

 LISTEN AUDIO BOOKS, PODCASTS, MUSIC, PLAYLISTS

 READ CHAPTERS, EXCERPTS, SNEAK PEEKS, RECOMMENDATIONS

 DISCOVER BLOGS, EVENTS, NEWS, CREATIVE PARTNERS

 SHOP LIMITED EDITIONS, BUNDLES, SECRET SALES